L

For Mom and Dad

Forgiving Tess

Kimberly M. Miller

Forgiving Tess
COPYRIGHT 2018 by Kimberly M. Miller

Contact Information: titleadmin@pelicanbookgroup.com

Scripture quotations, unless otherwise indicated are taken from the King James translation, public domain.

Cover Art by *Nicola Martinez*

Prism is a division of Pelican Ventures, LLC
www.pelicanbookgroup.com PO Box 1738 *Aztec, NM * 87410

The Triangle Prism logo is a trademark of Pelican Ventures, LLC

Publishing History
Prism Edition, 2019
Paperback Edition ISBN 978-1-5223-9846-2
Electronic Edition ISBN 978-1-5223-9844-8
Published in the United States of America

1

For ye were sometimes darkness, but now are ye light in the Lord: walk as children of light.
Ephesians 5:8

The doors squeaked open and Tess Carson stepped outside where a wave of heat hit hard, making her want to dive back into the air-conditioned safety of the bus. She wondered whether her skin was melting already as sweat trickled down her arm and dripped onto the pavement.

Tess was annoyed at everything and yet trying desperately not to be. The trouble was that her life, the humidity, the stiff-backed bus seats, and especially Uncle Stu—who'd dragged her along on this mission trip—seemed bent on reminding her of all that continued to war against her. It was the first time she'd been away from Maple Ridge in nearly two years and she wasn't sure she was ready. Not that she was given a choice. Uncle Stu made sure she was coming along; otherwise, he promised he wouldn't bail her out again.

And she believed him.

"Come on, let's get settled." Uncle Stu walked by, his backpack shouldered on one side of his body. He wasn't a tall man, but his presence made up for it. He was kind, firm, and lately the only person remaining who was willing to give his niece another chance.

Tess drew a deep breath, certain her hair was

1

rapidly turning to thick and unruly frizz in the humidity. As if she cared what anyone thought of her appearance anymore.

"I still don't get why you hate me," Tess muttered as she tugged her backpack higher on her shoulder. While she didn't care that she'd left a majority of her minimal wardrobe at home, it did bother her that this pit stop after graduation from nursing school meant she was forced to wait even longer to begin applying for work that would take her away from trouble, and into the rest of her life.

It was a move she needed desperately.

"That's not how you change, Mouthy," Uncle Stu said, using his nickname for her—one, he insisted, she deserved.

Humph. Tess never cared much for Uncle Stu's wisdom, no matter how right he always was.

"I can change without frying to death."

Stu glanced at the group of people from his church who volunteered to go from Pennsylvania to the small town near Cocoa Beach to help rebuild a youth center for their sister church there. Tess slowly followed him toward the bunkhouse.

"You won't fry to death," he muttered. "And I'd stop complaining. Nearly everyone else took time from work—some of them vacation time that they could be spending lying on a beach instead of working near one."

Tess searched her uncle's deep brown eyes and nodded. Everyone else danced around the subject instead of getting to it, but not Stu. He'd told Tess the truth and refused to hold back even when it was hard.

Maybe that was why she trusted him.

"You're right. I'm working on it. I promise."

Stu nodded and reached out to give her a big hug. "Love you, kid. Come on." He started walking toward the large building. They'd arrived at a church campus that wasn't far from the church they'd come to help rebuild from the aftermath of a tropical storm. The neighboring congregation offered to allow the use of its activities building to feed the workers, who would sleep in bunkhouses that were situated behind the main church building. Since it was only a short walk to where they'd be working, it was a great set up.

Tess followed her uncle until she realized she'd left a bag in the cargo hold of the bus. "I'll catch up," she said. "I forgot the extra Bibles."

Stu nodded and kept going as Tess turned and ran back to the bus where several members of the team were divvying up their luggage. She hung back, waiting for a chance to grab her bag. She wasn't likely to make friends with many of the people on the trip, which was better anyway. Tess burned a lot of bridges in the last few years, and making amends was difficult. Besides, if she didn't make friends, there would be no problem keeping them.

"Need a hand?" a deep voice asked behind her.

Tess turned and found herself facing a broad chest. She raised her head and was stunned to find the familiar blue eyes of her childhood friend, Joshua Thorne, a man she hadn't seen in over twelve years. What was he doing here? Tess blinked rapidly as her knees went weak. She drew a breath in an effort to find strength. Inwardly she groaned. Those distracting dimples were even sweeter now.

Josh had lived next door to Tess and her family for seven years of their childhood, and he'd been best friends with Tess's brother, Brody. The boys played on softball and basketball teams together—and of course a little football too, while Tess, who was five years younger, trailed after them trying to keep up. But the friendship was so much more. They'd hung out together. And if there was anything to be said about kids, the real learning and bonding took place in those moments when they were doing nothing. That was when they were doing everything.

In a flash, Tess remembered that his birthday was August tenth, he loved her grandmother's blueberry muffins, and he hated when Tess taunted him about his terrible pitching record from his sophomore year. All in all, not bad for not having dreamt of him in so long. There was a time when he entered her dreams every single night.

Tess's mouth opened but she was unable to form any words. Instead she stared up at him stupidly, thinking that he'd gotten even more handsome since he left—when he was eighteen and heading to college and she was mourning the loss of the guy she was certain would one day be her husband. He'd been a cocky boy, followed by a gaggle of giggling girls who were certain he was in love with them all. It made Tess so jealous that she'd gotten into more trouble than she wanted to remember ruining his dates, as only a smitten teenage girl could. Tess worked to say something, cursing herself that the words still refused to emerge.

Surely Uncle Stu knew about this. Why hadn't he warned her?

"Um, hi…" she said weakly.

"I'm guessing Stu didn't tell you this is my church?" Josh asked with a smile.

Tess shook her head. Why did it appear as if he'd

walked straight off a movie set? She swallowed hard, now wishing her hair didn't look like she'd taken a bath with her toaster.

"He...didn't mention it," she said softly. Josh nodded as Tess turned to grab her bag, glad for the distraction. Her childish love for him was the stuff embarrassment was made of—complete with foolish, homemade gifts and ridiculous gestures. Surely he remembered it all as well as she did. Her stomach tied itself in knots as image after image of her pranks played in her mind. It was pointless to hope he'd forgotten. Reluctantly, Tess turned back to find he was still smiling.

"You look great," he said, eyes twinkling.

So, he was a liar. At least he wasn't completely perfect. There was some solace in that. Tess shook her head. Had he grown after he left for college? Staring up at him was giving her a painful neck cramp. "Your dimples look great too," she said, cursing herself when Josh laughed. She blew a stray piece of hair from her eyes and continued, hoping he would be distracted. Maybe a flash hurricane would make something fall on her. "Wait," Tess rambled. "I mean, you go to church here?"

"Kind of. I'm the youth pastor."

Tess's stomach sank. Another score for him and another strike for her. "Youth pastor? Wow. Congratulations, that's...impressive," she said awkwardly. "Um...yeah. So, I better go. I'm sure I'll catch you later." Tess started to walk away.

Josh took her arm and swung her back around, and she nearly dropped the Bibles she was holding. He grabbed them to steady her. "Hey! We got a lot of catching up to do." Josh kept hold of her elbow.

Tess prayed he'd let go and she could melt into the pavement.

Instead, he steered her past a group of girls who were wearing matching green t-shirts, probably members of his youth group. They watched Josh territorially before turning back to each other with whispers and giggles. They'd made themselves comfortable at a picnic table and seemed uninterested in moving. "You girls could help the team with the luggage." Josh called over his shoulder. "Clarissa…Lydia…Taylor…Lila… get a move on."

The girls scrambled off the picnic table and went to the remaining ministry members who were struggling with various items.

"You sure do have a way with them," Tess said as he led her into a tiny office and closed the door.

Where did Uncle Stu go?

Tess gulped as she drank in the walls, covered in sports memorabilia and pictures of Josh and his family, as well as a few that included Tess, her brother Brody, and even their parents. She peeked up at Josh and smiled, aware that there wasn't one picture of him with anyone who could be mistaken for a wife, fiancée, or girlfriend. Interesting. None of her business. But, interesting. "Um…what's up?" Tess asked, reminding herself that she was a grown woman, not a kid sick with puppy-love.

Josh pulled her into a hug. "I can't believe you're here. Stu said you were coming but I asked him not to say anything, so it would be a surprise." He stepped back, his hands still on her shoulders. "So, surprise!"

He smelled amazing. Tess wondered if it was possible for her entire body to be on fire. Or maybe she was getting a glimpse of what hell was actually like.

Although she was certain of her salvation, it never hurt to be reminded of how far she'd come. "Yeah..." Tess tried to sound cheerful as she watched Josh go behind the desk and flop into his chair as if exhausted and relieved all at the same time.

He was still grinning. Would it kill him to stow the dimples for a while?

"Please sit," he said. "I've been so excited you were coming that I hardly slept."

"Really? You were that excited about *me*?" Now Tess smiled as she lowered into a worn chair and tried to wrap her mind around what he'd said. She'd spent years pining for him. Granted, back then things couldn't possibly have worked out. The words he'd spoken were ones she once longed for, but likely ones that were based on his idealized view of a childhood that long since passed them both.

Surely, she could hold him at a distance and run away before he discovered all the ways she was no longer an innocent child.

Tess squirmed while Josh continued staring at her, grinning goofily. She drew a deep breath and tried to assess the situation. There were a few options. She could run and hide, hitch her way back home, and be gone to who-knows-where before Uncle Stu even got back. But of course that meant when Stu did find her— and Tess was sure he would eventually—he'd wring her neck and disown her. Since he was the only family left who still had any faith in her, that plan wouldn't work.

Of course, Tess could simply tell Josh everything and get on with it. Although it might embarrass him, at least Tess wouldn't have to lie. And that was exactly what she might do if this sickeningly sweet reunion continued.

With a smile that could win her an Oscar, Tess met Josh's eyes and decided to ignore the problem entirely. She was going back home when her work on the youth center was complete, and Josh would be staying in Florida. They'd never see each other again, or at least not for a long time, preferably after Tess moved as far away as possible and Josh and the rest of the world forgot about her so she could start her life over.

"It's great to see you, Jed. But it sure is a...surprise." Her childhood nickname for him slipped out so easily Tess hoped he didn't catch it.

Josh laughed. "No one's called me that in a long time, Tornado," he said with a wink.

Tess blushed. Josh often called her a 'pig-tailed tornado' when she'd made yet another mess he and Brody were forced to clean up. It was one more reason she'd fallen hard for him. Well, that's what her childish brain concluded anyway.

"And no one calls me tornado either." Even if they still thought of her that way. She glanced around his office. "Listen, this is great and I do want to catch up but shouldn't we get back? I need to give someone these Bibles, and isn't there a barbecue?"

"Oh!" Josh stood quickly. "I'm sorry. I wasn't thinking." He took the Bibles from her and set them on a chair nearby. "I'll take care of these," he said. "Come on. You must be hungry."

"It's not that..." Tess said. "I figured you'd need to work." She didn't understand what went into being a youth pastor, but she was certain it didn't include reminiscing with your old friends while the team that came to help you re-build a youth center waited for dinner.

Josh smiled and Tess warmed again, blaming the heat on embarrassment.

"You're right," he said. "How 'bout we eat, and once things quiet down you and I can slip away for a cherry ice cream cone? There's a great place not far from here."

Against her better judgment, Tess nodded. She never could turn down cherry ice cream. "Sure. I'll harass you in private." Where did that come from? Already she was flirting with him? Tess mentally kicked herself while Josh chuckled.

"Great. I can't wait to find out what you've been up to, and Brody...your grandma." Josh opened the office door. "Let's go get you some food so you don't faint. I'll bug you for information later."

Tess smiled and nodded as she slipped out of his office. "Yeah. Let's go get dinner," she muttered.

2

The Lord is my light and my salvation; whom shall I fear?
The Lord is the strength of my life; of whom shall I be afraid?
Psalm 27: 1

Josh was certain he'd lost his mind the minute Tess arrived. He'd acted like a complete idiot lacking any self-control. How many times did he insist on tripping over himself before she gave him the kick he deserved? He wished Stu warned him.

The pig-tailed tornado with skinned knees and a sassy attitude was a stunning, grown-up, full-fledged woman. He wasn't sure why he didn't expect it when he heard she was coming, but it never once occurred to him.

Josh shook his head as he walked with Tess toward the activities building where much of the team was already making themselves at home with plates full of barbecue chicken and cheesy potatoes. While it smelled wonderful, Josh barely noticed. He couldn't manage to think straight as he desperately tried to quit staring at the beautiful woman who was walking beside him.

Sure, he'd expected Tess to grow up, maybe into a bigger version of the child who'd caused so much trouble. But to find she'd become the exact representation of everything he'd ever found to be attractive seemed astoundingly unfair. Her dark hair fell in graceful waves around her neck where it didn't quite want to stay up in the makeshift bun she'd swirled it into on top of her head. And her eyes…Josh couldn't help but stare. They were deep brown pools of chocolate he could get lost in. And when she smiled Josh's heart skipped. That never happened before with anyone else.

Why would God blindside him this way when all he'd wanted to do was reminisce over old times and make a connection back to the only community that ever made him think he was home? This was definitely not part of his plan. But of course, God was aware this was coming. And what's more, Josh was now certain that God had a sense of humor.

"I'll get Uncle Stu." Tess's voice shocked Josh into remembering he was still standing right next to her. His cheeks grew warm, but he hoped she didn't notice.

"Sure. We'll catch up later."

Tess smiled. "Sounds good."

Josh didn't tear his gaze away until he noticed a familiar presence beside him.

"Maybe you should get your jaw off the floor. The kids all think you've been hiding a girlfriend."

Sheepishly Josh hung his head to mask the warmth creeping up his cheeks. "That bad?" he asked Tom Fisher, his senior pastor, boss, and dear friend.

The older man nodded as he patted Josh on the back. "I know that expression well—see it all the time in our boys." Tom continued, "I take it that's the friend you were telling me about?"

Josh nodded as Tess and Stu walked to the food line. He couldn't be sure, but he thought her face was flushed, as if she was giving Stu an earful for not telling her she'd be running into him on the trip. As she gestured her hands wildly, Josh grinned. She was every bit the wildcard he remembered. At least some things about Tess stayed the same.

"I'm anxious to meet her," Tom said as he followed Josh's gaze. "She's...passionate."

Josh chuckled as she continued ranting to her uncle, who appeared bored by his niece's latest tirade.

Stu glanced in Josh's direction and winked before turning to get a piece of chicken.

Tess continued talking and swinging her arms. Had she even taken a breath?

"I think she's taking her uncle to task for not warning her I'd be here," he said, not bothering to take his gaze off her. "It's been about twelve years since we've seen each other."

Tom whistled as he watched the scene. "Shouldn't she be happy you're here?"

Josh laughed. "Maybe, but not without warning. She was...how should I put it?" He searched his mind for words that would soften the blow. The truth was, Tess was a mischievous child, prone to trouble of all sorts. But what kid wasn't, really? Josh cleared his throat. "She was convinced from the day we met that she would marry me, and she pulled a lot of tricks to get my attention over the years."

"Such as?"

Josh laughed. He'd opened the can of worms and could only blame himself. "Whoopee cushions under seats, chalk drawings for me in the driveway, hiding my deodorant and hair gel. Oh, and there was the time she got creative with a garden hose and doused my prom date. It wasn't pretty." Josh turned to his friend.

Tom's green eyes danced with laughter. "And how old was she?"

"Probably twelve or thereabouts."

Tom chuckled and clapped Josh on the back again as he handed him a microphone. "You'll want to greet everyone in a minute, once the food line runs through." He leaned toward Josh confidentially. "Doesn't look as if she's changed any." The older man walked away, still chuckling as he headed for the food line.

"Sure doesn't," Josh muttered.

~*~

"You aren't eating your chicken," Stu said as he tucked into his potatoes, skillfully avoiding Tess's murderous glare.

"I'm still waiting for you to answer me." She drummed her fingers on the table top, not at all concerned with her growling stomach. They'd sat far away from everyone on their team since Tess had scarcely taken a breath once she got rolling. And thankfully, Josh was busy with his usual group of high school girls. It didn't matter that he'd never pay them any mind, Tess was sure he still enjoyed the attention. She pitied those girls. Joshua Thorne was easy to fall for and tremendously hard to get over.

"You knew he would be here, didn't you?" Tess demanded.

Stu shrugged as he reached for his drink. "It didn't matter. This is part of the process, Mouthy."

Tess growled to keep herself from saying what she wanted to. Now that she was renewed and reformed she knew she couldn't resort to angry name-calling no matter how much she wanted to. "I'm not sure I buy into your process anymore," she muttered.

"Eat or you'll pass out." Stu finished his potatoes and wiped his mouth.

Irritated, Tess took a bite to appease him. She glanced at Josh who was talking and laughing with a group of students.

Stu watched her watching him and smiled. "Josh is a good man. He's grown up, Tess, same as you."

Tess regarded her uncle, horrified, when it hit her. "You're trying to marry me off, aren't you? No one worthwhile at home will take me so you've dragged me all the way to Florida because Josh is so good he might be game. How many cows did you offer him?"

Stu rewarded her hysterics with a laugh. "He doesn't seem like the farming type," he said. "But you could do worse than to be a pastor's wife."

Tess raised an eyebrow. "Are you trying to give my father a heart attack?" She dropped her forehead into her palm and shook her head. "I. Can't. Be. Here."

Stu reached across the table and gently placed his hand on her arm. "This is moving on. You got no choice in it, kiddo."

Tess raised her head. She drew a deep breath and nodded as Stu went back to eating. She'd spent enough time in church and studying the Bible with him to be sure her uncle believed she was ready to be pushed ahead in her faith.

"Can't blame your old uncle for dreaming about your childhood wishes coming true. Besides, I did work out a dowry—I mean, in case. I figured a few rental properties should be a fair trade."

Tess groaned, even as she was beginning to calm down. Uncle Stu wanted the best for her. He didn't possess an ulterior motive except the one he honestly shared.

"He's not interested in me," she muttered as she lifted her fork. "And I'm not interested in him. It's been a long time."

Stu snorted. "The man has no poker face. He was interested as soon as he looked at you, whether he admits it or not."

Tess met Stu's gaze as they shared a smile. "He never did have a poker face," she said. "That's why we always got caught." Tess's hope that she might enjoy herself—really and truly enjoy herself—for the first time in two years, began to take root.

But 2 Corinthians 5:17 came to her mind. She still struggled to remember verses, and yet when it came to that one, it was etched somewhere deep inside her, a lifeline she clung to daily. Quietly, she recited to herself, "Therefore if any man be in Christ, he is a new creature: old things are passed away; behold, all things are become new." She mulled the verse for several long moments as she stirred the ice around in her cup. "But wouldn't it be wrong to...not tell him? I mean...if he talks to Brody..." she began.

Stu shrugged. "If anything needs to be said it will come out in due time, the way any other topic would."

Tess smiled as she considered not living in fear. Despite being paranoid she'd slip up again and disappoint everyone. Maybe the trip to Florida would be exactly what she needed to move to the next place in her healing. She could hardly fathom that something she'd so dreaded might in fact be the best thing to happen to her in a long time. "OK. I'll enjoy being myself for a while. No worries, no drama, no apologies."

Stu winked. "Good. Now, eat up and go get your ice cream. We'll be pounding nails tomorrow."

3

For all have sinned, and come short of the glory of God.
Romans 3:23

Tess stuffed her back pack and small duffle bag under the bed and gave them a kick for good measure. Before he'd left to change his clothes, Josh promised he'd be back in under an hour to take her for ice cream. Although Tess trusted what Uncle Stu said, that didn't mean her confidence was back. She still feared she'd say something stupid. Or that Josh would call her brother before he saw her again.

Tess probably should have made more of an effort with her appearance but all she could manage was to get a shower and change into a clean pair of jeans and a T-shirt. What good would frills do? Not that she brought any frills with her anyway. She'd only packed essentials, thinking that a mission trip meant she was supposed to be roughing it.

"You're not going like that, are you?" Morgan Farrell asked, startling Tess into turning away from the mirror, where she'd been yanking her damp hair into a messy bun.

Tess shrugged. She and Morgan were friendly in high school, but lost touch in the years that followed. They'd reconnected recently, and to Tess's relief, Morgan was very encouraging with regard to her new faith. They'd drawn closer as they both worked at the same assisted living facility and were often paired for leading workouts or crafts with the residents.

Tess enjoyed Morgan's positive and kind attitude, and yet she dreaded talking to anyone about Josh lest the whole thing fizzle like a dream.

Morgan pushed Tess's hands away from her hair and reached for a hairbrush.

"We're only going to talk…" Tess whined as Morgan shoved her onto a nearby chair.

"*Pshhh!* Right. I bet he only wants to talk to you." Morgan gently took Tess's hair out of the bun and began brushing it. "A little lipstick and eyeliner go a long way."

"I'm aware," Tess said.

"Tess…"

"Oh, come on! He's a pastor! They don't…"

Morgan laughed. "They don't? Please. They're people, Tess. And many pastors are even married." She feigned shock before muttering, "Besides, it was written all over his face what he was thinking."

"He asked how my brother was!" Tess exclaimed, her words tinged with doubt.

"Right." Morgan began working Tess's long hair from its messy waves into a loose braid. Tess squirmed as Morgan pulled lip gloss from her stash and began applying it to her friend's lips.

Tess grimaced. "I don't want him to think I'm trying to impress him."

Morgan shook her head. "Shh…" She waved her hands to get Tess to be quiet.

Tess glared at her friend as she finished the lip gloss.

"Now, some eyeliner…"

"Nope." Tess stood to signal she was done playing

dress-up. She loved Morgan and what she was trying to do but not only was it a waste of time, Tess refused to morph back into the demon of her past. And that was exactly what make-up did to her. "I realize you're more...experienced in dating." Morgan blushed before continuing. "But sometimes you can be completely blind."

Tess grabbed her purse from the bed as the door opened and their bunkmates, middle-aged sisters, Sharon and Shelley Parsons, entered.

Sharon smiled as she yanked her red, but graying, hair into a ponytail at the back of her head. "I ran into that handsome pastor you were talking to earlier, Tess," she said. "He's out there as though he's waiting for his first date, pacing back and forth with his hands stuffed into his pockets."

Shelley gave her a whack that was only appropriate from one sister to another.

"Ow!" Sharon exclaimed. "What was that for?"

"Because it isn't our business," Shelley hissed. She tossed a wary glance at Tess, who was already aware what the woman was thinking.

"I was just telling Tess that he..." Morgan began, but quieted quickly when Tess shot her a murderous glare. Morgan cleared her throat and grabbed her bag to unpack.

"Thanks," Tess said. "I need to go."

Sharon nodded.

Morgan grinned. "Have fun. Remember they said the doors lock automatically at eleven."

Tess laughed as she stood in the doorway. "Pretty sure he can open the door if we're late." She glanced at the horrified faces of the Parsons sisters as her face warmed. "Not that we'll be late—never mind." She exited quickly, wondering when she'd start thinking before talking.

~*~

Josh's mouth went dry when Tess emerged through the doors of the women's bunkhouse. While she was dressed casually, something about the way her long hair was pulled back, and the slight bit of lip gloss shining on her lips told him that she, too, considered this encounter to be bigger than the promised ice cream. "Hey," he said, willing his racing pulse to slow down.

Tess nodded toward the helmet tucked under his arm. "You ride a motorcycle? Since when?"

Surprised by her interest, Josh smiled. "I rode a scooter all the time when I was in the mission field with my parents. Always missed it so I bought a bike when I got settled here."

Tess nodded, thinking. Finally, she held up her hands. "Please don't say it's a three-wheeler."

Josh burst into uncontrollable laughter. "Why would I ride a three-wheeler?"

Tess shrugged. "You are five years older than I am," she said, her face serious. "Usually older men go for that sort of thing."

Josh laughed again and gave Tess a playful shove, as he often did when they were kids. "I didn't buy a three-wheeler, you goof."

"Sidecar?" she asked, eyebrow raised.

Josh laughed openly, shaking his head. "No sidecar either."

Tess sighed with relief as she tossed her purse strap over her head cross-wise. "Thank goodness. I would definitely go back to the bunkhouse to get some of the old ladies for you, otherwise."

Josh had yet to stop smiling. He couldn't remember the last time he was able to carry on a conversation that didn't involve listening to someone's problems in an effort to help solve them. Not that he minded being a pastor. But he was always "on" and so rarely got the opportunity for unguarded moments. The time with Tess was already a breath of fresh air.

"Come on, Tornado. Let's see if my bike is up to your high standards."

"So if you're not into three-wheelers or sidecars, what do you like?" she asked as she followed him toward the parking lot.

"I'm pretty old school. But I like British bikes." He gestured toward his cycle. "We could walk, but…"

Her eyes lit up when she saw his motorcycle.

His chest puffed with pride.

"No way," Tess said. "I love to ride. Besides, I'm dying to see how you handle your chopper, wimpy."

Tess walked confidently toward the motorcycle, not tentatively or with any fear. Most women were fascinated by the idea of the bike, but it was more about the fantasy than the reality of the machine itself. Tess's approach showed that she wanted to appreciate the motorcycle, not what others would think of her. She knelt and began giving the bike a thorough inspection from tire to tire. "You lower it? And custom handlebars?" She whistled and shook her head. "Didn't know pastors made that kind of money."

Josh chuckled, amused by her adoration of his beloved motorcycle. "Birthday present to myself. I got a good deal on the bike, so I figured a few modifications, the saddlebags, new paint job, and seat were a good start for now. I plan to do some other work later if I can get the time and money. Make it a little more classic, vintage."

Tess nodded in appreciation and stood. "Nice," she said and accepted the helmet Josh offered her as he tucked his own under his arm with a smile.

"So you ride?" he asked.

"Yep. Haven't taken it out yet this year... still too cold. I'll get it ready for summer when I get back."

Josh couldn't mask his surprise. While Tess had always been a rebel, it shocked him that she owned a bike and understood them. Neither Brody nor her father drove one that he remembered. Still, he'd been gone for twelve years. A lot could happen in twelve years. It sure had for him.

"So, what do you have?" Josh asked.

Tess laughed. "If it was a dog it would be a mutt. I have a little bit of everything in it. Whatever I can afford that's awesome makes it mine," she said as she went back to inspecting Josh's bike.

"What modifications have you done?" Josh asked.

Tess smiled. "I monkeyed on the engine a little, got some new wheels. We'll see what she's like when I pull her out. I'd love to jazz up the paint this year if nothing else," she said, lifting her helmet with a wicked grin. "So, can a straight-laced pastor drive this thing properly?"

"Oh, I'm looking forward to surprising you, Tornado," Josh said with a laugh.

Tess deftly pulled the helmet over her hair, but not before Josh caught a glimpse of her grin. "All right, let's go," she said. "Take me for a ride, Jed."

"Yes, ma'am." Josh pulled his own helmet down and got on the motorcycle, waiting for Tess to get on behind him. He started the bike and drove down the road, ready to show her what he could do.

~*~

Despite the ice cream shop being a short walk away, Josh drove through the streets for nearly twenty minutes anyway. It was the first time he'd been on the bike with a passenger and he was enjoying it. Having Tess cling to him as he steered into curves and onto busier streets where he easily maneuvered around slower cars seemed natural. It was with disappointment that he finally parked outside the small ice cream shop called Dips that sat immediately off the beach. Josh got off the bike, yanking his head free of his helmet. He ignored a nervous twitch as he nodded toward the motorcycle. "Well?" he asked.

Tess pulled her helmet off and gave a reserved smile. "Not bad," she said. "But I could show you a thing or two."

Josh laughed as he set their helmets on the bike. "It's been a God-send down here. I can get wherever I need to be a lot faster."

"And you don't need to put it away for the winter. I'm crazy jealous there." Tess followed him to the ice cream shop.

"Oh, but I miss the winters. All that snow for skiing and sled riding, tubing..." Josh smiled and she smiled back as he held the door open. "Besides, the constant heat and humidity are murder on my hair."

He winked.

"I know what it's doing to mine," she muttered.

Josh tugged on her braid. "You could always go back to pigtails."

Tess laughed. "No, thanks."

They stepped into line and Josh placed his order— a large cone with peanut butter ice cream.

Tess made a face. "A small cherry cone please."

"I was sure you'd be a sucker for the cherry," he said. "Which will only make it easier to get you talking."

"Some things don't change, Jed. Give me cherry ice cream and I'll spill my deepest secrets." She sobered and cleared her throat, her face clouded with something Josh couldn't identify.

What happened?

Josh accepted his cone and paid while Tess appeared to be lost in her reverie. He nodded toward the door. "We could walk on the beach."

Tess shrugged. "Sure."

She allowed Josh to hold the door for her, and then he followed her outside, wondering what deep secrets she was already afraid to share.

4

And be ye kind one to another, tenderhearted, forgiving one another, even as God for Christ's sake hath forgiven you.
Ephesians 4: 32

"So, you went to nursing school?" Josh asked. "Still looking for a job, or are you already working?" He bit into his huge ice cream cone.

Although she tried to avoid staring at him, Tess found the task impossible. Josh Thorne was, in a word, breathtaking. This wasn't handsome like 'wow, what a guy', but handsome like 'the cars are stopping so women can gawk and throw themselves out at his feet' handsome. Her memory didn't do him any justice— probably because now she understood that his appearance was only part of his charm, and she possessed adult experience that told her he was more than his perfect hair, sparkling white teeth, or those show-stopping dimples. She'd always been smitten with those lousy dimples.

At the same time, there was a peace that emanated from him, putting Tess at ease in a way she'd not experienced with anyone recently except Uncle Stu. She was certain that all Josh wanted was to laugh and enjoy her company, to be himself and embrace her being herself. It seemed too good to be true. Tess spent much of the previous two years trying to pretend she had it all together. She was exhausted.

"Nothing solid yet. I graduated recently, but Uncle Stu pulled some strings to get me into Pine View. It's not hospital nursing in the emergency room like I want, but it's OK for now." She licked the outside of her cone to contain the drips. "I've got resumes out pretty much everywhere."

"Not worried about staying near your family?"

Tess shrugged. "Not really." Josh didn't need a messy explanation, so she stopped short of giving it.

He appeared to be thinking as he continued eating his ice cream. "Ever consider Florida?"

Tess laughed. "I mean, I guess anywhere is possible," she said. "But I was thinking more California, Alaska, Hawaii, Montana…"

Josh met her eyes. "Anywhere but home? What about your family?"

Tess grimaced. It was only a few minutes and already Josh was too insightful. "I'm ready to move on," she said simply. "What about you? Why did you come back to the states? I thought you wanted to be a missionary like your dad."

Josh took another swipe at his cone before answering. "I tried for a few years," he said. "There's a lot I love about it and a lot that tells me I'm supposed to be in one place with one congregation. I prayed for a long time and God led me back."

"You like Florida?" Tess drew a deep breath of the sea air and was convinced anyone would love being so close to the ocean, even if it did mean bad hair days.

He bit into his cone with a shrug. "I like it right now."

"Does that mean you aren't staying?" Tess asked. "So where do you want to go next?"

"No clue, but I am working on my resume. I like

the kids and the church well enough, but I'm not so sure I'm supposed to be a youth pastor. My soul's too old."

Tess nodded as they walked to the water's edge and finished their cones. She sat in the still-warm sand, removed her shoes, and rolled up her pants. She dipped her toes into the water and smiled, loving the coolness of it on her feet. She'd been trapped for so long that the feelings of freedom the sea brought almost overwhelmed her. Tess closed her eyes to stop the grateful tears that threatened. *Dear God, let me enjoy this moment. Let me be a blessing to him. Keep my thoughts pure, my actions true to Your will and nature, and my words honest and kind. Help me to continue healing. Most of all, help me to accept Your grace—grace that I will never deserve. Amen.*

"What are you thinking?" Josh asked softly. He'd taken off his shoes too and was standing beside her. He was focused on the expanse of the ocean.

"Sometimes I'm completely overcome by God's forgiveness." She whispered the words, hoping he didn't ask her to elaborate.

Josh glanced down at her, surprised. "Me, too."

Tess turned her attention back to the ocean, aware of Josh but not really caring that he was there. "We should probably go back," she said. "It's a long day tomorrow." Tess walked slowly back to sit in the sand. She was grateful that the attraction she'd sensed earlier had already passed. It was replaced by contentment at being near a good friend again. This was an emotion she could embrace.

Josh flopped nearby but made no move to put his shoes on. Instead, he glanced at his phone. "We've still got two hours."

"Wow. OK," she said. "So, what happened to you after you left Maple Ridge?" She leaned back on her elbows. "You went to…was it Florida State?" Tess was trying to be cool, as if Josh wasn't already aware that she remembered where he went to college since she'd spent the better part of his freshman year sending him care packages full of doodles, pictures, and even his favorite muffins. She once feared he would forget her, and now she was afraid he would remember.

Josh lay back on the sand. "Yep. But I found out pretty quick I was in the wrong major, which meant that by the middle of my sophomore year I was also at the wrong school. I dropped my baseball scholarship, my physical education major." He laughed. "Dropped my girlfriend too—and switched to philosophy and ministry, which led me to California."

Well that explained why Tess's last care package was returned. "California? You've gotten your share of warm weather." Better to keep him talking about himself so he couldn't ask her any questions.

"Yeah. I graduated a few years later and headed into the field with Mom and Dad."

Tess ran her hand along the grainy sand. When she'd left Pennsylvania, it was snowing and she was wearing gloves. Holding sand was so much more pleasant than holding snow. "So where did you go?" she asked as Josh rolled onto his side, propping his head on his hand.

"Oh, Asia, for a little while. We spent some time in Thailand and Vietnam, and the rest of the time I was in Africa. That's where their hearts are."

"Is that where your parents are now?"

"They'll probably never come back." Josh met Tess's gaze and pointed at her. "I see what you're doing."

"What I'm doing?" She picked up a seashell and pretended to inspect it.

"You're asking me questions, so I can't ask you any."

Tess laughed. "Whatever." She tossed the shell into the ocean. "Ask away, Jed." But even as she said the words she wanted more than anything for him to stick to superficial topics so she wouldn't be forced again to own any of what happened over the last few years.

And yet if he asked, Tess hoped she was ready to answer.

~*~

Josh considered Tess, aware that she was guarding something very carefully. He was curious as to what it was. He would tread lightly. "Um…" Josh sat up so he could clear his head. He focused on the ocean as he spoke. "How's Brody? We lost touch when I switched schools and we haven't talked in a while. I miss that big oaf."

"Brody's good. He got married about three years ago."

Josh remembered receiving the invitation, but he wasn't able to go since he was in Africa. Yet another reason he was glad to be home; he could be included in all that he'd missed being away. "Yeah. I remember. I wanted to be there. Stell sounds like a great lady."

Tess was stoic as she turned her gaze to the ocean again. "It was a nice wedding…but we don't spend much time together now. Everyone's busy."

Josh began stacking shells in a pile. He found a large one and handed it to Tess who smiled as she accepted it, fingering the rough surface on one side before closing her palm around it.

"Life happens that way," Josh said. "I mean take us; I haven't talked to you in something like twelve years. I'm having a hard time wrapping my mind around you without pigtails." He reached out and gave her long hair a tug.

"And you're a pastor. I'm half afraid of talking to you." She smiled. "I'm not so great at memorizing scripture…"

Josh sobered. "Don't. It's hard enough as it is. Talking to you…well, it's nice to just be Josh and not 'pastor' sometimes."

"Don't worry. I'll still give you a hard time this week. I wouldn't want you to think I've grown up." She stood, tucking the shell he'd given her into her pocket. "Come on. I'll race you down to that umbrella."

Josh squinted and finally caught sight of a blue dot in the distance. He turned back to Tess. "You've got good eyes."

She grinned. "And you should get checked for glasses. It isn't that far."

"I left the glasses at home," he said. "All right. I'll smoke you, Tornado."

Tess snorted. "Good luck, snail." She drew a line in the sand with her toe. "Ready?"

Josh stood next to her and made a show of pretending to stretch his arms, legs, and neck.

Tess rolled her eyes. "You're pathetic."

"And you're about to lose." Josh drew a deep

breath. "Ready? Set. Go!"

And they ran as fast as their legs would take them, neither caring to let the other win.

~*~

Tess dropped to the sand near the umbrella, winded and laughing as Josh fell beside her, clutching his sides.

"Dang," he gasped. "You're still a tornado."

Tess laughed. "So, I'm told."

"I haven't raced anyone in a long time."

"Some youth pastor you are."

"It'll be a fun week, won't it?" Josh's voice softened with the nostalgia of being with a childhood friend.

"Yeah, pounding nails and getting sunburn instead of laying on a beach or surfing sure sounds like loads of fun."

"Touché." Josh smiled. "But I won't make you work the whole time. We'll get some fun in too. What would you say to a softball game? You still play?"

Tess's stomach clenched. "Not really," she said. "I hurt my shoulder. I don't play much anymore."

Josh's eyebrows raised in surprise. "Wow. I'm sorry. I remember how much it meant to you."

"Yeah. Play hard, get hurt," Tess said. "It doesn't matter now. I mean, not like the major leagues were coming for me." She forced a laugh. "I bet we can find some other things to do anyway. I always wanted to try surfing..."

Josh's eyes sparkled in the moonlight. "Now that

sounds like something I can help with. How about tomorrow?"

"Sure."

To avoid further questions, Tess stood and held out her hand. Josh took it and allowed her to pull him to his feet. He didn't let go as they started to walk back to where they'd left their shoes. Although his touch was amicable and familiar, not romantic, Tess worried that she found his hand so perfect in hers. "So, you like being a pastor?" she asked. "I bet the kids would be fun."

"They are. As I said, I'm wondering if I might be suited to something else. Not getting out of the ministry necessarily but...maybe being used in another way."

They walked in silence, still holding hands. Tess smiled up at Josh as they drew closer to their shoes. He squeezed Tess's hand before he released it and sat, gesturing for her to do the same.

"We should probably get back," he said reluctantly. "I want to get a good day's work out of you. You'll need your sleep."

Tess laughed as she reached for her shoes and began putting them on.

Josh did the same.

"How's Caroline?" she asked. Tess wasn't close to Josh's sister, an older, bookish girl, but it seemed polite to ask.

"OK, I guess. She's got a couple kids with that boring husband of hers." He tugged at his laces and finished tying his shoe. "I don't see them much, but we talk every month or so. I mean we weren't ever close, not like you and Brody."

Tess nodded, hoping her face didn't give anything

away. She and Brody weren't close anymore, but clearly Josh wasn't aware of that. Tess jumped to her feet to avoid the explanation. "Ready?"

He smiled and nodded, grabbing her hand as they walked back toward the parking lot. Josh stopped next to his motorcycle, lifting Tess's helmet and holding it out to her. "You want to drive?" he asked.

"You'd let me?" She was genuinely shocked by his question.

Josh pointed out at the street in front of them. "See this street?"

"No."

"Ha. Ha. Take this street to the light, make a right onto Palm and then a left onto Delina Way. The bunkhouse is at the end of the street."

Tess took the keys. "All right." She laughed wickedly and got onto the bike, patting the seat behind her. "Let's go, buddy. You're in for the ride of your life."

Josh groaned. "Maybe I should walk."

Tess tugged the helmet over her hair. "You do, and I'll take this bike all the way home."

Josh slipped easily behind Tess, but clearly wasn't sure where to put his hands. Tess glanced behind her and smiled. "Hang on." She started the bike and drove away, his hands on her sides.

5

And therefore will the Lord wait, that he may be gracious unto you, and therefore will he be exalted, that he may have mercy upon you: for the Lord is a God of judgment: blessed are all they that wait for him.
Isaiah 30:18

The next morning Josh made sure Tess was on his work team. He told himself it was only because he wanted to catch up with her, and because Stu assured him she'd gained a lot of construction experience thanks to helping often with his rental properties. Josh knew his limits and would admit freely Tess was likely more adept at construction than he ever hoped to be. But in reality, he was keeping her close because he was hoping to sort out his strange and unexpected reaction to seeing her again.

"Hey, Jed! Do you want us to finish the baseboards in the rec room?" Tess stood in the doorway with her hands on her hips.

Josh couldn't help but smile at the way her messy hair fell in waves where it refused to stay in the bun on her head.

"I think you should play poker with me sometime, pastor," one of the kids muttered as he handed Josh a toolbox.

Josh glanced away from Tess toward Dylan, a high school wrestler who'd recently started attending the youth group.

"Why is that?" he asked.

Dylan chuckled. "Because I'd beat you." He leaned close to Josh conspiratorially. "If you want to win the lady, you might not want to make it so obvious that you like her—know what I mean? They like that mystery, hard-to-get stuff."

Josh fought the smile that desperately wanted to come out. "Really?" he asked.

Dylan shrugged. "Works for me. I can hardly keep 'em from calling." As if on-cue, the student pulled his phone from his pants and held it up. The display indicated a young woman named "Sarah" was calling.

"I'll keep this in mind, Dylan," Josh said. "In the meantime, go tell Dana her group can get started on painting the women's bathroom."

"Sure thing, boss." Dylan glanced over at Tess, who was still waiting for Josh's answer. "You two deserve each other." He shook his head and walked away as Tess came over.

"Meeting of the minds?" she asked, folding her arms.

Josh laughed. "Something like that," he said. "I need to grab another box of nails before we can deal with the baseboards."

Tess shrugged. "OK."

Stu came over. "You two gabbing all day or do you plan to work?" His smile said he didn't care about the answer.

Josh grabbed two boxes of nails and hammers, handing one of each to Tess. He leaned toward her with a smile. "Game night later. You in?"

Tess smiled. "Wouldn't miss a chance to gloat when I beat you."

Josh reminded himself he was surrounded by kids who were watching his every move or he might have kissed her right there on the spot. Instead he took a step back and smiled. "Good," he said. "I entered us in the three-legged race. Be ready."

"I will."

Josh winked and nodded for her to follow him. Even if he was forced to lie on the floor to work on baseboards all day, he didn't care. With Tess around, it would be fun.

~*~

Hours later Tess was tied to Josh and hobbling toward the finish line while students screamed all around them.

"You're like dead weight!" Josh complained. "We'll lose!"

Tess snorted, trying not to laugh. "Well maybe if you'd get in my rhythm instead of following your own we wouldn't be losing. Besides, what is with your long legs? You're dragging me, Jed."

"I can't help it!"

They finally stumbled over the finish line, second to last, and fell in a heap laughing as the kids cheered around them.

"You're the worst racer I've ever seen," one girl complained. Others laughed and shook their heads at their youth pastor and a woman they all seemed to be convinced was his secret girlfriend.

"OK, all of you go find Dana or Brian for the ice cream we promised earlier. They're in the kitchen,"

Josh muttered as he began untying his leg from Tess's.

She smiled at him and moved away as soon as she was free. "You really do stink at that game. Even I couldn't help you."

Josh snorted and gave her a playful shove. "Well at least we won charades."

"A minor victory," Tess said as Josh got to his feet and held out a hand to her. "Ice cream?"

She raised an eyebrow. "I get the idea you're trying to fatten me up. Ice cream two days in a row is more than I've eaten in months," she said.

"You could stand to add a few pounds," Stu said as he walked by.

Tess rolled her eyes. She pretended it was annoying but in reality, she was already sad that her time away from home would soon be at an end. Josh would merely be a fond memory.

"So, ice cream?" Josh asked again. He yanked her in the direction the kids were going.

Tess tried to pull away, but he held firm. "They already think something's going on," she whispered.

Josh glanced down at her with those silly dimples, one eyebrow raised. "Pastors are allowed to have lives. I'm only getting that now, Tornado. Come on."

And against her better judgment, or maybe because she hadn't met most of the kids or the adults who were helping—she went along, not letting go of Josh's hand until much later that night.

~*~

Like most times in Josh's life when things were at

their best, the week he spent with Tess went too quickly. Each day they drew closer as they found many things they shared in common, from their love for their motorcycles to Tess's newfound passion to learn all she could about the scriptures.

Most days they did so much talking and laughing that the youth group students started teasing them and doing 'hand checks' and asking when Josh would propose. Uncle Stu even took Josh aside and told him to slow down.

Despite standing several inches taller and broader over Tess's uncle, Josh didn't doubt the man would introduce him to a fist if he didn't behave, so he assured Stu that his intentions toward Tess were honorable. Stu gave Josh his blessing, ending with "You're getting the best. You better treat her that way, especially considering how long she's waited."

With only two days to go before Tess left, Josh decided they should spend as much time together as possible, so he could figure out if his newfound dreams were worth exploring.

"You forgot one."

Her voice startled him. Josh glanced up from his toolbox as Tess held a hammer in his direction. "I'm finished," she said as Josh took it from her. He placed it with the other hammers in the toolbox before closing the lid.

"Where are you headed now?"

Tess grinned. "Don't get too close or you'll figure out that I need to get to the shower."

"Yeah. Me, too." He rose to his full height. "Some of the leaders are taking groups to the movies or over to the beach for a bonfire, but we can go on our own if you'd like. Maybe take a ride? Get dinner? Maybe see a movie or go back to the beach?"

Tess grinned. "Are you asking me on a date, Jed?"

Josh swallowed hard and forced a smile.

What was he doing? It was one thing to playfully tease her all day long, and even wish he could date her, but it was another to act.

"I am," he said. "Will you go on a date with me, Theresa Carson?"

Tess kicked the toe of her work boot against a piece of wood, nudging it aside into the pile of scraps. "Why?" she asked suspiciously, avoiding his eyes.

Tess was not making this easy for him. "Why does a guy usually ask a girl on a date?" he asked, giving her a gentle nudge.

Tess reached up to release her hair from its ponytail only to fuss with it again until it was back in a messy bun on the top of her head.

Josh said a quick prayer she'd agree.

"I probably shouldn't," she said carefully. "Uncle Stu was asking me what was going on between us and the kids think…"

Josh laughed. "Those kids try to marry me off every day. Who cares? It's a free night and it's obvious you're dying to hang out with me." He gestured to himself as if he was a fantastic prize. "You always did like me, remember?"

Although Josh knew he was splattered with sawdust from his head to his toes, and he was wearing a dirty, sweat-stained work shirt, and a pair of tattered jean shorts, Tess squinted at him, one eyebrow raised. "All right, Jed. Gimme an hour to make myself pretty again."

Josh nodded.

Tess ran off toward the bunkhouse.

What was he doing?

~*~

After taking a shower, Tess was in the room brushing her hair when Morgan entered.

"I'm exhausted," she whined.

Tess smiled.

Morgan raised an eyebrow and made an "mmm-hmmm" noise as she set about putting her things away.

"Don't even," Tess said as she went back to her mirror.

"I didn't say a word...Mrs. Thorne."

Tess turned to her friend. She smiled, embarrassed. "I tried to say no..."

"What for? Goodness! I might smack you if you said no."

"But I shouldn't go," Tess's voice drifted off as she turned back to the mirror.

"Tess."

Tess went back to fussing with her hair before she answered. "Morgan."

Morgan started to dress. "You like Josh. The real Josh. The adult one, and he has no idea about any of what you went through. Don't you think you should trust him enough to level with him? He could be really supportive. There's nothing wrong with having more people around to love you."

Tess grunted. "You say it as if I overcame a disease." She stood and grabbed her purse. "I appreciate what you're trying to do but I want to forget it for a while. It will be waiting for me when I get home."

Morgan tugged her red hair into a tiny ponytail. "Josh is a good guy. You should trust him, especially if you really are interested. Besides, I've seen how he looks at you. I doubt the truth would change that—I mean, if you tell him now."

Tess's stomach fluttered as Morgan's words resonated deep inside her. It was sound advice whether she wanted to acknowledge it or not. She hugged her friend. "Pray for us? I'm sure we could both use it—no matter what happens."

~*~

A short time later, Tess picked at her dinner, wondering how she could tell Josh the truth about her life—or if she should. "So, what are we doing tomorrow?" she asked, in an effort to keep the conversation on a safe subject.

Not that it mattered. Tess was falling back in love with Josh as fast as if the twelve years that separated them had never passed at all. But this time it was the actual, real love that happened between adults—not the impetuous, idealized love of kids.

It didn't help that she could tell in his eyes and his actions that he seemed to feel the same. Already he was often holding her hand, sharing private jokes, and calling her 'Tornado'. It was no wonder his youth group students could see right through the charade.

"I'm thinking we could go do something fun tomorrow. After a long, hard day of painting, of course. What do you say?"

"I say you should stop asking me on dates when I came here to work." Tess paused. "But I do like painting. And having fun."

"Me too," he said, as his eyes lit up. "Oh! I forgot to tell you I talked to your dad this morning."

That one sentence made Tess lose any hope of control over the conversation. She and her father were once almost as close as she was now with Uncle Stu. But since her rocky life took over, she could only say that he still claimed her as his daughter—and barely that.

"Oh? What did he say?" The fear inside Tess remained silent since she'd come to Florida. But in that moment, it resurfaced, turning her insides around so quickly she wondered if she might lose her dinner right in front of Josh and the rest of the people in the restaurant. She couldn't tell him. She shouldn't tell him. But maybe now that decision was out of her hands. To Tess's surprise, Josh was smiling at her.

"Tess?" he said softly.

She swallowed. "Yeah?"

"I wanted to talk to Brody but all I knew was your parents' number so I talked to your dad instead."

Tess nodded, as Josh reached across the table and captured her hand in his. The warmth of his palm reassured her, and her mind quickly settled. "So, your dad was happy we're spending a lot of time together. He kept asking me if Stu was hanging around or leaving us alone. Any idea what that was about?"

Tess took a drink and tried to squelch her nerves as she shook her head.

Josh held her gaze for a moment and took his hand back to resume eating. "Anyway, he said you were doing a good job taking care of your grandma," he said.

Tess filled with pride at the indirect praise. Her father hadn't said anything positive to her in what seemed like years. Not that she deserved any accolades. But to get them now meant he'd noticed all of her hard work, and maybe she'd turned a corner in her relationship with her family. Tess set her fork down. "I have Brody's number," she said before switching gears. "Is this really what you wanted to talk to me about?" she asked. "My dad?"

Josh shook his head but he still seemed to be nervous.

Tess wondered if she should change the subject before he told her she'd need to get lost, so she didn't ruin his reputation. Surely her dad told him something. Any of her sins could be enough to make a pastor run away. With a sigh she lifted her fork and went back to eating. "I'd, um, keep an eye on Susannah. She's a little too interested in boys. It'll end badly if someone doesn't keep close tabs on her."

Confused, Josh smiled lopsidedly. "What?"

"Trust me."

Josh continued to smile, the dimple in his right cheek teasing her into smiling back at him, except this time it was against her will. She'd listened to the fifteen-year-old talk about boys, watched her dress inappropriately, and she'd asked all sorts of ridiculous questions over the last few days. Tess was certain she was right about what Susannah was up to since she'd once been there herself.

"Tornado...you just met her."

"Trust me."

Josh nodded, reluctantly. "All right." He wiped his

mouth and set his napkin on the table beside his plate. "This isn't exactly how I dreamed this conversation would go," he said. "Um, do you mind if we leave?"

Tess shrugged and set her napkin on the table. "I'm finished. It was very good. Thanks."

Josh nodded and glanced at the bill before he tossed some money on the table. He nodded toward the door as he stood. "Come on. I want to talk."

"We were talking," she said.

Josh leaned over and kissed the top of her head as a brother might. "I'd like to talk about something beyond work and families," he said as they got to his motorcycle. He handed her a helmet. "Don't worry. It will be painless."

Tess raised an eyebrow and silently slid the helmet over her hair, certain that Josh was clueless to the pain that awaited when they finally talked as they should have all along.

~*~

A short time later Josh slipped the motorcycle into a parking lot that was close to the beach. He stood and yanked his helmet off before extending his hand to help Tess.

She removed her helmet and handed it to him, her smile slipping as she stepped off the bike and stood next to him.

Josh reminded himself to stay focused on what he wanted to say despite the fact that she looked as nervous as he felt. He set their helmets on the motorcycle and reached for Tess's hand, astounded at how natural it was.

They walked together in silence.

As Josh opened his mouth to speak, his cell phone rang, disrupting his daydream. With a heavy sigh, he yanked the phone from his pocket and checked the screen. "Sorry..." he muttered. "I've got to take this."

Tess shrugged.

Josh pressed a button and held the phone to his ear. "Hey."

Tess walked ahead of him and sat to take off her shoes.

"Hello, Joshua. Any word on the job front?" His father's deep voice questioned.

Tess left her shoes on the sand and walked toward the water. She made a show of sprinting through the waves, the bottoms of her pants now completely soaked through as she tried to entertain him.

He smiled. Her carefree attitude was another reason he turned to mush when she was around. Josh waved her off with a laugh. "Nothing solid yet," he said. "But I'm thinking Pennsylvania might be an option."

"Really?"

Josh wasn't sure how he should say it, or even if it mattered. "Well, I was applying everywhere. But..."

As his father cleared his throat, Josh imagined he was already bored. The man never sat still. "But?" he asked.

"Well, you remember the church you served there?"

"Sure...are they in the mix?"

"I heard there was a position available. Maybe I can look into it," Josh said carefully.

"And you want my help."

Tess was staring out at the ocean, eyes closed, lips moving.

He felt breathless as he watched her pray. "The team is actually here now helping us rebuild the youth center and the more I'm around the people…"

"Hmm…finally. What's her name?"

Josh could hear his father smiling. His parents had been pestering him to find a wife for several years; they wanted more grandchildren and they feared that as a single pastor Josh would be chewed up and spit out of the ministry without a strong woman beside him. But Josh wasn't convinced. He understood what his mother went through in ministry with her husband. He didn't think he wanted to put his wife through that, but he also couldn't stop thinking about Tess since she'd arrived. To act as if it wasn't happening might be turning his back on God's will for his life. Josh cleared his throat, not bothering to deny it. "She's, uh, here now," he said. "Dad, you won't believe this…but do you remember the Carsons?"

The long pause on the other end of the phone told him his father was going through his memory carefully. Finally, he spoke. "You mean our old neighbors? Your friend Brody and…what was that little spitfire's name? The one who colored our driveway in chalk with your name all the time?"

Josh smiled at the memory of Tess's little hands and face covered with all colors of chalk as she tried to impress him. "Tess," he said.

"And there it is…" Paul said with a sigh. "Be careful you don't focus so much on her that you fail to address God's plan in this. It has only been a week."

"But what if she is God's plan for me?" Josh asked.

Now, Tess lay on the sand, her eyes closed, her

lips still moving. She'd done that several times already, as if she was talking right to God without a care of anyone else's presence.

She was so strong in her faith that it inspired him. Before his father could say anything, Josh said, "I gotta go, Dad. Please…check on it, OK?"

"I'll do what I can," he said. "Tell Tess we said hello."

"I'll do that." Josh hung up and went to Tess, who was still quiet and praying. He sat beside her, not disturbing her.

She finished her prayer and opened her eyes slowly, embarrassed. "Sorry," she said.

Josh shook his head, still feeling tongue-tied by her strong faith. "Please don't apologize," he said. "I love how close you are with God."

Still embarrassed, Tess pushed up. "I can't get through an hour without praying."

"Anything I can do?" Josh asked.

Tess shook her head, blushing. "I…need to check in a lot," she said. "You remember that verse…?" Tess rubbed her head as if trying to recall what she wanted to say. "I'm not very good with memorizing verses," she said apologetically. "It's the one about…not worrying, but praying instead."

"Philippians 4:6," Josh said. "Do not be anxious about anything, but in everything by prayer and supplication with thanksgiving let your requests be made known to God."

"That's why you're the pastor," she said with a chuckle.

Josh shrugged as he took her hand, delighted when she squeezed his fingers against her own. "Well, tell me if I can pray for you." Josh sounded calm despite his raging nerves.

"You can always pray for me," Tess said. "So, how's Papa Bear?"

"He said to tell you hello."

"He remembers me?" she asked, surprised.

"Sure. Asked if you were still covered in chalk."

The sun was beginning to set, but that didn't hide Tess's flushed face. She covered with a laugh. "I retired the chalk years ago."

Josh squeezed her hand as they stood and started walking. "This week has been amazing. It's been the first fun I've had in a long time."

Tess smiled, gently bumping her hip against his side. "Me too, Jed. You're not half as boring as I imagined."

He laughed. "And you're—" he paused. "—You're not anything like I thought you'd be."

"Hmm...twice as tall and only half as annoying?"

"I'm serious. I...I think there's more than friendship between us." He finally met her gaze with his own. "Please stop me if I'm making a complete fool of myself."

Tess visibly gulped, his words seeming to end the jokes. "What?"

"Don't tell me you...I mean...don't you think about...?" Josh stopped as fear set in. Now it was his turn to gulp. "I am making a fool of myself, aren't I?" Josh started to pull his hand away, but Tess held firm and shook her head.

"You aren't." She glanced away and said, almost too quietly for him to catch, "At least not for the reasons you think."

Josh wanted to be relieved but sensed it was too soon.

Tess stopped walking and drew her hand from his. She sat rigidly, gazing at the waves.

Josh was unsure what he was supposed to say or do. He sat and gently placed his arm around her shoulders, scooting closer when she shivered. "We can leave if you're cold," he said.

She shook her head.

Josh paused for a long moment as they sat quietly, each lost in thought. "So, um, what do we do?" Josh asked. "Is there any chance you could stay a little longer?"

Tess sighed. "Definitely no. I need to get back to work."

"And I can't leave either. So, what does that mean?" Josh asked.

"This was a bad idea." Tess looked up at him. "It's been amazing. I really needed this. Just working and being myself has been a nice change of pace."

Josh nodded as disappointment filled him. "Can we still talk? And maybe you could come back, or I could...come and spend time with you?" His nervousness was apparent, but he didn't care. "It would help us decide if there's anything between us."

Tess smiled and shook her head even as she leaned into him, her warmth making his arm tingle. "I...can't. I shouldn't." She turned so she could gently kiss his cheek. "It would only hurt you, Jed. I'm sorry."

The spot on his cheek burned where she'd kissed him, and Josh was as sorry as he'd ever been about anything.

~*~

49

Tess wanted to tell Josh the truth but something deep inside held her back. What purpose would it serve to ruin the fun they'd been having? She wished he could simply enjoy their time and not force something that could never be. But even as she separated herself from him and stood, it was clear the conversation wasn't over. It wasn't fair of her to drop him with no explanation when all signs during their time together pointed to a relationship beyond a mission trip or ministry.

Josh jumped up and followed her to the edge of the water. "Hey…" He took her arm and gently turned her, so she was focused on him. "Tell me what you mean."

Tess's shoulders dropped, and the air escaped her lungs. "I'm not…a good girl. I've…my family is ashamed of me. Justifiably ashamed. There aren't many people at home who trust me…even if I am working on that." She understood that it was time even as she prayed for deliverance from what she was about to do. "You can't get mixed up with me. Not right now, when no one trusts yet that I've changed. The timing is bad and…"

Josh continued studying her face as if the secrets were there for him to discover.

But Tess buried them deep inside her, pushing it all further down into her soul so nothing would be found by him or anyone else. Tess hated apologizing, but she couldn't stop herself. "I'm sorry," she said again, the words practically choking her.

"What are you apologizing for?" Josh asked gently. "I'm not asking you to marry me. I only want a chance to figure out what this thing is…" Josh put his hands on her shoulders and met her eyes. "Is your past in the past?"

Tess nodded firmly. "Yes." She could hardly believe it when Josh moved his large hand to cup her cheek.

"What are we talking about? You've already been forgiven." Josh stared at her, and all the love Tess had felt for him since the day they met was reflected now in his deep blue eyes.

"I really want to kiss you," he whispered. "But things are going so fast..."

Tess's stomach jumped. She wanted to kiss him too, but it would make things worse. She swallowed, not sure what to say, glad when Josh saved her the question by nervously running his fingers through his hair as he stepped away from her.

"I'm sorry. I shouldn't assume..."

"No..." Tess didn't want him to apologize for liking the woman she'd become after all the work she'd done to make it happen. "Don't be sorry," she whispered. "But, Josh...I'm not...a good girl, a church girl. I'm...tainted, I'm struggling to move past what I was and...a man like you..." She laughed. "A pastor. It's ridiculous..."

The concern slid from Josh's face, transforming into a lopsided smile. "You're not a church girl?" he stepped closer and took her hand, tugging her to walk with him as he continued. "You don't attend a church and you aren't here to help rebuild a youth center? You didn't admit to me five minutes ago that you were bad at memorizing scripture—which means you try to memorize scripture?" He chuckled. "Didn't you say you're always praying?"

Annoyed, Tess shook her head. "You know what I mean..." She turned from him slightly, frustrated that he didn't comprehend what she was talking about and yet he was willing to ignore her problems all together. "I've done things that…church girls don't do."

"I think that's a warped vision of what church is for, Tess," he said. "Isn't it for the sick, hurting, and lost? And aren't we all in that category, if we're really honest?"

Tess groaned, wishing she could shake him into understanding. "You're being difficult."

"So are you." Josh pulled his hand away, pretending to be angry with her.

"I'm not a good girl, Jed!" Tess wailed, throwing her hands into the air.

Again, Josh laughed, this time loudly. "You weren't ever a good girl, Tornado."

Tess was shocked he would be so blunt. "What?" she asked weakly as her heart slid down to her toes. Stu likely told him the truth, or worse, he'd lied and her father…

Josh's head tipped to the side as he looked down at her. "You were always grounded for something—breaking a window, being somewhere you weren't supposed to be, ruining my prom date…" He paused. "You live in the moment. That doesn't make you a bad person. If you've made some choices you aren't proud of, well, welcome to life. I make mistakes all the time." Josh brushed a piece of hair away from Tess's face before resting his hand on her shoulder. "But right now—what I've witnessed this week, tells me who you are. I'm not interested in digging up your sins unless you think we need to talk about them because they might impact the possibility of a future for us."

Tess met his gaze, her head still spinning at the ease with which he accepted her admission. Maybe she was being too hard on herself. Maybe she should drop it. Even if everyone else supposed she was on a one-way ride to hell. She shook her head, still wishing there was nothing to tell, nothing to admit. "Jed."

Josh smiled. "I'm not playing games. And there's no guarantee this will all amount to anything once we go back to our lives."

Tess could hardly think since Josh was still touching her. All the memories of her family laughing at her and how 'cute' her infatuation with him was still filling her mind. She wished they could see her now.

"Listen. I deliberately didn't get involved with anyone because I wasn't sure how a pastor is supposed to maintain a life outside of the church. I mean, if I mess up, everyone will find out, right? But with you being far away, we can talk, get acquainted again and find out if there's anything there to pursue. And if so, well, we'll figure that out later."

And of course, Tess maintained silently, there was the added benefit of Josh continuing to be kept in the dark about who she really was. Neither her family nor his, or his congregation, should be dragged into the muck of her life before it was time. And when it was...Tess shoved that notion aside. If this moment was all she ever spent with Josh, it would be enough. She smiled at him and nodded. "Let's see where it goes," she said. "One day at a time."

"Right. One day at a time."

~*~

Josh drove pensively, taking the long way back to

the bunkhouse so he could keep Tess with him longer. He wondered what her brother would say about all of this. Part of him was relieved Brody was in Pennsylvania and couldn't punch his lights out. Although, if he was being honest, he didn't care. He'd endure any pain thrown his way if it meant he got to be with Tess in the end.

Josh slowly steered the motorcycle into the parking lot near the bunkhouse. He stood, lifting his helmet off, only slightly worried that the long drive was giving Tess time to come up with another excuse to push him away.

She removed her helmet and stood, stepping off the bike and closer to him. "Well, pastor," she said, handing him her helmet. "I guess there's only one thing left to say."

Josh grinned, waiting. "Yeah? What's that?"

Tess raised an eyebrow. "I'd say you've been warned." She started walking toward the bunkhouse. "Thanks for dinner!" she tossed the comment over her shoulder as an afterthought as if she wasn't at all impressed by him.

"You're welcome...and I can handle it," he said loudly, causing her to turn and glance at him.

Her smile wavered. "You're sure?"

Josh walked closer to her and nodded. "Oh, I'm sure."

"Well, Jed, I guess it's game on."

He nudged her playfully. "So it is."

Tess nodded. "So, I'll catch you at breakfast."

Josh stuffed his hands into his pockets. "I'm counting on it."

Tess went inside.

Josh smiled, certain his last day with Tess would

be the best he'd ever had.

6

Hear instruction, and be wise, and refuse it not.
Proverbs 8:33

Josh woke early the next morning and jumped into the shower, his mind consumed by Tess and her response to him the previous evening. He'd been surprised that whatever she'd been through in the last few years appeared to be enough to make her hold back from getting too close to him. He was relieved he'd convinced her otherwise, though he was incredibly curious about the details. While he was sure it would come out eventually, he also believed that whatever the problem was made Tess unnecessarily upset. She had a past. So what?

None of it could be a real problem. Tess was a bit rambunctious growing up but people matured, and it appeared to Josh she'd done exactly that. Besides, the physical distance between them would be perfect for him to get her comfortable enough to tell him what was on her mind, without the distraction of physical intimacy and the drama of his church family or hers being involved.

As he brushed his shaggy hair and ran his fingers through it to make himself presentable, he wondered if he might try again to call Brody—not to tell him about the situation with Tess, but to find out if some of her reservations might naturally come out through the person she was closest to—besides Stu.

Josh sat heavily on his small couch and tried to pray, but something about the situation continued to nag him. Was he pushing forward too fast? It was only a long-distance relationship. Surely, he was doing the right thing since he'd have time and distance on his side. Before he could answer his own questions, the phone rang. Without opening his eyes he pressed it to his ear. "This is Pastor Thorne..." he said, leaning his head back against the wall. A faint chuckle caught his attention

The deep and familiar voice said, "That sounds like an oxymoron. Still can't believe the guy who filled my locker with shaving cream is a pastor. The church must really be in trouble."

Josh's eyes flew open and he grinned. "I think I'm talking to the moron," he said. "How's it going, Brody?"

"Are Stu and Tess behaving?"

Josh continued smiling as he remembered his good friend. It didn't matter that they'd not spoken in years. It was as if no time at all passed between them. Josh was quickly taken back to the makeshift softball field behind the Carson home where he, Brody, Tess, and even Josh's know-it-all sister, Caroline, spent many hours hitting and fielding balls.

"They've been quite a help actually. The workload is light today, so maybe we'll do something fun as thanks after all of the hard work."

Brody grunted. "Don't give Tess too much fun or you'll be stuck cleaning up the mess."

Something in Brody's voice caught Josh's attention but he wasn't sure how to ask what his friend meant.

Instead he laughed. "I'll keep that in mind. So, what's going on?"

"Well, my dad said he talked to you yesterday and he got the wild idea that you were interested in my troubled sister...and not just for her construction skills."

Josh's stomach fluttered. "What gave him that idea?"

"He said a father knows. So, are you interested in her?"

Josh swallowed, surprised, but not shocked by his friend's direct question. "I, um, guess I'm not really sure. She's nice and this week was fun, but it's a bit fast to..."

Brody interrupted his stammering. "You won't hurt me," he said. "There isn't an easy way to say it but she's been in a whole lot of trouble the last few years. I mean, she's getting better—the church thing seems legitimate, but it's a little soon to call it a complete transformation."

Josh let his words sink in. Trouble? Transformation? Although Tess was trying to tell him something the previous night, Josh didn't want to consider it. Maybe he'd been too quick to squelch her confession. Then again, he'd observed enough over the week to be sure that her actions revealed her as a caring, hard-working, and fun woman. "Hey, whatever she did is in the past. I believe that, and I think you should too," Josh said.

"Wait. You don't know?" Shock was apparent in Brody's response.

Josh wondered what that meant, and yet he'd always been one to take the easier road when possible. He was having fun, but their time together was too short. Hearing about Tess's past when she would soon be leaving and already showed her true spirit to him seemed an exercise in pain he didn't want to endure. Josh ran his fingers through his hair. "She tried to tell me, but I told her it didn't matter, and I believe that, Brody. The person she is now is amazing, fun, helpful, and growing in her faith. What more is there?" The long pause on the other end of the phone told Josh there might actually be something else to this quandary he was in. Regardless, he pressed on. "Don't worry. She isn't hiding anything," he said.

Brody snorted. "Watch yourself," he continued, sounding reluctant to go on. "She's not an innocent little girl anymore. I'd hate for you to get hurt."

"I appreciate that, but we're adults. We got this."

Brody paused again. "All right. So, when will you get back up here? We miss you. I mean, I don't but my parents go on and on…"

Josh laughed and settled back into the couch. "I'm committed here for a little while longer at least, but…" he paused for a long moment realizing his next words might mean a commitment he'd never considered making. "…I'm open to whatever God has for me after that."

"Well, whatever happens between you and that sister of mine, remember that we'd love to get you back home where I can kick your butt on the court or field anytime I want."

It was Josh's turn to snort with laughter. "I'll remember that," he said. "But I'm glad you already think Maple Ridge is the only place I've always thought of as my home. Man, it's good to talk to you."

"Same here."

The men talked for several more minutes before

Brody had to go.

Josh hung up and set his phone aside, bowing his head and praying for guidance. He prayed it wasn't too late to stop being blinded by his feelings and be completely open to the truth of whatever was going on with Tess Carson.

~*~

Tess sat across from Morgan, her plate loaded with a breakfast that smelled so wonderful her stomach was having its own conversation with the food.

"Hungry?" Morgan asked, amused. She bit into a muffin as Tess grinned and nodded.

"Starving. All this hard work every day has me eating too much," she said, glancing around. "Where's Uncle Stu?"

Morgan shrugged. "No idea." She smiled. "So...we didn't get to talk last night with the two eavesdroppers sitting there...what happened? How was your date?"

Tess laid awake for a long time after Josh dropped her off, unsure how much—if anything—she should tell anyone about what happened since she herself wasn't even clear on it. She shrugged. "We went for a ride."

Morgan raised an eyebrow as she set her coffee cup aside. "And? Did he kiss you? Come on, Tess. I can't live vicariously through you if you don't tell me anything."

Tess chuckled and shook her head. "Of course, he didn't kiss me," she whispered.

"Liar."

"He didn't. Said he had too much respect for me. He didn't want to resort to physical stuff when we hadn't even really talked. It was kind of strange." Tess paused as she took a bite and chewed thoughtfully. "I mean, to be treated like that—as if he actually cared about me—I don't think a man has ever been so sweet to me."

Uncle Stu arrived with a full plate and sat next to Morgan. He glanced between the two women and sighed dramatically. "Dare I ask what you two are up to?"

Tess smiled at her uncle, hoping she could fool him, realizing the chances were slim. When her own parents didn't see what she was up to or what kind of trouble she was in, Uncle Stu always put it together. "We're enjoying this delicious breakfast, Uncle Stu," she said, averting her eyes as she stirred her coffee.

Stu cleared his throat. "Where's your boyfriend?" He dug into his meal before Tess could respond.

Morgan giggled.

Tess flashed a warning with her eyes. "Where's your girlfriend?" Tess asked.

Stu swallowed and shook his head. "You can't meet her yet, Mouthy—and you never will if you keep that up."

Tess gawked.

Morgan giggled again. "I'll, um, leave you guys to it." She stood. "Tess, I'll catch you at the youth center."

Morgan was gone before Tess could even acknowledge her. "You're dating? When did that happen?" she asked, dropping her fork. How had she missed such a thing? Uncle Stu was barely past fifty years old and while he was handsome and successful, he'd never married, despite often having some woman or other calling him. He'd always said he wasn't interested in drama, so he didn't need a woman in his life. What changed?

"Eat your breakfast and tell me what's going on with the pastor," Stu said evasively. "The truth, please."

Stu continued eating. Clearly, he wasn't troubled about what was going on. Of course, after the things she'd already done, dating a pastor was the least of his worries.

"He talked to Brody and your dad." Stu paused long enough to take a drink of coffee. "I imagine your mom's already got the wedding plans started."

"What are you talking about?" Tess pushed her eggs around her plate before taking a sip of coffee, hoping it would calm her nerves. "Jed's my friend."

"Your dad said he's interested in something besides friendship. Said he could tell and he's miles away." He snorted. "Heck, I'm here and I can tell you he's on to something."

Tess was seething inside but doing her best to squelch the anger. "Why is it that my father doesn't call me to ask what's going on?"

Stu met Tess's gaze. "No one's upset. It's a great idea. The best one in a long time, honestly. I only wonder if you understand what you're in for—him being here and you being so far away."

Tess sighed heavily. "There isn't anything going on."

Stu grunted. "Right. The way you two stare at each other gives me heartburn."

Tess groaned. "Do you think I'd willingly let him try to attach himself to me with my past? He's a pastor!" Tess shook her head and went back to rearranging her food. "It wouldn't be fair...no matter how handsome, sweet, funny, or dimpled he is..." Tess took a drink of coffee.

Stu was grinning at her. He reached across the table and squeezed her hand. "One day at a time."

"You've said that before..." she muttered.

"Good morning!" Josh appeared, balancing a plate full of food along with a cup of coffee. "Mind if I join you guys?"

Stu grinned as he shook his head. "Not at all, Pastor. I was just telling Tess I wanted to check out the building before we got started. I saw something with the shingles that needed a second glance."

Josh looked worried as he sat across from Tess. "Nothing bad, I hope."

"Nope. I'll catch up with you two later." Stu left them.

Josh smiled. "I interrupted?"

Tess took a quick bite of food and chewed slowly to avoid answering. She swallowed as Josh started eating. "I should get over to the youth center too," she said.

"Hey."

Tess met Josh's eyes. He smiled, and she melted into her seat.

"It's all right," he said gently.

"Is it?"

Josh nodded reassuringly as Tess's pulse quickened. "I shouldn't still feel like I'm six-years-old around you," she muttered. "You're...you and I'm..."

Josh smiled. "You're just as you should be. A tornado," he said, leaning toward her confidentially. "Slow down. I'm just a guy with a crush."

Tess exhaled slowly. She needed to trust. As her reservations began to diminish, she took a bite of her breakfast.

Josh calmly changed the subject. "I'm not sure I've done a very good job pastoring the kids this week. I'll make up for it when you're gone." He took a drink of coffee. "We're showing a movie later and need to get some snacks. Think you'd be able to help me pull it together after lunch?"

"You're letting us go after lunch?" Tess asked, shocked. "But we're not even..." While they'd made significant progress over the week, Tess was sure they could get some painting done and at least get the carpet ordered.

Josh shook his head. "We got a lot done. We wanted to do something fun with you guys before you leave." He changed the subject again. "So, you didn't tell me that Brody's a full professor now."

"What? Oh. Right. He is." Tess sighed as she went back to pushing her food around her plate. "Sorry. We...don't talk like we used to. He's busier now."

"And you are too. He said you work all the time."

Tess glanced up, surprised. "I guess I do," she said with a smile. "Lots of loans."

"Yeah." Josh resumed eating. "You better eat. I don't want you fainting from hunger. I need to get the most out of my crew before you head home."

Tess's cheeks warmed as she smiled and shook her head. "I'm no wilting flower," she said. "I'll be fine."

"No doubt."

Tess thought for a bit. "Jed?"

"Hmmm?" Josh lifted his coffee cup and took a drink.

"Why aren't you already dating someone?"

The ever-present smile faded from his face, and Josh set his cup down. He leaned back in his chair, stretching his long legs under the table so that his feet brushed hers.

He shrugged. "I haven't dated in a long time. Didn't know anyone worth spending time with," he said. "Why?"

His answer was solid but almost too simple and perfect. "Don't get a big head or anything but you're a great guy with a good job. Maybe you're commitment phobic or secretly in the mafia...there has to be something wrong with you. And I'd like to know it up front before I get involved. I mean, you may not care what I've done, but I'm really not sure what you've been into over the last twelve years."

Josh laughed. "Well, you aren't lacking in the imagination department. The truth is, Tornado, I was engaged when I was in college. It didn't work out. I switched schools and went to the missionary field as soon as I graduated. After that, I guess things got even messier."

Tess relaxed enough that she managed to eat a little of her now-cold food. She nodded. "Messy, how?"

"Messy like I'm not sure how a pastor dates without hurting his whole congregation if it doesn't go to marriage...and then there's my parents who remind me constantly what my mother went through when they led a church. It might surprise you, but people can be really judgmental."

Tess bit her lip. That was one thing she understood too well. She ignored the second part of what he'd said, fearing it was too close to her own life, and went for the first part instead. "I would hope that your congregation would recognize that sometimes relationships aren't meant to be, and it's better to find that out before you get married instead of after when it's even harder."

"You'd think that," Josh said. "What about you? I wouldn't want you to get a big head either but you're a beautiful, intelligent, kind, and spontaneous woman who is in love with the Lord. Why aren't you involved with anyone?"

"We sound like a mutual admiration society," Tess said, as her insides churned. She set down her fork, hoping her face gave nothing away. The problem, of course, was that she'd had too many boyfriends to count—some she could barely even remember because they'd only been a passing distraction in her search for fun and love. She forced a smile. "I don't want to tie myself down. I wanted to get out and make my own way." She didn't elaborate and was relieved when Josh didn't ask her to.

He nodded and began collecting his things. "Want to go for a ride after the movie tonight?" he asked. "One more ice cream?" He reached across the table and squeezed her hand gently.

The familiarity of the gesture reminded her that she was wanted by someone who believed she was something she wasn't. The idea both pained her and gave her peace. She wasn't sure what to do with her warring emotions, so she squeezed his hand back. "I'd love to," she said as she downed the last of her coffee. "But only if I get to drive."

"I already let you drive," Josh said as he stood. "Besides, it's my bike."

"And you drive it like my grandma," she said, following him to the garbage can.

"I think Violet would give us both a run for our money…"

"Hey, Josh." Fred Sullivan stepped next to the garbage can where Josh and Tess were tossing their plates.

He was another pastor with Josh's church. "Keith's trying to find you. Something about the paint."

"Oh, right. Thanks, Fred." Josh smiled at Tess. "I'll see you over there?"

Tess nodded and headed for the door alone, hoping to sort her thoughts before that ride with Josh.

7

*Because you know that the testing of your faith produces
perseverance.*
James 1:3

"Your phone's ringing again," Morgan said a few hours later as the sun beat down on Tess's shoulders, reminding her that she would be sorry she forgot her sunscreen in her earlier rush to find Josh.

Tess sighed heavily and yanked the phone from her pocket, glad for a distraction. While she'd hoped it would be an easy day, that wasn't the case.

Some of the teens made a few mistakes when they were putting shingles on a portion of the roof.

Tess was now following Morgan as she yanked them off while Tess replaced them.

Uncle Stu came by every so often to be sure all was well. It was slow and tedious work.

Tess had been ignoring her ringing phone all morning.

Morgan grabbed her water. "Break time," she said with a smile.

Tess pressed the phone to her ear. "Yeah?" She plugged her other ear with a finger as she listened, trying to ignore the loud music and yelling from the teens and other workers.

"Theresa? It's your mother."

"Mom?" Tess sat to keep from falling over the

shock of her mother calling.

Morgan made a face that showed her worry as Tess rolled her eyes in an effort to deflect her friend's concern. And yet that didn't stop her own stomach from fluttering. Tess was never close with her mother, so if she was calling now it could only mean one thing.

"Your father mentioned he spoke to Josh Thorne the other day and that he was quite interested in you," Karen Carson said sternly. "What's going on?"

Tess sighed. "I'm on a roof, Mom. It's not really a good time."

"You're on a roof?" Karen squeaked. "Stu truly needs to get the notion out of his head that you're a boy."

Her mother would prefer her daughter to be getting a manicure rather than building a youth center. Yet another reason they weren't close.

"Did you need something?" she asked, hoping to end the call quickly.

"What? Well, no, I...wanted to remind you that I'm sure Josh is interested in a lady, not a buddy, but it appears I'm too late for that," Karen said. "Please tell me you're wearing a bra."

Tess groaned.

"Well it wouldn't be far-fetched, would it?" Unfortunately, the statement was true. Or it was a short time ago.

Tess rolled her eyes anyway.

"I'm completely naked and helping Morgan put the roof on while Josh watches. He's one of those free-love, 1960's kind of pastors," she said. "I gotta go. I got a splinter in my..." she hung up and stuffed the phone into her pocket.

Morgan had dissolved into a fit of giggles. "You're

terrible!"

"I'm terrible? My mother just asked if I was wearing a bra after I told her I was on a roof!" Tess shook her head as her phone rang again. With a heavy sigh she yanked it from her pocket and pressed it to her ear. "I'm wearing a bra, Mother, I promise."

"Ehem. Well." The distinctive voice of her boss, Ashley-Marie Hinton crossed the miles and practically pulled Tess's ear into the phone and stomped on it.

Tess made a face as her insides plummeted. She really should remember to check her caller ID when answering the phone. "Oh. Sorry."

"I certainly hope you are wearing a bra," Ashley-Marie continued. "I was wondering if I could put you on the schedule for a double shift next Saturday. I'm strapped."

"Um, sure. That's fine."

"Excellent. And please, in case this bra thing is a pattern, be sure to wear one to work. I don't want the residents or their families to get the wrong idea…or should I say the right idea, about you…"

"Thanks, Ash. I can always count on you for words of wisdom."

"Now, listen here. The only reason I gave you this job is because your uncle has been a real peach when it comes to making repairs for us—and we can't afford anyone else with his level of ability. But that does not mean that I am afraid of cutting you loose."

Tess made faces that sent Morgan into giggles again. When she was finished, Tess drew a deep breath. "I understand, Ashley-Marie. My apologies."

"Humph!" the phone was dead before Tess could even say good-bye. She hung up, turned it off and stuffed it back into her pocket.

"Why was our favorite boss calling you?"

"Overtime," Tess muttered. "She plays it as though she's doing me a favor when it's obvious that she loves having me around to torture." Tess took a long drink of water and smiled. "But of course, more time together means I can torture her too—and I'm much more creative."

Morgan laughed as they went back to work.

"Are you working up there or gabbing?" Josh asked, shielding his eyes as he looked up.

Tess rolled her eyes. "Lighten up or I'll make you cry like a little girl when I drive your motorcycle tonight."

Josh grimaced. "I never said you could drive it."

A few of the teens stopped working, chuckling as they listened in on another flirtatious conversation.

"Mmm...maybe not, but I never said I'd ask permission either." Tess adjusted her tool belt as she prepared to get back to work.

"Oh! She got you!" Denise squealed with laughter as the others joined in.

"Yeah, yeah, she got me all right," Josh muttered, shaking his head. He winked.

Tess sensed a warm flush crawling up her cheeks which made her grateful for sunburn.

"Watch yourself up there," Josh said, worry creasing his brow. "Oh, I was supposed to tell you guys we're wrapping it up in the next hour. Lunch at one—movies and pizza."

Tess went back to hammering. "Better be mushrooms on that pizza," she muttered.

"You're demanding. I'm second-guessing myself about you."

The kids were still listening.

Josh was still grinning, clearly smitten with her.

She shook her head and went back to work, glad they weren't in Maple Ridge since his acting skills needed work. "I warned you," Tess murmured.

Josh smiled, nearly blinding Tess with his white teeth and dimples. "And I told you I could handle it. Mushrooms it is, Tornado."

~*~

A few hours later Josh waited anxiously in the parking lot. That Tess was leaving weighed heavily on him. There wasn't time to develop anything between them and he wasn't sure a long-distance relationship was the answer. He might even consider accepting that she would be a pleasant memory if something more wasn't mean to be, but even that was too difficult to figure at this early point in their relationship.

When Morgan walked out of the bunkhouse alone, Josh smiled, hoping to appear casual.

"Tess is almost ready," she said. "I'm taking a walk over to the beach with some of your kids."

"Oh? Good." Josh nodded stupidly.

Morgan was sizing him up, deciding if he was worthy of her friend.

His respect grew for the short redhead. He didn't know Morgan well when they were younger. In fact, it struck him that he wasn't even sure she and Tess were friends in school. In his memory, Morgan was a rather serious, studious girl who'd kept to herself and her schoolwork. She wasn't the kind of girl Tess would have been friends with, though she'd always been ready with a smile and encouragement for the students who'd been picked on or abused. Was that what her relationship with Tess was about now?

"She could really use someone like you to believe in her," Morgan said gently. "I...don't think she's been here long enough to be sure if you're serious. So...are you serious?"

Josh shrugged and smiled. "Week-long serious? Or are you asking about life-long serious?" he asked before dismissing the words. "Either way, I don't know. Is she serious?" The conversation was making him think he should check a box about his intentions.

"She's figuring herself out—doing the teenaged thing a little late, I guess."

Josh nodded and drew a deep breath as he glanced at the door of the bunkhouse. "Is she...OK?" he asked gently.

Morgan smiled and nodded. "She's the most amazing person I've ever met. I'm not sure she believes it yet. The worst is behind her."

Again, Josh nodded, a sense of relief slowly settling over him.

Morgan gently touched his arm. "Whatever she tells you, she's doing her best to make it right now. She's changed. Completely."

The door to the bunkhouse opened and Tess stepped outside wearing a pair of jeans and a cute T-shirt. Her long hair flowed behind her in waves and it appeared she'd taken the time to put on make-up.

Josh's stomach fluttered. Morgan's giggle brought him back to reality.

"Go get her, Pastor," she whispered before smiling at Tess. "You two kids have fun."

Tess stopped in front of him, one hand on her hip

the other held out as if she expected him to give her something. Her grin was sassy.

He watched her stupidly, unsure what to say. "You look beautiful…" he stammered.

Tess sighed heavily and shook her head. "Give me the keys, grannie."

Josh shook his head with a huge smile. "No way." He handed her a helmet and straddled the bike, patting the seat behind him. "You're in for the ride of your life." Josh fought the desire to steal a glance at her and instead tugged his helmet on. He caught her heavy sigh as she sat behind him, placing her hands gently on his sides. "This better be good, Jed, or I swear I'm not giving you my phone number," she whispered.

He laughed. "Oh, it'll be good. It'll be really good. I may even get my own special ringtone."

"Mmm…cocky, aren't you?"

"You always said I was." Josh didn't wait for her response as he started the motorcycle and drove away.

~*~

An hour later, Josh pulled into a crowded parking lot and stepped off the bike. There was a freshly-written speeding ticket in his pocket and a huge smile on his face as he yanked his helmet off, tucked it under his arm and reached a free hand to help Tess off the bike. "Well?" he asked proudly. "Will I get your number now?"

Tess took her helmet off. She was smiling. "We'll see." She raised an eyebrow and assessed their surroundings. "What are we doing here?" she asked, taking in the numerous softball games going on around them.

"A lot of my kids play so I figured we might as well watch a while. Something fun to do."

Tess nodded as Josh took her helmet and placed it, along with his, on the motorcycle. A bit shyly, he reached for her hand and took it in his. "Shall we?" he asked.

~*~

Tess's hand tingled in the warmth of Josh's as they walked toward the games. He followed her up to a high place on the bleachers where they got comfortable.

"Sorry you got a speeding ticket," Tess said as the crowd cheered for a player who was rounding the bases after a homerun.

"I think the officer enjoyed it when I told him I was a youth pastor trying to impress a young lady," Josh said with a chuckle. "Think I converted him?"

Tess laughed. "He did say you'd see him at church on Sunday."

Josh laughed and pointed to the young man who'd scored. "He's one of ours. Doesn't come to youth group much but I'm working on him." He paused. Tess was trying not to watch the game. Too many memories. She turned her attention to Josh as he continued.

"I really wish you weren't leaving," he said sincerely.

"Me, too," Tess answered with a slight smile.

"Don't worry. I'll give you my phone number. If you can catch me between jobs we might even be able to talk sometimes."

"Good." Josh grinned. "Remember how we used to play catch for hours behind your parents' house?"

Tess nodded as he took her hand.

"You and Brody used to make me go after all the lost ones." She playfully nudged him. "And for some ridiculous reason I still followed you like a puppy."

Josh nudged her back. "Aww, you were cute...and we felt bad for you. We didn't think you could get any friends..." He laughed as Tess smacked him again. "And Stu told us he'd beat our backsides if we weren't nice to you. So..."

"Ha...ha...," Tess said wryly as she scooted away from him. "It goes to show what a dumb kid I was."

Josh slid closer. "I think you were the smartest of us all," he said.

"Please." Tess rolled her eyes. "So, Stu said we're leaving at six in the morning to get a good start on driving back. Maybe I better give you my number now in case you don't make it that early, princess."

Josh scoffed. "I'll make it. I might even kidnap you and make you stay longer."

Tess laughed, wishing that were an option. She reached into her pocket anyway and drew her phone out and handed it to him.

"OK. Give me yours and I'll give you mine. Just in case."

~*~

A short time later the game was winding down and the home team was way ahead.

Josh handed Tess the box of popcorn they'd been sharing and stood. He held out a hand to her. "Ready to go?"

"Sure." She accepted his help rising.

Josh loved that she kept holding his hand as they moved down the bleachers. "Can I ask you something?" he asked as they made their way back to the parking lot.

"I guess."

"What made you so sure you would marry me when you were little?"

Tess snorted. "I was a dumb kid," she said, though her reddened cheeks told a different story.

Josh squeezed her hand as she tossed the popcorn container into a nearby garbage can. They continued walking. "A dumb kid would take all of my hints to get lost, but you didn't." Josh was embarrassed to say it, but he pushed on. "I wasn't exactly nice to you — especially when you ruined prom."

They stopped walking when they reached the motorcycle.

Tess lifted her helmet and leaned against the bike. "It's different now," she said. "You want to call me and you're holding my hand. I'm not sure I can answer you."

Josh cleared his throat. "And, we're both adults." He shook his head. "It was a dumb question."

She kicked his shoe with her toe. "It was probably the dimples."

"Come on..." he said. "Really?" He raised an eyebrow but smiled widely to enhance her favorite feature.

Tess groaned as she looked away. "It's the weirdest thing. As if it was my mission in life. I can't quite put my finger on it. But, the more I was with you the more sure I was."

Although he wanted to drag her into his arms and kiss her like crazy, Josh reluctantly released her hand and lifted his helmet. "Big head," he said. "You better stop."

Tess playfully smacked him and continued talking. "I liked when you gave me a nickname."

Josh laughed as his phone rang. "You named yourself," he muttered. He yanked the phone from his pocket and regarded the screen, his smile slowly melting to confusion. He didn't recognize the number. Without glancing at Tess, he pressed the phone to his ear. "This is Josh."

"Pastor Josh? It's Susannah. I'm…I was on a date and I…" the teenager's voice was strained and she was crying. "He tried to make me do things. I got away though. I'm safe now," she took a deep breath, and obvious effort to calm herself. "It scared me so bad! Can you get me?"

"Take a breath, Susannah," Josh said. "Are you OK?" He paused. "Where are you?"

"I was afraid to call my mom. She's working late. I'm at the convenience store not far from the junior high. On the corner."

Josh nodded. "I can be there in fifteen minutes. Don't move." He hung up and stuffed the phone into his pocket. "We need to get Susannah."

Tess wordlessly yanked her helmet on as she threw her leg over the back of the motorcycle.

Josh started it and was off quickly, flying down the road.

8

We love because he first loved us.
1 John 4:19

Tess ran after Josh as he ditched his bike and hustled to a dark blue van where he yanked the passenger door open and nodded for her to jump in.

"Yeesh, Jed. You want another ticket?" she muttered as she dove into her seat.

He slammed the door, ran around to the other side, hopped in and shoved a key into the ignition.

His haste reminded her of the time he'd actually agreed to sneak out of his house with her and Brody, so they could go to their "secret" hideout. Their parents found them before they'd even lit the lantern in the tree house. "What did she say?" Tess asked as they sat at a red light.

Josh ran his fingers through his hair. "Said she went out with this guy and he..." Josh stole a glance at Tess and shook his head.

"Oh...is she all right?" Tess asked, praying immediately for the girl's safety.

He nodded. "I think so. She ran to a convenience store nearby and is waiting there."

"Good," Tess said. She reached over and squeezed Josh's arm. "I'm glad she called you. You must have a special relationship with the kids."

Josh slowed and turned into a parking lot. "I hope

so. I've told them a million times if they get into trouble, no matter what it is, I'll come for them. Some of their parents won't say that and the kids need someone who will be there for them regardless of the situation." Josh set the car in park.

Tess kissed his cheek, the emotion nearly overwhelming her. "You're a good man." Her voice was thick with tears she held back, so she hopped out of the car and went into the store. "Susannah!" Tess said with relief when she spotted the girl inside. She hugged her close. "Are you OK?"

Josh stood nearby silently, placing a hand on Susannah's shoulder.

"I'm sorry I called, but my mom was working late and she told me not to go out but I went anyway and he..." she glanced at Tess. "...underestimated me, I guess. I'm glad I took that self-defense class with my friends."

Tess hugged the girl again. "Come on. Josh wants to buy us a drink before we take you home."

"Thanks for coming," Susannah said to Josh.

He bought their drinks and gestured for her to follow him to a small table with benches outside. "You really put yourself in a dangerous situation," Josh said as he passed out their sodas. "You're very blessed that nothing worse happened."

"I know..." Susannah took a sip of her drink. She peeked sheepishly at Tess. "I guess you never did anything so stupid."

Tess laughed and tried to ignore that Josh was standing nearby. "Are you kidding? I've done too many stupid things to count. But, I realized that no man would respect me if I didn't respect myself enough to make better choices."

Susannah nodded silently and took another drink, a young girl ashamed.

Josh caught Tess's gaze and smiled before mouthing 'thank you'.

She nodded and put an arm around Susannah's shoulders. "Did he hurt you?" she asked gently. "We can take you to the hospital if…"

"No. He didn't get that far…" but even as the words escaped she began to cry with increasing intensity. Susannah was more frightened than she'd let on.

Tess took the girl's drink and handed it to Josh, so she could fold Susannah into her arms, quietly soothing her by stroking her hair. Tess understood exactly what she meant. She'd been there herself—ashamed, alone, embarrassed. "Listen," Tess said. "You should talk to your mom or Josh, OK? This won't go away overnight."

Susannah nodded as she wiped at her nose with a tissue Josh handed to her. "Can I call you?"

"You can call me anytime, day or night."

Susannah smiled tentatively before her face clouded over and another tear fell. "I probably deserved this. I wanted him to like me and I didn't want to be a…tease."

Tess took the girl's hands into her own. "I've been there. But you didn't do anything wrong. You said no."

Susannah sniffed. "I did. And I won't do this again. I promise."

Tess wiped the girl's cheeks. "Good girl. You did the right thing. You stopped it before it went too far, and you called for help. You're a smart girl, Susannah."

"How about we get you home?" Josh asked. "I

don't want your mom to worry when she figures out you're gone."

Susannah stood to give him a hug, surprising Tess by doing the same to her. "When you two get married, you better invite me," she said casually as she went to the trash and tossed the remainder of her drink.

Josh winked at Tess who laughed.

"You'll be the first to know," Josh promised as he took Tess's hand and walked toward the car.

~*~

A short time later, Josh left Susannah with her grateful mother. To say the young girl would be grounded for a long time was probably an understatement. But that wasn't Josh's worry. He smiled at Tess as he held the door for her, closing it when she was safely seated inside.

"I get why you brought the motorcycle out first," Tess said as Josh got into the van and slammed his door closed.

He grinned as he started the vehicle and backed out of the driveway. His minivan was probably the nastiest vehicle he could find but it served a number of purposes—one, he could haul a lot of kids in it, and two it was ugly, so it was super-cheap—a definite plus for a poor pastor. "I wanted this thing so I could pick up more women," he said as he drove down the road toward the church and bunkhouse. It got late quickly, and he was concerned with what everyone would think when he brought Tess back.

"Maybe soccer moms and grandmas," Tess said.

Josh laughed. "Not you?"

Tess groaned. "Your dimples will only take you so far."

"Yeah—but the bike and cherry ice cream will get me the rest of the way." Josh smiled and nudged her arm. "I'm impressed with how you handled things back there. Ever think about youth ministry?"

Tess snorted and shook her head as her cell phone rang. "No..." she pulled her phone from her pocket and glanced at the number. She held up a finger to signal she needed to answer. "Hello?"

Josh drove silently as he tried to avoid listening in.

"Hey...what's up?" she listened for several long moments, her face pinched as if the conversation hurt. "No, but...I will. Sure. Right. Bye." She hung up the phone and stuffed it back into her pocket. "I'm not sure why I bother to turn that thing on."

Josh stopped at a red light and glanced at her. "I think the same thing all the time. But at least when you get home I'll be calling so it won't always be bad." Josh turned the van into the parking lot and pulled into a space before he glanced at Tess again.

"So...that was Brody," she said with a sigh. "He's...concerned that I'm corrupting you or something. So...sorry." She shrugged as she opened the van door. "Thanks for tonight."

Confused, Josh grabbed her arm. "What?" he asked. Tess smiled, but Josh refused to release her. "Close the door, Tess. We should probably talk about this or I won't sleep."

Reluctantly, Tess closed the door and waited.

Josh did his best to meet her eyes though she appeared to be intent on fussing with something that was on her lap. "Maybe you should tell me what happened," he said.

"No." The statement was simple, final. Tess sat, hands folded primly, waiting.

"But if we..." he cleared his throat. "Do whatever it is we're doing here—talk, get acquainted, it may eventually come out with our families and I'd need to...I mean...hear about it before that, don't you think?"

Tess sighed heavily, appearing resigned to her fate. "What do you want me to tell you first? The promiscuity, the drinking, the smoking, or maybe the jail time? No, I can start gently with the piercings. Oh, wait, working at the 'gentlemen's' club. Let's get that out of the way. That was priceless. The list is endless, Jed." Tess looked resigned, as if she was telling someone else's story.

Josh hoped his face masked the shock inside him. He gulped. "That's not funny."

Tess raised one eyebrow. "My family didn't think so either. They all bailed me out at one time or another until the only one left who was willing to do it was Stu. I think even he wondered whether it was worth the effort." Her gaze met his.

Josh understood that she feared he would pull away from her, disregard her as everyone else in her life had done outside of Stu and Morgan. He reached over and took her hand.

Tess tried to pull her hand away, but Josh held firm and refused to let her go. "Tell me."

She sighed, her hand limp in his. She'd already given up.

Josh blinked, fighting a wave of nausea as he waited for her to explain.

Tess drew a deep breath and began. "I've only

been great at a small number of things in my life, Jed. I mean where I didn't mess it up by being difficult, usually on purpose." She sighed. "Softball was my thing. Scouts came from everywhere for me, the town loved me. No one went to girls' softball games before I came along." She didn't say it to brag—it was a fact Josh remembered well—even when she was barely a freshman in high school she'd been amazing—striking out everyone who stepped into the batter's box.

Tess fiddled with the hem of her shirt before continuing. "Well when I was in college I got cocky, trusted the hype," she paused, drawing a deep breath. "I blew it. Hurt my shoulder bad. Three surgeries and tons of physical therapy went by. I lost my scholarship because I didn't really care about my major, so I got kicked out of school because without softball, what was the point? I ended up back at home with all the other losers who couldn't hack it...and it wasn't long before I became one of them."

Josh was shocked and sympathetic to what she'd gone through. When he remembered Tess as a child, it was usually an image of her pigtails and softball glove that came to his mind. Softball was her life and she'd always played hard. Of course, she'd also been told repeatedly that she was the best. It crossed his mind that perhaps there wasn't anyone to keep her humble until it was too late. "So, what happened?" he asked gently.

"When I was recovering from my last surgery, I was lost. Brody was finishing grad school and he was so focused on Stell I could barely get him to talk to me. Dad and Uncle Stu were off working on a big development in Ohio, so they were never home, and my mom?" She laughed wryly. "We were never close. I was alone. It didn't exactly help me make better choices." She paused, her eyes on her hands. Her face became a mask. Gone was the sweet, fun, full-of-life Tess. She'd been replaced by someone who was removed from her life, ashamed of what she'd been and unable to accept what she'd become.

"So that's what made Brody think he should warn me about you?"

Tess shrugged. "I made embarrassing my family an Olympic event. If you can imagine it, I probably did it."

Josh's stomach clenched. "I don't need details," he said.

"I told you I wasn't a...good girl."

Josh reached over and turned her face so she met his eyes. "And I told you that I see who you are, Tornado. I don't care about the past. In fact, I'm kind of done talking about it."

Tess's eyebrows lifted in shock. "Um, OK."

"Stu thinks you're the most amazing niece on the planet. He's a good judge of character." He smiled. "Your family will catch up. So will everyone else." With a shrug he kissed her hand. "I'm not worried. And I won't change my mind. So, I guess you and Brody can both stop trying to tell me I'm wrong."

Tess's face revealed she wasn't convinced. "Oh. Right. OK," she said reluctantly. She reached for the door, but Josh shook his head.

"Not yet." He released her hand, got out of the van, and ran to the other side to open her door for her.

Again, Tess appeared to be surprised as she swung her legs out and stepped in front of him. "You don't need to do that," she said. "It's only me."

Josh nodded as he leaned against the door. "I will

continue to do that because it is you." He leaned down to kiss her gently. "And I'm glad you trusted me," he said.

Tess nodded and stepped toward the bunkhouse door. "Good night, Jed," she said softly.

"Catch you tomorrow, Tornado."

Tess nodded and went inside.

Josh got in his van, still thinking of all she'd said and wondering if he was making a mistake.

~*~

Tess didn't sleep all night. Even if her past was behind her, she'd moved on and even went on some dates, all of which were disasters since the men she chose remained the same. When Josh held back from kissing her, or opened doors for her, Tess was reminded that he was the kind of man every woman wanted, but not someone she deserved.

"Knock it off," Morgan whispered when Tess tossed to her other side for the millionth time.

Her phone told her it was nearly three o'clock in the morning and they'd be getting up soon enough anyway. "Sorry," she whispered back as her phone vibrated with a text. She opened it and smiled as she read the words.

I think my ringtone should be something like 'bad to the bone' or 'born to be wild'.

With a deep and intense yawn, she text back: *And what will my ringtone be?*

Immediately a text came back. *What are you still doing up?*

She smiled. *I'm waiting...*

Moments later his text came: *Your ringtone is either 'blowin' in the wind' or 'don't get me wrong'- now go to bed.*

Tess bit her lip to muffle her giggle. She quickly text back. *You too—you thorn in my...*

Hey! ;(

Good night.

Night.

Tess smiled as she tucked her phone under her pillow and again tried to fall asleep, certain it would be a long two and a half hours until she needed to get up.

9

A man's heart deviseth his way:
but the Lord directeth his steps.
Proverbs 16:9

"So, what were you giggling about at three in the morning?" Morgan asked as she and Tess dragged their bags toward the bus the next day. The plan was to pack the bus before eating breakfast and visiting with the staff and pastors until it was time for the ministry team to head home.

Tess tried not to smile as she tossed her larger bag into the bus's cargo hold and handed her smaller one to Stu as he walked by.

He pretended it was too heavy for him as he got on the bus to reserve their seats.

She grinned and turned back to her friend. "Jed was texting me," she said. "I hope I didn't keep you up."

"No." Morgan smiled. "Maybe you ought to stay here and date him. Heaven knows going back to work is enough to make me want to stay."

Tess snorted. "I can't. This was fun but once reality sets in tomorrow for both of us, it will be nothing but a great memory."

Morgan shook her head sympathetically. "Tess."

"It's all right," she said. "Let's get some breakfast."

Reluctantly, Morgan followed Tess into the dining hall and they got in line.

"Mind if I cut?" a deep voice asked.

Tess glanced up at Josh. His blond hair flopped over his eye as he smiled, dimples popping deeply in his cheeks.

She gestured for him to step in line wishing her face didn't go warm every time she was around him.

"You're surprisingly awake," he said with a nudge. "Considering how late you were bugging me."

"I was about to say the same thing."

Josh took a muffin followed by scrambled eggs. He grinned mischievously as he continued to load his plate. "I set your ring tone."

Tess raised an eyebrow. "Do tell."

Morgan gave a fake gag. "I'm going to go...over there," she muttered and headed off to a table where Stu was already seated.

"You first," Josh said as he handed her a cup of coffee.

Tess set the coffee aside and yanked her phone from her pocket, quickly pressing Jed's name.

His phone immediately began to buzz in his pocket and he laughed, shaking his head. "It's on vibrate, Tornado." He continued laughing as she ended the call.

"Come on, Jed!"

"OK..." he sighed and pressed a few buttons, and an obscure song about a tornado began to play.

Tess shook her head, disappointed. "That's the best you could do?" she asked. "You're an amateur." She nodded toward his phone. "Call me."

Josh cleared his throat and pressed the buttons on his phone until Tess's began to ring with the theme song from an old television show about hillbillies moving to the big city. As the words from the popular television show rang out, Josh began laughing until tears were running down his cheeks.

Tess smiled with victory and shoved the phone back into her pocket. She started toward the table, Josh close behind.

"I concur with your judgment, Tess. I believe I am, in fact, an amateur. I'll keep working on it."

"Next time better be good." Tess set her things down.

He leaned down and whispered in her ear. "Maybe I should change yours to 'It Had to be You'."

Tess stopped cold and looked up.

Josh winked and started whistling as he set his things down and gestured for her to sit.

Stu didn't notice Tess's blushing face as he shoveled his breakfast down. "Didn't you sleep?" he asked, glancing at her as she sat. "I guess we'll be listening to you snore all the way home."

"I'll lay my head right on your shoulder, so you can get the full experience, Uncle Stu," she said with a smile.

He groaned and gestured to Josh with his fork. "You sure you're interested in her? She's pretty mouthy."

Josh smiled and nudged Tess gently. "It's one of the many things I like about her."

Tess focused on her food to avoid the conversation.

Stu raised an eyebrow. "You two deserve each other," he muttered.

Morgan smiled at Tess, and Tess was grateful her friend realized her need for a change of subject.

"So, Tess...will you start teaching that exercise class when we get home?" she asked.

Tess nodded and smiled. "Yeah. Grandma Vi and her friends are really excited about it. I was thinking of asking if it would be OK for me to go into the memory care side with it as well, maybe in a few weeks."

"That's a great idea. I was reading a study about that the other day, about how movement and music can affect memory." Morgan sipped her juice.

"I read that too." Tess stole a muffin from Josh's plate which she broke in half and ate, returning the rest to him without a glance his way.

He sighed heavily before switching their plates and finishing off her eggs.

"Come on," she mumbled. "It was like half of a muffin."

"It was the half I wanted."

Tess ate the other half of the muffin.

"Should I ask if one of the pastors wants to do the ceremony before we leave?" Stu asked as he finished clearing his plate.

Tess chuckled.

Josh's cheeks went pink and shook his head.

"The six-year-old me would be thrilled," Tess said. "But the twenty-six-year-old me has yet to be convinced. So, you're safe for now, Jed."

Josh took a drink of coffee, winking at Tess as he did.

She smiled in return. Since she was leaving, it was easier to flirt with him and be herself. If they were back home, Tess was certain she would be hiding in her apartment and staying as far away from Josh as she could to preserve his reputation—as Brody wanted her to do. Tess took a drink of coffee and stood. "How much time before we go?"

Stu glanced at his phone. "I'd say about twenty

minutes or so."

She nodded and cleared her place. "OK. I'm going to find out if Susannah stopped by."

Josh stood too as he collected his plate and cup. "I'll come with you."

Stu nodded and waved them off. He tossed a grin in Morgan's direction. "I predict that before this year is out those two will be walking down the aisle."

Morgan's jaw dropped. "A year? But, how…?"

Stu shrugged. "God has a way of working these things out, and from what I can tell, He definitely wants them together."

Tess pretended not to hear, but her heart did a funny little flutter.

~*~

Josh followed Tess outside to a nearby picnic table. She sat on the bench as he leaned against the top of the table. He towered over her as he scanned the parking lot where the busses waited. "Susannah texted me sometime late last night that she couldn't make it. Still grounded," he said. "But I gave her your number. I didn't think you'd mind."

Tess squinted up at him. "I don't mind, but why did we come out here?"

Josh nudged her with a shy smile. "So, we could get a few minutes alone before you leave, dummy."

"Oh." She met his gaze. "This week's been fun. I'm glad we got to reconnect."

"Me, too." He heaved a sigh as he sat beside her. "I wish you weren't leaving yet."

"Me, too."

"So, um, I'll call you..." he began with a chuckle. "This feels like summer camp."

Tess chuckled. "I'll send you muffins, Jed. The blueberry ones you love."

"Don't you dare tease," he said sternly.

Tess pressed her hand to her chest. "I would never tease about blueberry muffins."

"Ten minutes!" someone yelled. "Busses leave in ten minutes!"

Josh smiled and stood. "Come on. I want to show you something." He nodded toward his church.

"But we're leaving in ten minutes," Tess began.

"Oh, please...as if you ever worried about being late." He gestured for her to follow him. "Come on!"

Tess jumped to her feet and sprinted toward the church. "Race ya!"

"Why, you...!" Josh ran after her and made it to the door before her. He leaned against it as she nearly crashed into him, laughing. He caught and steadied her with one hand as he opened the door with the other.

"So...what is it?" Tess asked as she followed him down the hallway toward his office.

He opened the door and stepped inside.

Tess was right behind him.

"I didn't want you to go without saying that...I've been praying and I trust that God is doing something amazing in your life and that He has great plans for you, even if I'm not completely sure yet if that includes me." He smiled softly. "But I hope it does." He obviously meant every word of it.

Tess smiled, her heart full. "Thank you," she whispered. "That means a lot."

Josh blushed and nodded. "And I wanted to pray...together, I mean, if you don't mind."

"I don't. I'd like that."

They sat together on the couch at the far end of his office. Josh clasped her hand in his and closed his eyes as she did the same.

"Dear Lord," he began. "I thank You for the amazing gift You've given us this week—a week full of friendship and maybe...something more. In Your name, Father, I ask that You guide our steps as we get to know one another better. Be with Tess and the rest of the team as they travel home, but especially....dear Lord, I pray that You help Tess to see and accept that she has been forgiven and is now a new creation with a future You laid out for her. Help me to be an encouragement and a blessing to her. In Your holy name, I pray. Amen."

"Amen." Tess slowly lifted her lids and met Josh's gaze.

He cleared his throat and stood, pulling her with him.

Tess was bursting with what she was certain was Josh's love for her. Uncle Stu was the only man who'd ever prayed with her. No man or boyfriend ever bothered to think highly enough of her to even consider doing so. Josh was special, and she silently thanked God for bringing him back into her life, even if it was only for a short time.

"Here," Josh said as he opened his office door, holding out an envelope. "My team was taking pictures the whole time and they got a few of us together. I thought you might want them." He smiled sheepishly. "I kept a few for myself too."

Tess smiled as she accepted the envelope.

"Thanks." With her other hand she reached up and squeezed Josh's arm. "Thank you for believing in me."

Josh seemed surprised but nodded as he stepped closer to the door. "We'd better say good-bye now. I wouldn't want anyone to get the wrong idea."

Tess nodded and reached up to hug Josh. If ever she'd wanted to avoid her life it was that moment. Going home might be the worst punishment she'd faced so far, and yet she was certain Uncle Stu would not leave her in Florida when she still needed to make amends for all her wrongs.

Josh held Tess tight for several moments before finally kissing the top of her head. "I'll miss you," he whispered.

"Me, too," Tess said as she took a step back from him.

Josh kept his hands on her arms and slowly leaned down to kiss her. "Come on," he said reluctantly as he took her hand. "We better go before I beg you to stay."

Tess smiled and squeezed his hand. "I might even be tempted to say yes."

Josh tugged her toward the door with sadness in his eyes showing that he didn't want to.

They walked silently until they got to the doors of the church where Josh squeezed her hand one last time and gave her another kiss on the head. He pushed the door open and they stepped through.

She looked up, hoping he didn't notice the tears forming in her eyes. "Bye, Jed."

He nodded as they walked toward the busses, saying nothing the entire way.

Tess stepped up onto the bus and smiled through her tears at Josh, giving him a small, final wave.

He nodded.

Their time together was over.

10

I can do all things through him who strengthens me.
Philippians 4:13

Tess trudged to the back of the bus, stepped over Stu's legs silently and flopped down next to him as traitorous tears flowed down her cheeks. She hastily wiped at them in annoyance. She hadn't felt this horrible since she'd been devastated by losing softball to an injury that was her own fault.

"Hey." Stu leaned close to her and wrapped his arm around her.

She turned her head into his shoulder, so no one would catch her crying.

Stu nudged her gently. "Come on. Sit up and give him one last smile."

Tess sniffed and sat up, glad her red face would be masked by the slight tint of the windows.

Josh was staring directly at her window and he smiled though it appeared he was in the same sad shape as she was.

Tess smiled back and placed her hand on the window.

Josh glanced around and, since no one was paying him any attention, he reached up and touched her hand through the glass briefly before pulling his cell phone out and pressing a button.

Her phone rang. Tess grabbed for it and pressed

the button.

Stu chuckled and shook his head.

"Hello?"

"Open the window."

He gestured to her, still glancing around to make sure no one was watching.

She hung up and stuffed the phone back into her pocket before putting the window down. "Miss me already?"

"We'll be OK." Josh said with a forced smile. He gulped. "There's a reason for all this—and I'll visit. Maybe soon."

Tess nodded, wanting to believe him, even if his intention to visit Pennsylvania made her feel nauseated. "Ride that bike like you mean it, OK?"

"As long as you promise to do the same." Josh offered her another dimpled smile and reached his hand out to take her fingers from where they rested on the window. He lifted her hand and squeezed it, his gaze fusing with hers. "Good-bye, Tornado." His voice cracked on her nickname.

Tess nodded and tried to memorize the way their hands felt joined together. Reluctantly she squeezed his fingers one last time. "Bye, Jed." She put up the window and waved again as the bus pulled away.

Stu placed a comforting arm around her shoulders. "He won't let you down."

Tess closed her eyes and relished the expression on Josh's face as the bus pulled away. He wanted her to stay. Her. The girl who was hated by an entire town. A man of God was falling in love with her. It was almost too much. Tess was suddenly so overwhelmed that she started chuckling.

Stu nudged her closer with the arm that was still

around her shoulders. "Are you OK?"

Tess opened her eyes and shoved his arm away as she continued laughing. "It's hysterical," she said. "I can't believe you weren't laughing this whole time."

Stu's eyebrows knit together in concern. "Maybe you should take a drink of water," he said, reaching for the bottle beside him. "You got too much sun yesterday and…"

Tess shook her head and pushed the water bottle away, as she continued smiling. "No! How can you not find the humor in a man like Josh…a pastor, for heaven's sake, finding someone like me…an ex-con…"

"You are not an ex-con," Stu said impatiently.

"I might as well be." Tess calmed down and rolled her eyes at her uncle. "Seriously—you don't think this is kind of funny?"

"I don't think it's funny at all." Stu held out the water bottle to her.

She reluctantly took a drink.

"And I think you're ducking your feelings so you can avoid dealing with them. They'll catch up with you eventually."

Tess sighed heavily and shifted in her seat. "Yeah, well none of it matters because even if he calls me a few times and we text, it won't matter. I mean, his intentions are fine, but it won't be long until he realizes I'm…not cut out to be a pastor's wife." Tess leaned back in her seat and closed her eyes.

"Tess."

"I don't deserve him." Tess yawned as the disappointment filled her. As much as she wanted to believe it didn't matter, her words were true. She shouldn't be with Josh. She'd assumed that he was taking a sincere interest in her. She'd hoped that her life would dramatically change because of their reunion, and more because Josh believed in her so deeply and transparently. But it wouldn't happen. Some dreams were simply too outrageous to entertain.

Tess's phone buzzed with a text message. She yanked it from her pocket and hit the button.

What'd you think of the pics?

Tess pulled the envelope from her back pocket and opened it. A picture of Tess and Josh laughing together during a game they were playing with the youth group kids was on top of the stack. Immediately Tess smiled. They were sitting side by side at the front of the church in the next picture, dressed for a service where Josh blew Tess away with his sermon about the need for continued growth in Christ. Another picture showed them working hard and again laughing together as they pounded nails. She flipped through the rest of the stack and realized that forgetting Josh or pushing him back into the recesses of her mind would no longer be possible. She was in love with him.

And this time there was no growing out of it.

~*~

Josh walked back to his office, wondering how long he should wait before he called Tess. She wouldn't be home until the next day, so he should probably stick to texting if he tried to communicate with her at all.

Maybe he was idealizing her. She'd said there were serious problems and even Brody tried to warn him, so it was possible Josh was pushing ahead too fast, something that was very much against his typically cautious nature. But he couldn't stop himself—it was as if the situation was beyond his control. And yet even as he considered it, he couldn't help but wonder when or if he'd be able to take a vacation, so he could visit her. His phone rang, and he smiled to himself hoping it was Tess.

"Hello?"

"Surprised I caught you so early." His father's voice reached through the line and brought Josh back to the moment.

"What? Oh, um the Maple Ridge team left a little while ago."

"So, you were saying good-bye to Tess."

Josh grimaced. "Yeah, something like that."

"Well, it's good I caught you. I spoke to Harrison Flynn, who said the board met and was beginning a preliminary search for a new pastor. John Williamson is retiring shortly. Because of my relationship with the church they were happy to put your resume at the top of the stack, as soon as they receive it that is."

Josh smiled, shocked at this sudden sign. "Wow. Thanks, Dad. I'll be sure to do that."

"Your mother and I are concerned about how fast this is happening. We always liked the Carson family, but you remember what it was like when we left missionary work for a full-time church ministry."

"How could I forget?"

It was the time of his life, settled in one place for seven years when all he'd experienced to that point was the transient, often unstable life of a missionary. He and Caroline loved those seven years. Unfortunately, it was painful for his parents, especially his mother, who found out quickly that shepherding a congregation was nothing like ministering to a village in Africa. As soon as Caroline and Josh were off to college, the Thornes went happily back to the mission field.

"We don't regret staying as long as we did, and of course being settled in one place did have its good points but..."

"But...?"

"But your mother wanted to remind you that any pastor's wife should be aware of what she's in for before she signs up for that job. Keep that in mind as you move ahead. Even if Tess is above reproach someone will find something to criticize, and she'll need to be very self-assured so as to not be overcome with loneliness and doubt."

Josh ran his fingers through his hair. If there was one thing Tess possessed, it was the ability to move past peoples' opinions—or at least the confidence to work through it. Still, he wasn't yet convinced he was supposed to marry her. They'd only reconnected a week ago. That wasn't nearly long enough to even think about marriage.

But then again if people really were being as rough on her as she'd said, maybe moving ahead with the relationship wasn't a great idea.

Josh sighed heavily. It was easier to be delusional when she was in front of him, smiling while her big brown eyes sparkled. Now that she was gone, reality was hitting him like the tornado he accused her of being.

Irony.

"This is an amazing pep-talk, Dad."

Paul laughed. "Sorry."

"And she went home."

"Your mother and I were long distance for nearly two years."

Josh groaned.

"What? Honestly, Joshua, we've been hoping for this for a long time. You can recognize that the answer to prayers often comes in ways for which we are not prepared." Paul paused. "Keep us posted?"

"I'll do that. Thanks again." Josh hung up and opened his own envelope of pictures as his cell phone buzzed with a text. *You're so vain; you probably think this text is about you. Nice pics.*

Josh laughed and set his phone aside. Now that Tess was gone the loneliness was already beginning to consume him.

~*~

It was nearly five o'clock in the morning before Tess got into her bed at Uncle Stu's house. She didn't want to go home to the nearly-empty apartment she'd moved into only a few weeks earlier. She still spent most of her time at Stu's place anyway. And regardless of his occasional nudge toward her own home with promises of a television or a new couch, Tess preferred to stay close to her uncle and his constant positivity and encouragement. Now she wondered if he was, in fact, hiding a girlfriend and so honestly wanted to be rid of his niece. In a nice way, of course.

At the moment Tess was too tired to think about it. And she needed to go to work in a few hours, which wasn't a pleasant idea either. As she tossed off her shoes and pants and fell into bed, Tess noticed her cell phone vibrating on the nightstand. Jed. She grabbed it before it woke Stu who was already snoring in the next room. "Hey," she whispered.

"You home safe?" The sound of Josh's deep voice warmed her.

"Sort of. I'm crashing at Stu's. I was too tired to go home."

"Well, I'm glad you made it," he said.

"Go to bed, J." Tess stretched out on her bed and yawned. "You won't be any good for your kids if you're up all night talking to me."

"Yeah, yeah. I wanted to make sure you were safe."

"I'm safe," Tess said, trying not to smile. "Are you?"

"My neighborhood's questionable, but I think I can handle it."

"Glad to hear it."

"When is a good time to call again?"

"How about not at five in the morning?" Tess asked.

"You'd answer."

Tess smiled, glad her expression was hidden from him. "Sadly, you're right. But I do need to work in a few hours and my boss isn't my biggest fan. So, I better go. Exercise class and crafts."

"Sounds riveting."

"Hater."

"'Night, Tornado."

"'Night, Jed." Tess hung up and tossed her phone aside, glad to be home but dreading what the next day would bring.

~*~

"Mouthy!?" Uncle Stu's voice reached through the bedroom door.

Tess was trying to hide from the inevitable. She groaned but made no effort at conversation.

Uncle Stu pounded a fist against the door. "I made pancakes." He would be relentless.

She groaned again. "It's not even nine o'clock."

He laughed wryly. "You're almost lazy." He pounded on the door again. "You better not make me come in there…"

"Fine…" Tess tossed aside the covers and tried not to shiver in the cool air, which only made her miss Florida. She yanked on her robe and went to the door to find Uncle Stu grinning at her, victorious, his arms folded over an old T-shirt with the words 'Carl's Motorcycle Warehouse' across the front in faded yellow lettering.

"Nice shirt," Tess muttered as she pulled a hair band from her wrist and piled her long hair high on her head into a messy bun.

Stu laughed. "Nice hair."

"No comment," Tess said as she trailed down the creaky stairs and into the kitchen where a plate of steaming pancakes waited for her beside the stove. She grabbed it and headed for the small table on the other side of the room.

Stu refilled his coffee mug. "My whole crew doesn't eat as much as you do."

Tess grunted. For nearly six months, she'd spent time on his crew doing everything from laying carpet to painting and reframing walls. It made her more valuable in Florida—even Josh was impressed with how much she could do despite her stiff shoulder. She poured a generous swirl of syrup over her pancakes. The inviting, warm smell filled her nostrils and made her stomach grumble.

Stu laughed. "Very lady-like."

"I never pretend to be lady-like," Tess said as she dug into the pile.

Stu went to sit by her. "I hate leaving again when we just got back," he said. Stu was on his way to Massachusetts to talk to a friend about more investment properties. He cut back on his travelling to keep an eye on Tess but told her right before their trip to Florida that after they were home he would resume his normal schedule.

Tess stopped eating, not caring that a drip of syrup made its way down her chin. She swiped at it with a napkin, her appetite suddenly gone. She swallowed the heavy lump of pancakes and nodded, trying to remember if Josh was a dream or if he'd really happened since everything else appeared to be going right back to the pits where they'd been before. "You'll only be gone a few days or so," she said unconvincingly. "Besides, I can't hide here forever. Of course, I could go back to Florida."

Stu smiled.

Tess prepared for what was coming.

He reached out and pulled her into a bear hug. "Not until you're done here," he whispered into her hair before he leaned back, the smile on his face reaching up to his deep, chocolate-brown eyes. "I'm proud of you. You're coming out on top—and I'm sure Josh will be right beside you."

Tess blinked back the tears and reached out to

punch Stu in the arm as hard as she could. "Knock it off."

"Ow!" he winced.

"Girl," Tess said, turning away from him so he wouldn't notice the single tear that managed to escape and fall down her cheek.

Stu grinned and stood, going to lean against the counter. "Finish your pancakes or I'll put you to work again."

Tess stuffed another mouthful of pancakes in and chewed as she nodded. "I gotta go," she said. "Grandma Vi will be wondering if I don't show before her exercise class."

Stu glanced at his watch. "And I should get to the airport," he said. "My phone will be on…"

Tess waved a hand at him in dismissal. "I'll be fine. Promise. No drugs, no boys, no drinking…but maybe a little bit of speeding?"

Stu laughed, shaking his head. "Don't get caught. I'll try to be back for church but if I get held up, you make sure you go to Sunday dinner at your parents' house, all right?"

Tess groaned, her mouth full of a fresh bite of pancakes. Sunday dinner with her family was certain to be torture. She would refuse to answer any questions about Josh or anything else. She hoped Brody didn't talk to Josh again. The less he knew of the situation between them, the better. "Really?" she whined.

Stu pointed at her. "Paying back the money you owe is only one part of getting things back on track."

Tess snorted in irritation. She still owed thousands of dollars. Despite working two jobs, getting a discounted rate on her apartment, and eating only what she needed to survive, she wasn't digging her way out of the hole quickly enough. And taking the trip to Florida only set her back further.

Of course, if she had stayed home Josh would still only be a childhood memory.

"My only goal in life is paying that money back and getting out of this town."

"And making your way back to Florida?" Before Tess could respond, Stu grabbed an apple from the counter and bit into it with a nod. "Life has a habit of changing the game right when you think you figured out the rules."

Tess resumed eating with a vengeance, aware that the time was ticking away, and she was soon to be at work. As a staff member who worked mostly with resident activities, Tess's day was full of exercise classes, administrative duties, and keeping residents out of their rooms and engaging with others, all while trying to avoid her boss. Even if the job didn't pay as well as she would like, she thoroughly enjoyed bringing life into Pine View and spending time with people she'd come to adore.

"Well, one thing I'm sure won't change is how much the people in this town hate me," Tess said, not bothering to finish chewing before she spoke.

Stu rolled his eyes but said nothing, as the conversation took a turn Tess was sure he wasn't interested in following. They'd already talked about this enough times, and found there would be no agreement between them. Tess wanted out. Stu was convinced that once people saw her actions they'd conclude she was different.

"You get Harrison Flynn repaid and things will change," Stu said.

Tess groaned. "That man will never let it go, whether I pay him in full this month or three years from now," she muttered. "If you'd loan me the money I'd pay you back...I'd be out of your hair, and everyone else's too."

"Nope." Stu tossed his apple core into the garbage. He'd already explained enough times that he wouldn't bother doing so again. Stu was of the opinion that everyone already knew how many times he'd bailed her out and they wouldn't believe she'd changed if he did so again.

Tess snorted in irritation. Harrison Flynn was one of the most judgmental people she'd ever met. The fact that she and her band of hooligan friends spray-painted his family's pharmacy with graffiti was unlikely to ever be forgotten. Of that Tess was certain. It would never matter to him how much time passed or how many ways she'd repented or paid her debt.

"Right," Tess said wryly, giving up on enjoying any of her breakfast. She went to the garbage where she tossed what was left of her uneaten pancakes, depositing the empty plate to the dishwasher. "He'll never change. Ruining his property was one of the dumbest things I've ever been part of."

Stu nodded. "You all did pick the wrong man."

"It wasn't exactly my choice," Tess said. "They wanted to. I went along, and was the only fool to get caught. Forget it. I don't need to tell you." She exhaled, annoyed. "Maybe if he wasn't such a bad rep for Christianity we'd have picked on someone else." Tess could be frank with her uncle, even if he didn't agree with what she was saying.

"He can be," Stu said. "But that's not our problem, is it? He'll come around. It'll take time and effort on your part if you want things back to how they used to be. I can only do so much. You don't come by your stubborn, salty nature any way but through that awful brother of mine." He winked at her.

Reluctantly, Tess nodded. "I get it."

Stu smiled, satisfied that she understood her life wasn't the lost cause she sometimes tried to make it into. "Lock up before you go. Tell Vi I said hello."

Tess nodded.

Stu went out the side door to his old truck, his luggage tossed into the bed like garbage.

She smiled. Uncle Stu might not be the classiest guy, his face usually covered by an unruly beard, the dirt under his fingernails his reminder to the world that a man should work for a living, but he was pure, forgiving, and the exact illustration of love that she needed when no one else was willing to help her.

Tess would be forever in his debt.

11

I will praise thee, O Lord, with my whole heart;
I will shew forth all thy marvelous works. I will be glad and
rejoice in thee: I will sing praise to thy name, O thou most
High.
Psalm 9: 1-2

The door to Viola Westmont's apartment was open when Tess ascended the short staircase to Pine View's second floor. It wasn't unusual to find the self-appointed social director flittering from one apartment to the next in an effort to make the residents of the facility connect with one another. The transition to this arrangement wasn't entirely smooth and Tess was glad she'd still been on the outs with her family at the time, so she'd not been part of the difficult decision to move Grandma Vi from her home of fifty-three years to the assisted living facility.

Tess peeked inside the apartment and found her grandmother digging through a drawer as if for treasure. So as not to scare the eighty-four-year-old woman, Tess knocked lightly before entering. "Hey, Grandma," she said softly as she entered. "What's going on?"

Vi raised her head. The sparkling eyes that always greeted Tess were a bit less intense than normal. Tess squelched the nagging idea that her grandmother was slipping away.

Vi shook her head and gave a deep sigh as she went back to digging through the drawer. "I lost my keys again," she muttered. "I always put them here, but now I can't find them." She paused and gasped as she turned to Tess. "So, tell me, how was Florida? Did you forget your sunscreen?"

Tess smiled and went to the drawer where she began digging. "Florida was great. Hot and sunny most of the time so I did get a little sunburn."

"Well, put something on it or you'll peel." Vi sat and stretched her legs. "Find anything?" she asked calmly.

"No. Where were you going, Gram?"

"Um...exercise class," she said, standing and gesturing to proudly display her jogging pants and matching sweatshirt.

"Did you check your pocket?"

Vi reached into her pocket and sheepishly removed her hand, which now held the keys. "Oh, goodness. I guess I got ahead of myself again," she muttered.

Tess smiled. "Well let's get down there. I'm teaching today."

"Oh!" Vi squealed and clapped her hands. "I love it when you teach us. Gets my blood pumping."

Tess took Gram's hand and led her out of the room, hoping she didn't run into Ashley-Marie any sooner than necessary. She was having a good day and didn't need her boss to ruin it.

~*~

Tess and Vi made their way to the activities room, a large area that doubled as a craft room and a gym depending on the day. Today the tables were pushed to one side, along with some of the chairs to make more room for exercise, whether sitting or standing.

"Theresa." The stern voice caught Tess right as she was about to set foot into the activities room.

Grandma Vi kept walking.

Tess turned, her stomach tightening at the sight of the statuesque blonde who'd made it her life's goal to harass her until she begged for mercy. That Ashley-Marie Hinton was stunning, well-paid, educated, and an experienced professional in the health care industry apparently wasn't enough for her. For some reason, the impact of a childhood prank years before when Tess was barely thirteen years old was enough to mean they would be enemies for life.

Regardless, it amused Tess until she considered the way it impacted her daily at work. Ashley-Marie insisted she was doing Tess some kind of favor allowing her to set foot in Pine View. That Tess got the worst hours, the jobs no one wanted, and was reminded all too often that Ashley-Marie would not let up, deepened her angst and yet caused her to remember she would work hard until she could escape and never turn back. Tess stifled a yawn and walked slowly toward Ashley-Marie, praying she was ready for whatever the woman wanted. "Yes, Ash?" A sick pleasure washed over her as Ashley-Marie cringed at the callousness with which Tess mangled her name. Both of them were aware she'd done it on purpose.

"Mr. Conders needs his meds by four-thirty each day. Yesterday's chart says he didn't get them until nearly five o'clock..."

"I wasn't here yesterday."

Ashley-Marie stared hard at the chart before turning her glimmering blue eyes to Tess. She pointed at her with the end of her pen. "I am the administrator of this facility, Theresa. You will not undermine my authority at every turn." She paused. "And I'm certain I needn't remind you about the many times you've been late with Mr. Conders' medicine. You can understand why I'd assume it was business as usual this time."

"Um, Ashley-Marie...?"

Tess and Ashley-Marie both turned at the voice.

Morgan was holding several sheets of paper. "I'm sorry to interrupt but there's some concern over tonight's dinner menu. Lydia said..."

Ashley-Marie groaned and clutched the clip board close to her chest before pointing her pen at Tess again. "I'm watching you, Carson. One slip up—one—and you are out of here. And don't think I didn't notice that you were five minutes late...again." She stomped off, her high heels clicking on the tiles as she grabbed the papers from Morgan and headed off down the hall toward the kitchen.

Tess smiled at Morgan and glanced at the clock. "Thanks. I, um need to get to exercise class."

"Yeah." Morgan glanced at the recreation room and smiled back at Tess. "How you holding up? Has he called yet?"

Tess shook her head. "He called this morning to make sure I got home. But I'm not counting on it going anywhere now."

Morgan waved her hand in dismissal. "Come on, Tess, be a team player. How will I live vicariously through you if you don't cooperate?"

Tess smiled. "I appreciate it but…"

"Save your energy for the class," Morgan said. "And make sure you tell me all the gory details about you and Josh later."

"Sure thing." Tess smiled and hustled to get her exercise class started. She was glad for the distraction work brought. It left her no time to think about the dimples that filled her dreams the night before.

~*~

Josh stared at his computer screen while he daydreamed about Tess instead of reviewing his resume. He still wasn't sure he wanted to be a senior pastor. Being close to Tess, and in a town he'd once viewed as home, was beginning to outweigh his doubts. He sighed and reached for his Bible.

The office door opened, and Tom entered. "Morning." He set a cup of hot coffee on the desk.

"Thanks." Josh accepted the cup gratefully. "Any word on the carpet?"

Tom settled into the chair across from Josh and took a sip before answering. He nodded. "Said they'd be here between nine and four."

"Great timeline," Josh said.

"Of course. How's Susannah?"

"It was good timing with that situation. I'm glad Tess was here. She really reached her in a way I doubt I ever could."

Tom nodded. He was a good friend and mentor to Josh over the last two years, and they'd learned to read each other well. So Josh wasn't surprised when Tom smiled at him over the rims of his glasses.

"You're leaving," he said.

Josh bristled. That his resume was on his computer screen at that exact moment was a bit too much. He shifted in his seat and took a drink of coffee. "I'm not making any decisions yet."

Tom set his cup down. "But she's it. I can tell by the way you acted around her."

Josh wished he could avoid this conversation. "It was only a week," he muttered, still trying to convince himself that his feelings were too rushed to be real.

Tom sighed heavily before smiling, the sincerity in his eyes reminding Josh that his friend would be honest with him—and more importantly that he was a true man of integrity, one Josh could trust.

"And yet women have thrown themselves at you and you've never blinked. This week we didn't carry on one conversation that didn't involve, or include, Tess." Tom shrugged. "That alone is telling me something."

Josh stood and paced for a moment before sitting down. The energy and anxiety were too much. "All I've wanted, for years, is a place to put down roots and call home. I grew up all over the place and I never thought I was home anywhere, but the seven years we spent next door to the Carsons was different. It would be a strange coincidence that Tess shows up and I'm entertaining feelings for her." Josh paused and finally said the words that were nagging him since Tess came back into his life again. "I could go home."

Tom drew a deep breath and smiled. "Have you told her what you're thinking?"

"Sort of, but not the extent of it."

"So, what's the plan?"

Josh laughed wryly. "There isn't one. I can't pick up and leave yet."

Tom laughed. "One thing you should learn now before you go any further. Love can't be planned and it is usually at least a little bit crazy." He stood and started for the door.

"Tom?"

The man turned to Josh.

"Would you mind keeping this to yourself? I wouldn't want anyone here thinking I'm not committed to this job."

"No problem. It's none of my business," he said before leaving and closing the door behind him.

Josh leaned back in his seat and closed his eyes. Clearly, he needed to pray.

~*~

Tess slipped into her truck and shoved the key into the ignition, glad another day was behind her. Although she was too busy to answer her phone, Stu and Josh both called and left several messages each. Tess planned to call them back soon, so they didn't worry. But first, she needed to stop and get groceries for her empty apartment. She avoided staying there much, choosing to hang out with Stu and eat his food, grateful for the company and the way it helped her save even more money.

And yet, at the rate she was going, it would take her almost a year to pay everyone back what she owed. With a heavy sigh, Tess steered her truck toward the grocery store, intent on filling her cart as quickly and cheaply as possible and getting home for an early night's sleep. After a day of avoiding Ashley-Marie, she was beat.

As Tess set the parking brake her phone buzzed again. She glanced at it, shocked to find her brother's name on the display. Her head dropped back. She sighed, pushed the button, and pressed the phone to her ear. "Hey, Bro, what's up?"

"What time did you get back?" Her brother didn't waste time with pleasantries, jumping feet first into the conversation.

"Um...about five this morning." Tess sat back in her seat, unwilling to talk on the phone as she shopped.

"Hmm. And Uncle Stu's gone?"

Tess watched customers going in and out of the store, wondering when her brother became such a master of restating the obvious. "Yeah. Why?"

"No reason." Brody paused for a long moment and drew a deep breath. "Anyway, if you didn't make plans for dinner, Stell and I wouldn't mind if you dropped by. We usually eat in about a half hour or so, but we could wait if you can't make it until later."

Tess cursed the knot that grew in her stomach. His invitation, while kind, appeared forced. Uncle Stu's voice rang clearly in her head telling her to go and not overthink it, but she shoved his phantom urging aside and cleared her throat. "Um...you don't have to..."

"We want to. I mean, if you aren't busy. It isn't a big deal."

Tess understood how hard the words were for him to say and that it was her fault things were so difficult. If she could be good, the kind of sister she *should* be, it would be normal for Brody to ask her to stop in for dinner. As it was, she'd not been to his home in months.

But Tess was sure her brother was offering her a chance for their fragile relationship to heal and that she would be foolish not to take it. She nodded. "Sure. I'm leaving work now and I need to grab some groceries. Once I change clothes I'll be over."

"Sounds good."

"I'll, um, bring dessert."

"All right. We'll see you in an hour."

"OK." Tess ended the call as the nervous sensation took root in the pit of her stomach. This should be interesting.

~*~

Tess finished shopping and was left with enough time to rush home to put the food away and change her clothes. She'd done it all fast to keep herself from thinking what she'd say to her brother and his perfect wife. Inwardly, Tess groaned.

It wasn't Estelle's fault she was petite, beautiful, intelligent and basically perfect in every way Tess wasn't. In fact, there was little Tess could dislike about her sister-in-law—well, except that since she'd entered Brody's life he'd given little time to his sister. They weren't close anymore and the cut was still deep. Of course, some of that wasn't Estelle's fault.

Before Tess could allow this line of thinking, her phone rang. She pulled over and pressed it to her ear. She could actually see Brody and Stell's house from where she parked. She bit her nail, already getting nervous.

"Hello?"

"You shouldn't answer your phone when you're driving."

Tess grinned at the sound of her uncle's voice. "You shouldn't call me when I'm in my truck. Actually, I pulled over."

Stu snorted. "Where you been? I called three times already."

Tess examined her nails. Her hands were rough from the hard work she'd done in Florida, her nails split and broken. She sighed. "Some of us work for a living…and since you didn't care enough to stick around to feed me I'm buying groceries now on top of it."

"What are you making?"

"I'm not making anything. Brody asked me to come for dinner, so I picked up pie for dessert."

Stu groaned. "You couldn't bake one? They'll never invite you back."

Tess shook her head. "I was working! I got one from the diner. It was the best I could do since he only called me an hour ago."

"Well, I'm sure it will be a nice meal. Stell's a good cook."

"I guess."

"Stop overthinking it. Go in there and have a good time. You gotta meet them halfway, kid."

"I'm on my way there, aren't I?" she asked. "How's it going there?"

"Good. Should be back early. At least that's the hope." Stu paused. "How's Josh?"

"No idea. Been too busy to talk."

Tess glanced up as Brody poked his head out the

door as if he was checking on her arrival. He waved tentatively, and Tess waved back, her smile plastic. He smiled back and nodded when she pointed to the phone in her hand. "Hey, I gotta go. I parked close enough that Brody's waving at me."

"OK. Call if you need anything, Mouthy."

"Sure. Love you."

"Love you too."

Tess hung up the phone, coasted to Brody's driveway, parked and drew a deep, shaky breath. She hoped her brother wouldn't bring up his old friend.

12

And be ye kind one to another, tenderhearted, forgiving one
another, even as God for Christ's sake hath forgiven you.
Ephesians 4: 32

"Hey!" Stell said as she threw the door open to greet Tess. "We're so glad you could make it! Sorry it was such short notice."

"Oh. Thanks for inviting me," Tess said tentatively as she held out the pie. "I, um, didn't get the chance to bake anything but I picked up a pie for dessert."

"That's perfect," Stell said as she accepted the pie and handed it off to Brody. "Set that on the table, will you?"

"I should throw it out the back door," Brody muttered. "Geez, Tess, you couldn't bake us one of your apple pies, for crying out loud? It's the only reason I asked you to come."

Tess glanced up at her brother and found his dark eyes sparkling in a way that made her tongue-tied. She remembered a time when his teasing was as normal as breathing, but those days felt like long ago.

"Stop!" Stell said with a laugh as she playfully swatted at Brody who managed to duck out of the way. "We hardly gave her any notice at all. Besides, I love pie from the diner."

Tess pinched her brother's side like she used to, hitting his weak spot hard enough that he nearly dropped the pie. "I will make Stell a pie anytime, but you only deserve store-bought."

Brody laughed as he left the room.

Stell smiled at Tess and gestured for her to follow into the kitchen. "Come on. Everything's ready. We can catch up while we eat."

Tess nodded and followed the tiny blonde with the pixie haircut through the immaculate kitchen and into the expertly-decorated dining room.

Stell was a wedding planner and as perfect as the weddings she prepared were, her home was even more so. Each room looked as if it should be featured in a magazine.

It was a talent Tess certainly didn't boast. Her own apartment was more like an abandoned rental property than any self-respecting woman's home.

"How was Florida?" Stell asked. "You sure did get a lot of sun…" She held out a tray of chicken to Tess who accepted it and began to fill her plate.

"Florida was hot. It went quick too. We were busy the whole time. There was a lot to do." She passed the plate to Brody who smiled.

"I'm guessing it only got hotter when you met up with old Jed again, huh?"

Tess's cheeks warmed. "We were there to work," she said.

"Right…" Brody filled his plate as Tess lifted the mashed potatoes and plopped a scoop next to her chicken. "He sure sounded as if he was working hard on you. Or was it the other way around?"

Tess bristled while Stell smacked Brody's arm. "We didn't invite the poor girl over here to harass her."

"Aww, I'm only kidding."

Tess set her fork down and turned to her brother.

"Were you kidding when you called Jed to warn him about me?"

Brody stopped chewing and his smile slipped. He cleared his throat as he swallowed. "What?"

Stell looked horrified. "You called Josh to warn him about her?" she exclaimed. "Brody…"

Brody threw his hands into the air and shook his head. "I did no such thing and I resent the accusation." He sighed, closing his eyes briefly before he continued. "Tess. You walked away from us years ago. I don't think you know me anymore at all. So, don't pretend you understand my motivation for that call."

Tess folded her arms over her chest and glared. "Well, please, oh great one, tell me why you did it."

A storm passed over Brody's face. "I called to find out if you told him…what you've been up to. Clearly you didn't."

"That isn't our business, Brody," Stell whispered. "It wasn't your place to get involved."

"Oh, come on, Stell! Don't take her side!" Brody tossed his fork onto the table in frustration.

Stell sighed and gave him a glance that only a wife could. "I'm not picking sides. I love you both, but you shouldn't assume…"

Tess contemplated her response but saw no way to win. "This was a mistake," she said, working hard to maintain her hold on her emotions. "I shouldn't be here." She paused, glancing at Brody. "Not that it's any of your business, but I tried to tell him…and he said it didn't matter because he knows who I am now…" She forced herself to stand on shaking legs. "Maybe it was nice having someone besides Uncle Stu believe in me for a change."

Brody tossed his napkin onto the table and shoved

his chair back in his anger. "I can't help it if I was worried, Tess."

Tess placed her hands on the table and leaned toward him. "Worried about what?"

"You. Him. Whatever." Brody sighed heavily and searched hard for the words he needed. "Dad said he talked to Josh and he sounded...well, interested in you. I guess I wasn't expecting that...after everything the last few years...and it scared me, despite what you've done lately — and even what Uncle Stu says."

Tess cleared her throat. "Right." She glanced at Stell. "Thank you both for inviting me but I think maybe it was too soon." She took a step toward the door and barely noticed as Stell rose from her seat.

"Stop. Both of you." Stell put a gentle hand on Tess's arm and smiled. "Please. Sit down. We didn't invite you here to berate you over the past." She glanced at Brody. "Especially when we both agree you've come so far in such a short time. We're proud of you and we want to support you — not question you."

Slowly, Tess returned to her chair and sat, wondering why she didn't run out the door. She clenched her napkin in her hand, unsure what to say.

Brody put his napkin back on his lap. "I'm sorry, T," he muttered softly. "It's still hard sometimes, that's all. Everyone went through a lot and it's still fresh. I didn't call Josh to warn him about you. Not like you're thinking anyway. I guess I was being an overprotective brother who didn't want his sister or his friend to get hurt."

Tess looked at him. "I'm still working on everything," she whispered. "And I overreacted. I'm...sorry."

Stell and Brody both smiled as relief filled Tess. It

was a small step and there was still a ways to go, but simply being invited over for dinner was a huge gamble on the couple's part. Tess had been drunk at their wedding and made such a fool of herself. Even in planning for the perfect wedding, Stell couldn't have expected the embarrassment of watching her inebriated sister-in-law taken out of the reception and forced to dry out overnight at the police station. Tess was surprised they even considered speaking to her again.

"The chicken is excellent, as always," Brody said.

Stell smiled. "Thank you."

"Everything is delicious." Tess took a bite of potatoes and smiled as the tension melted slightly.

"We're glad you came," Stell said as Tess's phone began playing Josh's ringtone.

Brody coughed.

Tess scrambled to silence it. "Sorry," she muttered as she stuffed the phone deep into her pocket.

Stell's eyes sparkled. "He has his own ringtone?" she exchanged a glance with Brody whose face was still red from coughing.

"Maybe I should be concerned," he muttered.

Tess picked up her fork. "We like talking," she said. "I gave him a ringtone that would make him laugh."

"And what ringtone did he choose for you?" Brody asked.

Tess avoided his eyes. "Um, I'd rather not say," she muttered.

Brody laughed. "All right, I'll drop the subject, but if our old friend decides to show up here, I swear I'm locking you in a tower. We barely got you back in our lives. I won't let him take you away from us."

Tess met her brother's eyes and realized her own were filling with tears. She and Brody used to be so close they didn't need words to communicate. But in the last few years, it appeared the chasm between them would never be crossed. But with those words, Tess was getting her brother back. "Thanks," she whispered. And even if she wasn't sure she could keep the promise, she said, "I'm not going anywhere. At least not yet."

~*~

By the time Tess left Brody and Stell's it was nearly ten o'clock. She was exhausted but her growing peace was worth the effort. Uncle Stu would be proud of her. Even when she'd gotten angry and wanted to walk away, she'd stuck it out and stayed for the meal. And she was glad she did. They'd spent the rest of the evening laughing and talking and Tess even managed to admit she was afraid of pursuing anything with Josh for fear he'd run once he witnessed the way everyone treated her.

It stuck in Tess's mind that there'd been no comforting words on that subject from either Brody or Stell. But she tried not to stay in that moment. They were all too aware that it would be some time before things could be normal again.

She'd missed several calls from Josh throughout the day as well as one from a woman at the church. She grabbed her phone, set it on speaker and played the messages.

"Hey, Tornado—I wondered how your day was

going. Give me a call when you get the chance. OK, bye." Tess smiled at the reluctance in his voice, like a teenaged a boy leaving a message for a girl he liked. It was almost too much. She waited while the second message began.

"Theresa." Tess laughed at the false sternness in Josh's voice. "I don't want to make a nuisance of myself, but you never called me back today. I wanted to check in. Didn't want you to think I'd forgotten about you. 'K. Bye."

And then... "Hi. This is Alison Gorman calling from North Street Church for Tess Carson. The ladies' missionary group gets together every Thursday at seven, and since you're back from the mission trip to Florida, I wondered if you'd be interested in joining us this week. You could tell us a bit about your trip. Um, give me a call at the church, extension six. Thanks!"

Tess wasn't sure whether to groan or laugh at the last message. They should ask Morgan or the Parsons sisters. She shook her head as she glanced at the phone long enough to press the button to call Josh. He answered as she pulled her truck into the driveway of the apartment she could loosely be called as renting from Stu.

"Hey, Tornado. Where you been all day?" The sound of Josh's voice immediately made Tess smile as she set the parking brake and turned the truck off.

"Don't you ever work?" she asked as she jumped out of the truck and headed for her apartment.

Josh laughed, and Tess imagined him running his long fingers through his hair as his dimples popped in both cheeks. "I was in meetings all day and youth group's tomorrow, so I'm covered for now. I'm on my way home actually and I passed Dips...almost went in for a scoop."

"You're evil."

"Miss me?" his voice suddenly turned serious. Tess was relieved at the miles between them, which kept her flushed cheeks private. She drew a deep breath. "I've been at work all day and afterward I went to Brody and Stell's for dinner so I guess there hasn't been much time to miss you."

"Ouch." Josh laughed. "I've been thinking...about everything..."

Tess gulped, certain his next words would be that he'd realized they were doomed. She braced herself for the inevitable. "Yeah? Me, too."

"Mind if I go first?"

Tess sank slowly into her couch and nodded. "Sure. Go ahead."

"Right. OK." Josh paused. "I might be off the mark but I had a great time when you were here. I mean...I told you what's been holding me back from relationships before. But it's different now." He cleared his throat. "With you so far away, I mean, we could keep talking like this. If things seem as though they're moving in the right direction, maybe I could come and visit or you could come back here for a while. What do you think?" he asked and released a deep breath she could hear.

"I think you're as adorable as the teenager who rescued my kitten when Brody was away at camp..."

"Really? Me? Adorable?"

Tess laughed at the hope in his voice, wishing she could be with him in person. "Yeah, really," she said as she tugged the pictures Josh gave her from her bag. She laid them on the table to remind herself to hang them on the refrigerator later. "But you're also delusional. Whatever happened should be a nice memory. I'm me, and you're—perfect you. I can't ruin that."

Josh choked. "Did you say I'm delusional?"

"Yes. And perfect."

"Tess," he dismissed one comment, still caught on the other. "I'm definitely not perfect...and I'm not even sure what you mean."

"I think you do."

"If I say I want to do this, it means I'm all in. I don't say it lightly."

Tess bit her lip. "If you ever think about coming back here—and you're involved with me..." her voice drifted off. "All I'm saying is that you should be careful with your reputation in a small town. That makes me the wrong girl for you."

Josh's sigh clearly told Tess how he viewed her concerns. "You are the only one worried about this. I'm not."

Tess gave him points for trying. She wanted to shake him, make him acknowledge that no matter what he wanted she cared too much about him to ruin his career. Of course, with no way to actually date him, what did any of it matter? "Fair enough. I mean, we can't really date anyway, so I guess there's no point arguing about it. Let's talk about something else. How's Susannah?"

"She misses you," Josh said. "But she's doing OK."

"Good. I'm glad we were there for her."

"Me, too. Hey, I already said this, but you should seriously consider youth ministry."

Tess laughed. "No way. But you're sweet."

"A little birdie said there's this girl who used to think that about me."

Tess smiled at the change in his voice. He was falling for her and part of her didn't want him to stop, despite what her mouth kept saying. "She still does," Tess whispered.

Josh was quiet for a moment. "Tess. I should be clear. I'm not out of reach any more, and…" he cleared his throat. "I'm already thinking about being with you again."

Tess's gaze fell on a picture of her and Josh laughing as she sat on his shoulders to paint a spot on the ceiling of the youth center. "I wish I could come there and forget this place exists," she said. She closed her eyes, imagining what it would be like to not fear the sting of the past biting into her everywhere she went. It seemed an impossible dream.

"You can't do that," Josh said. "Not because I don't want you to but because you should finish whatever it is you need to do there first. We'll figure it out, OK?"

"Yes," Tess nodded even though he couldn't see it, her confidence hanging by a thread.

"Would you like me to pray for you? For us?" His voice was filled with nervousness probably because he was serious about pursuing a relationship with her despite the miles and problems between them.

Her heart constricted. "I'd like that a lot. Thanks."

"Anytime." He drew a deep breath. "Dear Heavenly Father, thank You, so much, for this wonderful woman. Thank You for putting good, caring people around her to help guide her. I pray You continue to heal her spirit, Lord God, so she feels Your presence in her life every day. And Lord, I pray that You guide us as we move forward—" Josh cleared his throat. "—Together. Please make it clear to us both whether this is a relationship that is of Your will. Help us to serve You in all we do. In Your precious name I pray. Amen."

Again, Tess smiled as she opened her eyes, wishing she would find Josh standing there before her. Unfortunately, all that was there was an empty table where a television should be, dingy curtains that were left by the last tenant, and her favorite tennis shoes, abandoned near the door.

"Amen," she said, and in her soul, she was certain something wonderful and terribly frightening was about to happen.

13

Whatever you do, work heartily,
as for the Lord and not for men.
Colossians 3:23

Tess woke the next day with a fear she was late for something. It hit her like an oncoming train—work. "Oh no...." She leapt from her bed, dressed quickly and rushed out the door to the diner, arriving nearly a half-hour after the breakfast rush began. She cursed herself for staying up so late the night before talking to Josh when she'd barely recovered from the long trip home from Florida.

"You're late again," Brittany said as Tess struggled to get her apron tied around her waist.

"Did he notice?"

Their boss, Derek Patterson, made it his personal mission to harass Tess every chance he got. He was a few years older, and a spoiled man whose dad owned several restaurants across the state. He put his son in charge of the smallest, 'Roadside Attraction'. Since Derek held no fear of his own father firing him, he did whatever he wanted, little of which included actually managing the restaurant.

"It hasn't been too busy," Brittany said. "But if you could pick up C-5 I'd really appreciate it. They've been waiting a few minutes."

"You got it," Tess said and stepped away, but she

bumped into Derek who was standing much too close to her. She tried to go past him, but he straightened to his full height, towering over her and blocking any means of escape.

"I gotta get C-5," Tess said.

Derek smiled, his teeth gleaming.

His cologne wafted past the smell of greasy breakfast food, filling Tess's nostrils so she glanced away from him for a breath of air. She knew what he wanted. It was the same thing he always wanted, the same thing she would continue to deny him.

"What you got," Derek said, still smiling. "...is a real problem being on time, Tess. It's getting harder to overlook."

Tess sighed. "Derek. I need to work."

He reached out and touched her hair, lingering a bit too long for it to be innocent. "So I can count on you to go out with me tonight? I mean, I don't want to fire you, but you're starting to get tough to keep around. This is the second time you were late this month."

"I'm working at Pine View tonight," Tess said, stepping past him.

Derek grabbed her arm and spun her around before she could get away. "I don't mind staying up late."

Tess turned away. "No." She wrenched her arm free and headed to her table, wishing she could find someone besides the seediest managers to give her a job. Despite having been a good employee for nearly six months, no one wanted to bother with her yet.

Give it more time.

She stopped beside the table with a smile. "Good morning, folks. What can I get for you?"

After taking the first order, Tess was too busy to

even give Derek a passing glance most of the morning. And for that she was grateful. When things finally slowed down, Tess managed to pour her own cup of coffee at ten-thirty.

Derek held out his own nearly-empty cup and waited while she refilled it. "I'm tired of you putting me off. It's not as if you've been picky before."

Tess shoved the coffee pot back onto the warmer. She turned back to him with a forced smile. "Just because I was late today doesn't mean I'm willing to beg for my job by dating or," she couldn't bring herself to say what she was certain he was thinking. "Doing anything else with you."

Derek pointed at her. "I got applications from thirty girls like you that I could hire instead. Bet they'd be on time."

Tess gripped her coffee mug. "I won't be late again," she said as the restaurant door opened. "Excuse me. There are customers."

Unfortunately for Tess the day only went downhill from there. She finished her shift at the restaurant, hustled home to change clothes, and went back to Pine View to cover an exercise class and a craft class.

Before Tess even took off her coat, Morgan yanked her aside and said, "Watch yourself, she's on a real rampage."

Tess rolled her eyes. "I can't be in trouble already."

"Theresa!? Is that you?" Ashley-Marie rounded the corner, her hair slightly askew, her lipstick nearly worn off. It was an image none were used to, when typically the home's director was the picture of a polished executive.

Tess turned to the woman, hoping her face was

respectful. "Yep?" she asked.

Ashley-Marie cleared her throat and stared down her nose.

Tess squirmed and forced a smile.

"Three people quit in one day. Whether you like it or not, Theresa, I will need you to fill in. You'll be working double shifts for the next few weeks until I can get those gaps filled. Got it?"

Tess cleared her throat. "That's fine. I don't mind the extra shifts, but... um, I do work the breakfast rush and some lunches too at the diner..."

Ashley-Marie sighed heavily. "I'll get you the schedule tomorrow and you can make sure it doesn't interfere with your job at the greasy spoon." She turned on her heel and was gone before Tess could respond.

"Yeesh..." Morgan said. "What was that?"

Tess shook her head. "I'm not sure. And there's a class expecting me." She started to walk away.

Morgan stopped her. "Hey, any word from the good pastor?"

Tess had forgotten about Josh and their conversation the entire day. "Yeah, we talked last night." She glanced at the recreation room where residents were starting to gather. "Can we try coffee later? I'm here until eight anyway...I was planning to stay for 'classic movie night' but it's not critical."

Morgan smiled and nodded. "Sure. Your place? Eight-thirty?"

Tess nodded and turned back to her job. It was time to exercise.

~*~

Tess finished her classes before spending two hours reorganizing the supply closet in the rec room. She was so invested in her work that the deep rumble of a man clearing his throat nearly made her drop the last box she was about to shove to the top shelf of the closet.

"I didn't receive this month's payment, Theresa." The familiar condescension of Harrison Flynn's light southern drawl surprised her.

Tess flinched and turned, regarding him warily. That he took time from his work day to find her was not a good sign. Tess did her best to squelch the nervousness that bubbled up. Wronging him might have been one of the worst mistakes she'd ever made. Hate radiated from him so it was nearly palpable. "Mr. Flynn. I didn't get my paychecks yet. The way the dates fell and with my mission trip to Florida, I can't make your payment until later this week. But when I get the money I will drop it off at your office."

Tess despised groveling to this man who'd been anything but gracious toward her, despite her many apologies and the fact that she was working two jobs to pay back the money it took to fix his defaced property. Of course, when her friends wanted to do some 'art' on the side of his building right after he made a comment about her needing to get right with the Lord, she'd been all for it.

But now that she cared about her faith, Harrison Flynn appeared to be unable to consider that God's grace could extend to someone like her. Instead, he insisted on reminding her at every turn that she was beyond salvation.

Again, Harrison grunted, cleared his throat and

glared down at her in clear disapproval. "You agreed that you would pay me on the fifteenth of each month. It is now the seventeenth and I would like to receive payment from you. It is not my problem that you chose to go off on some trip…"

"It was a mission trip, one I told you about weeks ago," Tess said.

The man raised an eyebrow. "God will not be mocked."

Tess went so many rounds with Harrison already that it would serve no purpose to defend herself. Instead she smiled, unable to stop from saying, "You're right, sir. He sure won't."

Harrison didn't take kindly to joking. In fact, it was unlikely he'd ever laughed in his life. He grimaced at Tess and glared. "My aunt lives in this facility," he said. "And you can be certain I'll be keeping her away from you. I'm still shocked your uncle was able to get you into this place. They're usually so careful about who they hire."

Tess glanced at the clock over Harrison's shoulder and realized she was supposed to be helping the staff serve dinner. "I need to get to the dining room. I'll get you your money as soon as my paychecks are ready."

"I suppose that will do." Before she was out of earshot he said, "And it will be even better when you're out of this town."

Tess paused in the doorway and turned to him. "Trust me; it will be better for all of us."

He averted his gaze as she walked away.

~*~

Hours later Tess pulled into the parking lot near her apartment. Her feet were throbbing, her stomach was growling, and until she noticed Morgan waiting for her, she'd forgotten she'd promised to catch up with her friend. But there were two messages from Stu, one from Stell, and a text from Josh she was working on a snarky reply for, and still she was relieved she could avoid it all and hang out with her friend. One thing she was sure of, Morgan wouldn't care if she planned to come home and pig out on frozen pizza and chips. In fact, Morgan would be happy to join her.

"Hey...sorry. Ashley-Marie finished the schedule and wanted me to take it so she could approve it in the morning after I ran it past Derek." Tess popped the door to her apartment open.

Morgan followed her inside, flicking on the lights with a smile. "It's all right. I only got here a minute ago," Morgan said. She was dressed in a pair of old sweatpants and a grungy T-shirt which was partially-covered by a thick, half-zipped sweatshirt.

Tess smiled as she set the temperature on the oven, glad she needn't worry about impressing her friend. "You want pizza?" she asked. "I don't even remember when I last ate."

Morgan laughed. "Sure."

"I'll go change. Why don't you grab something from the fridge to drink? There's tea...not sure what else," Tess said as she yanked her hair up into a messy bun. She went into her bedroom, leaving the door open a crack so she could still talk.

"Thanks," Morgan said. Tess heard her open the refrigerator and root around before saying, "So, what's up with Josh? I'm dying!"

Tess grew warm thinking of him. Her long-distance, fantasy boyfriend. *Boyfriend?* "We talked forever last night. Which made me sleep in. I was a half hour late to the diner."

"Uh-oh. Did you get into trouble?"

Tess tossed her cargo pants aside and reached for a pair of sweats and a comfy t-shirt. "Derek tried to bribe me into going out with him to 'forget' I was late, but I told him no way."

"Yuck. I don't trust that guy."

Tess tugged her T-shirt on and went back to the kitchen. "I don't either but what can I do? No one will hire me, and I need Flynn off my back. Would you believe he stopped by Pine View today to remind me I'm late paying him? And that was after I told him weeks ago that this month I'd probably be late with my check. Not to mention the fact that he attends the very church I was on a mission trip with." Tess reached into the refrigerator and grabbed a bottle of iced tea. She popped the lid and took a long drink. "He's enough to make me want to go back to drinking."

Morgan looked at her sympathetically. "Tess..."

Tess waved her arms. "I know, I know. I won't...but it is tempting."

Morgan smiled. "OK, so we can talk about Mr. Flynn later. Right now, you need to tell me what was so important that Josh kept you up talking so late. What is going on?"

Tess rummaged through her freezer until she found the frozen pizza. She pulled it out and put it on a tray. "Oh, the usual..." Tess gestured from her messy hair to her bare feet. "Clearly the man is enamored of me. He's already asked me to marry him."

Morgan nearly dropped her drink. "What?"

"All right, maybe he hasn't proposed yet." Tess

laughed as she popped the pizza into the oven and set the timer. "But it does seem like we've switched roles. He's chasing me and I'm running the other way. I am disappointed though. No homemade gifts or chalk-drawings on my driveway yet."

Morgan sighed dreamily. "Why are you running away?"

"Oh, come on." Tess grabbed a new bag of chips from the pantry and tugged it open before placing it on the counter near Morgan. "Besides the obvious reason, what's the point of falling more in love with him when he's living in Florida and I'm living in hell...I mean, here."

Morgan reached to take a handful of chips. "This from the woman who's told me about a million times she can't wait to move away. What's to say you couldn't move to Florida and get everything you ever wanted—Josh, a new start, a dream job?"

Tess laughed. "You're funny. I think I'll keep you around." She glanced at her phone. It vibrated that moment with Josh's tune.

Morgan laughed. "Tell me that isn't Jed's ringtone."

Tess reached past her friend and shut the ringer off. "It's not Jed's ringtone."

"Right." Morgan paused. "You give a man a ringtone you might as well ask him to marry you."

Tess rolled her eyes, secretly aware that no matter how hard she was fighting it, she'd wanted to answer the phone more than anything she'd wanted to do all day. And she was certain things were too complicated for her to figure out yet.

~*~

Josh pressed the phone to his ear and wondered why Tess wasn't answering. Maybe he was too eager. Maybe she was busy. No matter the reason she never answered, Josh hated the fact that he cared so much. He was finding it increasingly difficult to do his job when all he wanted was to talk to her. She was the missing piece in his life.

"Hey, Tornado. Susannah committed to helping with the ministry we started with the retirement community. Anyway, she's already connected with this amazing lady there, Betsy," he laughed. "She's taken Susannah under her wing and I think it'll be good for both of them. So...I hope everything is good with you. Give me a call when you can. I also wanted to ask you a question. Something that might help you with—everything." He hung up and sat back on the couch. Before he could reflect on the events of the day, he took out his computer and opened the file he'd been working on. His resume was nearly complete and he was certain that getting it to the church immediately was critical. Still, it was a big step.

And it might freak Tess out if he showed up unannounced in Maple Ridge. How serious was she about moving on? Maybe he should talk to her about it first. Or maybe he should trust that she would like to find he'd come for her, for the town she'd once loved as much as he did, for the chance to put down roots in a place he'd longed to call home.

The ringing telephone made Josh jump, and he nearly knocked the computer over. He pressed the phone to his ear without checking the display. "Yeah.

This is Pastor Thorne."

"Hey, Pastor. You busy?"

Brody's voice surprised Josh, but he wasn't disappointed to hear it. "Hey, loser. What's up?"

"Not much. I, um, invited Tess over for dinner yesterday, and I was surprised to find she was acting like she used to. Actually it was kind of refreshing, considering."

Josh cleared his throat. "Considering what?"

"Well, everything… "

"Listen," Josh sighed. "If you're calling to find out whether Tess talked to me about her past, the answer is yes, she has. And I'm fine. I wasn't there, Brody. And I don't understand what it was like for you or anyone else who loves her, but I'm sure of what I've witnessed during her visit. And I can tell you, she's got a real passion for God. I don't have any reservations about getting close to her. I mean, I'm not proposing marriage or anything. I just want to, well, date, I guess."

Brody's laugh interrupted. "You need to calm down. Whatever is going on is none of my business. At least that's what Stell keeps telling me. I'm trying to keep out of it."

Josh cleared his throat awkwardly. "Oh, OK."

Brody chuckled again. "I said I was trying to keep out of it. That doesn't mean I will."

This time Josh laughed. "OK, so what can I do for you? I mean she's states away." Josh put his feet up on the coffee table and sat back, closing his eyes.

"I'm not sure," Brody sighed. "It's not even as if I got her back yet. I'm only starting to realize that she's back to what I remember—the fun, quirky, seat-of-her-pants girl. Not the dark, partying trouble-maker."

Josh smiled. "I imagine they're both different facets of her personality—only now she can use that energy in a positive direction. She's still tight as ever with Stu but how are things with your parents?"

Brody laughed wryly. "Mom barely speaks to her and dad acts as if he's clueless about what to do with her. They gave up after the last go-round. But Stu made her come to Sunday dinner the last few weeks. Everyone's working on it. Change isn't easy to come by. Tess is clear on that."

Josh opened his eyes. "Yeah. I think we all get it. So, what do you think about this? Me and Tess? I mean, maybe?"

Brody laughed. "I'm having a hard time thinking of both of you as adults and not Tess trailing after us to the ball fields swearing she'd tell Uncle Stu if we didn't let her play too."

Josh laughed, remembering. "Yeah, and really play not like she's a girl, Brody," he said, mimicking the voice Tess would whine with.

Brody laughed before exhaling. "So that's it. There's no agenda on my end. Just be careful and don't get hurt. And more importantly, don't hurt her. I got faith, not much, but some, that she's really coming back this time and I'll pretty much go crazy if you or this relationship ruins that."

Josh swallowed the hard lump that formed in his throat. "Yeah. I get it. And don't worry, I'll be careful. I think this is something that's really important for both of us."

14

*And be not conformed to this world: but be ye transformed
by the renewing of your mind, that ye may prove what is
that good, and acceptable, and perfect will of God.*
Romans 12: 2

Tess rolled clean silverware into a napkin and laid
it in the tray with the rest of the bundles. It was near
the end of her shift and it had been two days since
Derek asked her out on a date. It was practically a
record.

Two days also passed since she'd gotten enough
time in her schedule for a real conversation with Josh.
As much as she didn't want to admit it, she missed
him. Spending a few days with him was wonderful but
not nearly enough to convince her that she could
continue long-term with a relationship based solely on
a few phone calls and texts each week. It was wearing
her patience thin. She was even entertaining pleading
her case again with Uncle Stu, regardless of how
hopeless she knew it was.

"Hey," Derek flopped into the seat across from
Tess and waved the schedule from Pine View in her
face. "There's no way I can make this work. I got ten
other waitresses with problems too." He dropped the
paper on the table and shook his head. "This weekend
stuff is the real problem..." he pointed to the schedule.
"I need at least four waitresses on a Friday night, but

you can't work. Neither can Sheila or Deb. It's really sticking me."

Tess continued rolling silverware as she gave a quick glance toward the clock over Derek's shoulder. Her shift at the nursing home started in a half hour. "It's only for two weeks," she said. "Surely you can figure it out. I'll work doubles for you once Ashley-Marie gets things together at Pine View, OK?"

Derek stared at her. "Really? Why?"

"Because I need you to do me a favor. I'm not above doing one for you…" she quickly caught herself and qualified her statement before her boss could turn it into something inappropriate. "Within reason, of course."

"Of course," Derek ran his fingers through his hair. He sighed heavily.

Tess finished the silverware and stood. "I'm leaving," she said.

Derek glanced at her. "Hey, I'll work this out," he said. "But it sure would help if you'd do me a real favor."

Tess sighed heavily. "I will not go out with you, Derek. Please stop asking." The words sounded almost robotic to Tess's ears since she'd repeated them so many times before.

Derek smiled. "Wow. Thanks," he said. "Glad that wasn't the favor, but the offer is still open."

"I'm sure it is." Tess leaned against the end of the table. "All right, what is it?"

"Get me the number for that friend of yours. The one with the…" Derek glanced around. "Connections."

Tess's stomach clenched. Derek was referring to Justin Trapp. Tess was, at one time, what one might loosely define as 'friends' with the man a few years earlier. He was one of the first to get Tess into the messes she so readily found on her own shortly thereafter. Tess was not interested in reconnecting with him. She shook her head and stood up straight, ready to take on extra shifts or work until her arms fell off in an effort to avoid this. If she so much as even admitted she had a clue where Justin hung out or how to get in touch with him, Uncle Stu would find out and banish her from the family forever. "You don't want to be friends with him. Besides, he changes his number every other week to avoid the police."

Derek rolled his eyes. "Cut the bull."

Tess's phone began vibrating in her pocket. She shook her head. "No way." She yanked her apron off and walked away, tossing it angrily on the counter as she headed into the back room to answer her phone. "What?" she demanded.

"Well, that's some greeting." Uncle Stu's voice sounded both amused and concerned.

Tess grabbed her purse and headed out the back door into the cool spring air. Although the calendar said March, it was still felt like February most days. Thankfully, Tess was so angry she didn't notice that her breath was visible in the cool air. "Rough day," she muttered as she hopped into the truck, shoving the key into the ignition. When it roared to life she gunned it out of the parking lot, sending gravel in her wake. She popped the phone on speaker mode and set it on the center console.

"It's barely noon, Mouthy." Stu cleared his throat. "No trouble, I hope."

"I'm not in jail yet, if that's what you mean," Tess snapped, then softened her tone. "But it's still early."

"Care to elaborate?"

"Not now. I need to get over to Pine View. So, what's up?"

"Hmm. If you're on your way to Pine View and you just started the truck and you're angry, that would mean your other boss is giving you a hard time..."

"When isn't he? That isn't exactly your best detective work." Tess stopped at a red light and waited. Strangely, she spotted the man Derek was asking about moments before. She averted her gaze and made sure her doors were locked.

"I figured I should warn you I'm heading home soon. Wanted to make sure you're doing OK."

"Busy, but I'm behaving."

"You get the bike out yet?"

Tess sighed, wishing she'd been given enough time to even crave her beloved motorcycle. "No. Too busy working, and it's been raining and sleeting so..."

"We'll go over it when I get back."

"Sounds good."

Stu grunted. "How's Josh?"

Tess headed down the street toward the nursing home. "He's fine. I mean, I guess. We've talked a few times, and things are good." She pulled into a parking space. "I told him most of what happened. He doesn't seem bothered, Uncle Stu. Should I be worried?"

"Why? He likes you. It's good you two can talk and get reacquainted with each other. Besides, it gives him time to wrap his mind around how to move ahead if he wants—or if you even can. One day at a time."

Tess turned the truck off and grunted. "So you keep saying. Any chance I can quit the diner?"

Stu laughed. "If you already got another job or Ashley-Marie decides to give you a raise, I guess that would be an option. Otherwise, I'd say you need to stick it out for a few more months."

"Dang it."

"Go to work."

"You too. Careful coming home."

"See ya soon, kid."

Tess punched the off button and drew a deep breath. Before she could step out of her truck her phone buzzed again. She glanced at it to find a text from Josh that read: *Hope you're having a good day!*

She smiled and texted back: *Don't ask...call you later.*

~*~

"You know what I'd love?" Grandma Vi asked. She was sitting with her feet up, waiting for Tess to measure her medication.

"What's that, Gram?" Tess handed her grandmother a glass of juice along with her pills.

Gram shook her head as she took the pills, slugged the juice and handed the empty glass back.

Tess chuckled. She wondered for a brief moment if she'd gotten her drinking skills from her own grandmother.

"I'd love one of those blueberry muffins you make. Doesn't that sound good? With a nice cup of tea."

"It's your recipe, Gram."

"But they won't let me cook," Vi protested.

"Well, you could help me sometime. Maybe the cooks would let us do a little something in the kitchen."

Vi dismissed her with a wave of her hand. "Bring

me a muffin tomorrow. And while you're at it, make a whole batch and send them to Josh. He's still away at school, isn't he? Bet he'd love a care package from you. It would make a nice surprise." Grandma winked at Tess, who nearly dropped the pill bottles she was collecting.

"Um, what?" Tess was certain she'd never mentioned her renewed friendship with Josh and she doubted any of her family had done so either.

Vi pointed at Tess with a smile. "He's a nice young man. He'll come around eventually."

Tess laughed at her grandmother calling Josh a 'young man' when he was past thirty years old and well over six feet tall. "Oh, Gram..." she said carefully, neither confirming nor denying a thing.

Vi sighed, still smiling. "He'll marry you. He may not admit it yet, but he will."

Tess laughed as she went to the bed and began turning the blankets down. "Oh, I sure hope so," she said. "I've invested too much time in making that happen already."

"You said it." Gram stood and waved Tess away from the bed. "You teaching exercise class again tomorrow?"

"What? Um, yes, I think so."

Vi patted her cheek. "Good. Try working us a little harder, OK, kiddo?"

Tess nodded, not sure what direction the conversation would go in next.

Gram smiled again and waved toward the door. "Go on now. Give that boy a call and put him out of his misery."

Tess laughed and nodded. "I will, Gram." She kissed her cheek. "Love you."

"I love you too, honey."

~*~

Tess was so busy for the next two weeks that she scarcely got to talk to Josh, though they did text one another often. That he was thoughtful and sweet was making the situation more difficult. Tess still wondered if her life was a bubble about to burst. She'd managed to find the time to make her grandmother's requested muffins, sending half a dozen of them to Josh, knowing they were his favorite.

As soon as they were delivered he tried to call, but when he couldn't get her on the phone he sent her a text with a picture of the fresh muffins that said, "Is this a marriage proposal? If so, I accept."

Josh's words warmed her, but Tess never forgot reality. She was struck by the millions of reasons they'd never be together. In fact, she was well aware it would take years and distance before anything close to a relationship could happen. Still she burned for it. She was completely in love and sick with missing him.

"Where you been hiding yourself, Tess?"

The sound of Justin's voice immediately caused a bead of sweat on her forehead. She must have been too distracted by her busy morning to notice him sit in her section of the restaurant sometime between the breakfast and lunch rushes.

Justin smiled but his eyes glittered in a way that made her uncomfortable. He still resented the fact that she'd partied with him, and even dated him for a short time, but wouldn't let things go as far as he'd wanted.

She drew a breath, hoping no one would catch her talking to him. Brittany had to show up for her shift before Tess could leave to shower and go to Pine View to work a double. "I've been working," Tess said trying not to sound as cold as she felt. She drew her notepad from her pocket and held it up, pen poised to take his order. "What can I get you?"

Justin chuckled, shaking his head. "What you can get me is your manager. Apparently, he'd like to do a little business. Funny you wouldn't give me that message."

"He's in the back," Tess said. She turned to leave

Justin grabbed her wrist and yanked her down beside him forcefully despite his nasty smile. "Too good to talk to me?" he asked, reaching up to touch her cheek.

Tess pulled free and stood, glancing around. The other table was filled with senior citizens out for their monthly book club gathering. One woman stared in her direction and began to whisper to the others. Tess focused back on Justin, glaring. "Leave me alone."

Justin laughed again. "You forget that I know you. You'll need me again. You'll be back when all the glory of this working thing wears off. I got positions open."

Tess snorted. "I'm sure it's all perfectly legal."

Justin's eyes clouded for a moment before he schooled his expression, so it appeared he was friendly.

Tess wouldn't be fooled. She'd angered him and would, at some point, face his wrath.

"I run a legitimate business, providing for the needs of this community." He paused. "Get me some coffee."

Tess went behind the counter. She poked her head

into the small office next to the kitchen, where Derek was on the telephone. She gestured for him to wrap it up and come out front.

He nodded, but made no real effort to speed up his conversation.

Tess went back out to the dining room.

One of the gentlemen from the seniors' party approached the register.

Tess smiled as she took his bill. "I hope you enjoyed your breakfast this morning," she said.

The man glanced at her and grunted warily. "I thought this was a respectable place," he muttered as Tess collected his change from the register and held it out to him. "And then they hired you. No offense."

Tess's mouth went dry.

The man sighed. "Still you've been a pretty good waitress." He looked her in the eye. "My wife and I hoped you were cleaning up your act..." he nodded in Justin's direction. "But if you're still messing around with that trash, I'm afraid maybe we were wrong. You really should get it together."

Tess found no words that might convince him she wasn't getting back into that lifestyle. Instead she remembered the 'customer is always right' mantra and forced a smile. "You weren't wrong, sir. But I have a responsibility to wait on whoever comes into the restaurant."

The man nodded. "Well, if I were you I'd refuse that thing service. He's no good." The man went back to his table.

Tess grabbed a coffee mug and filled it, wishing she was in Florida.

15

Now faith is confidence in what we hope for and assurance about what we do not see.
Hebrews 11:1

It was only nine o'clock in the morning and already Josh had finished the lesson plans for this week's youth group meetings, answered five emails, and was about to research a fun outing for the kids at a local campground. Throwing himself into work felt right, even if he continued questioning his future in the youth ministry.

The ringing telephone interrupted his progress.

Josh cleared his throat and pressed the phone to his ear. "This is Pastor Thorne," he said, trying to force his mind away from the work on his computer.

"Josh? This is Dave Gorman from North Street Church in Maple Ridge."

Josh drew a deep breath. It had only been a few days since he'd sent in his resume. "Hello. How are you Dave?" He forced his voice to remain calm.

"Good, thanks. Hey, we were wondering if you'd be able to get out here in a few weeks for an interview. Maybe deliver a sermon for us and figure out whether we click."

Josh's insides quaked with the reality of the situation. He was clearly on the short list of candidates for the position. "Yeah, that would be great. I'm sure I can figure something out. Got a date in mind?"

"I'll put you on with the secretary in a minute and let you hash out the details with her. I think the board narrowed it down to a few dates but I'm not sure what they are."

"OK."

"We're impressed with your resume. I actually got the opportunity to work with your dad for a short time in Asia. He's fantastic."

"Yeah, he is pretty great," Josh said, fondly.

"So what makes you want to settle into a pastor's position over missions work?" Dave asked.

"I was in the field for a few years and of course growing up we were invested in it whether we wanted to be or not." He and Dave shared a quick laugh before Josh continued. "But I'm never settled in missions— even if I'm sure I'm supposed to be in ministry. Since I've started here in youth ministry things are coming together for me but I think that the next step is to find a home church. One I can serve long-term."

"And you think that's us?"

Josh laughed again. "Well, I'm not sure. I hope so," he said. "I think of Maple Ridge as my home since I spent the most consecutive years there growing up."

"Well, it's good to hear that. Your references are excellent and we're definitely anxious to meet with you."

Twenty minutes later the plans were set.

Josh would be in Maple Ridge in less than two weeks' time. The only question now was whether he'd surprise Tess or prepare her for his visit.

~*~

Tess hurried down the hall toward the rec room, kicking herself for being late to the exercise class. But it couldn't be helped. Ninety-five-year-old Doris Blackburn somehow escaped memory care and was wandering in the wrong wing of the building before Tess caught up with her.

"I kept them occupied as long as I could," Morgan said as Tess entered the room. She readjusted her off-kilter bun as she smiled at her friend.

"Thanks. Crisis averted, Blackburn has been returned to her nest."

Morgan laughed. "Mind if I stick around?" she asked.

"All right, but try not to break a sweat."

"I'll do my best."

Tess adjusted the radio at the front of the room before turning to her class. The usual suspects were there—Grandma Vi, her best friends, Betty and Helen, the never-satisfied and newest member of the group, Diana. And no one could miss the men who came mostly to ogle the women. Darryl, Bill, Martin, Larry, Steve, and Henry sat behind the women, talking and laughing as they waited for Tess to start. She smiled and cleared her throat, certain none of them heard her. She waved her hands and said loudly, "All right, kids, let's get this show on the road."

"It's about time," Diana muttered, shaking her gray head in disapproval.

"You said it," Tess said with a laugh as she hit the button on the radio. "Stand up everyone, let's get moving…"

~*~

Tess kept the somewhat rowdy group on track as she led them in stretches and basic exercises ranging in difficulty so everyone got a workout. But it was clear they'd accomplished enough as the group members started groaning and complaining that Tess was working them too hard. With a smile, she shut off the radio and said, "All right, let's call it a day. But you all better come back tomorrow."

Gram Vi smiled and waved to Tess as she left with her friends in tow.

"Great class," Morgan said, patting Tess on the back. "You sticking around tonight for game night?" she asked.

"Wouldn't miss it."

"Highlight of your week, huh?"

Tess laughed. "Well, the overtime is."

Morgan laughed.

Tess caught a motion by the rec room door. The tall man with dark hair turned in Tess's direction and her stomach dropped. Her father. "Crap," Tess muttered.

Morgan leaned close to Tess. "I need to run meds to the second floor," she said. "But I can stay a few minutes."

Tess shook her head and went toward her father. Her mother was talking to Grandma Vi on the couch across from the main desk. With a deep breath and quick prayer, Tess plastered a smile on and headed in their direction. She hadn't been in the same room with her parents since the last awkward and forced family dinner a few weeks earlier, before she'd gone to Florida. While it hadn't been a complete disaster, it was apparent that there was still a ways to go on the bridge Tess was trying to build back to her parents' trust.

Her father smiled as Tess approached. "Didn't realize you were working today." He awkwardly put an arm around her shoulders and hugged her, though he was quick to release his grip.

"I'm here pretty much every day," she said, relieved when she spotted Ashley-Marie heading in the opposite direction with a member of the kitchen staff, which meant that, for now, Tess was safe from further embarrassment. "So, what are you guys doing here?" she asked, trying to sound nonchalant even as her head began to pound with the many terrible ways this conversation could go.

Karen Carson turned from her mother and forced a smile. "We came to take Gram to get her hair done and afterward maybe we'll get something to eat. She's needed a day out for a while."

"Yeah. Why don't you bring her to dinner on Sunday?" Stan asked. "It would be nice for everyone to be together."

Tess tried to close her mouth when it fell open. The previous dinner ended when her mom asked if there was a middle ground in Tess's wardrobe between prostitute and bum. Tess stormed out, certain she wouldn't be invited again. That her parents wanted her to come back could only mean that Stu gave them an earful or that they were willing to move forward too, despite telling her that day that she still had a long way to go to be part of the family again.

She drew a deep breath. "I'll check the schedule," she said carefully. "Ashley-Marie is short-handed, and I've been doing doubles the last two weeks. I told her I want Sundays off, so I can get to church but it hasn't worked out for a while."

Stan nodded. "Well, come if you can."

Tess nodded too, wishing she could throw her arms around her father's neck. They'd been close once. Not like she was with Uncle Stu or Brody, but close enough that when she let her father down, Tess wondered if she would ever be able to forgive herself.

Her mother was another story entirely. Tess never pleased her and was certain she never would. Her mother wanted a little girl and she'd gotten Tess, a true loss in Karen's mind since her daughter always preferred softball and skinned knees over sugar and spice.

"Well," Karen stood, shadowed by Tess who was several inches taller. "It's time we get going. Gram's appointment is in twenty minutes and it is getting harder to get her in and out of the car."

Tess reached out to help Vi into her sweater. "Have fun, Gram," she said. "Good workout today."

Vi winked. "Got to keep this great figure," she said. "And don't you have any fun until I get back."

Tess laughed and impulsively hugged her grandmother. "I promise," she said.

Gram turned her attention to Stan, affectionately patting him on the cheek. "Well, let's get me prettied up so we can focus on my dear Tess. I'd like to dance at her wedding," she said.

Tess tried to laugh it off but she still grimaced. "How about we get you married off first, Gram?" she asked.

"Bah! Did that. I'm too old." She smiled at Tess with a twinkle in her eye. "But don't think I'm a fool. You're marrying Joshua Thorne." She shook her head. "Any girl who makes a man muffins…"

Tess cleared her throat as she tried to avoid the way her parents were staring at her. "OK, Gram, time to get to the salon. You don't want to be late, do you?" she urged her forward gently.

Stan looked at his daughter. "Tess?"

"I'll let you know about Sunday." Tess walked her parents out the door.

Ashley-Marie appeared. "Well, Theresa, I'll need you on the schedule double for another week. The new hires can't start right away."

Tess nodded as her phone vibrated in her pocket. "Sure. Is there any way I can come in later on Sunday? I'd like to…"

Ashley-Marie raised her hands to her temples as she closed her eyes, giving Tess her answer. "You understand what pressure I'm under right now," she said. "And between your waitressing schedule and now your personal preferences, I can't do it all."

Tess nodded, the fire burning inside again, telling her she needed to get out of town as soon as possible. She was tired to being beholden to everyone else's plans.

"Go get the trash on the third floor." Ashley-Marie lowered her hands. "I'm not sure why the maintenance crew failed to get it this morning."

"Right." Tess turned her attention to taking the steps two at a time in an effort to burn off the energy that woman inspired in her. When she reached the top, she yanked her phone from her pocket. A text from Jed.

You better make time for me tonight. I want a proper phone date. I miss your voice.

Tess smiled, glad someone wanted her.

~*~

"I'm beginning to wonder if I left you in jail long enough," Stu muttered as Tess glared at him. "Hand me that wrench."

Grudgingly, Tess grabbed the wrench, which she thrust into his hand.

Stu worked on her neighbor's plumbing with a couple grunts accompanying the twisting and banging of tools.

"I don't think I'm being unreasonable," she muttered. "I can't do this anymore. Justin showing up at work, Derek hitting on me, Ashley-Marie hates me. She gives me the worst jobs, and…." Tess groaned. "I went to the grocery store the other day and Mrs. Graham kept me in the produce aisle for something like twenty minutes telling me how if I really embraced God's love I'd be able to make better choices with my life."

Stu grimaced as he worked, clearly resisting the urge to explode at his niece for her constant whining. "They got nothing better to fuss about," he muttered. "Sometimes it takes people a while to admit there's anything different. Ever give any consideration to getting baptized? Maybe a public statement of your faith would…"

"Seriously?" Tess shook her head. The idea of getting up in front of the congregation to admit she was a sinner sounded as enticing as a root canal. Besides, everyone in town already knew her sins anyway. What help would it be to rehash them? "No way," Tess muttered.

Stu worked for another minute before he

responded with a grunt. "How much you got left to pay off?" he asked.

Tess kicked at the floor tile, annoyed. "I still owe Harrison around a thousand dollars, my parents five-seventy-five, and Brody three hundred. That doesn't even include the fifteen hundred I owe you."

Stu grunted again as he worked. "So…you need to drum up around thirty-five hundred. With what you make you'd need to work how long to do that…?"

A headache loomed. "Too long. Come on, Uncle Stu!" She stomped her foot. "Why can't I get out of here and send checks? They did invent the postal system a few years ago."

"Very funny, Mouthy." Stu poked his head out. "Turn on the water."

With a clenched jaw, Tess turned the water on while Stu listened, inspecting his work under the sink. He shook his head. "Turn it off." He went back to work before continuing. "Is this about Josh? You want to go back to Florida?"

"No," Tess snapped a little too quickly. She drew a breath. "I put resumes out everywhere. And I don't even think I should pursue Josh anymore. The whole idea is idiotic."

"What is?"

"Him and me."

Stu emerged from under the sink and checked the water again before beginning to clean up the mess of his scattered tools. "Did you say you sent out resumes already?"

"Yes. I figured it might take a while, so why wait?"

Stu squinted at her, irritated. "You figured your old uncle was such a push-over that if some hospital wanted to interview you and offer you a job in another state you'd get an easy out." He shook his head. "Nope. That wasn't our agreement when I bailed you out the last time."

"What?" Secretly Tess was hopeful that if something happened with her resumes she could get out of town faster. And since Stu rarely rejected her plans, she never gave the alternative any mind. "You wouldn't…"

Stu laughed and shook his head. "Maybe I wouldn't but do you think for a second Harrison Flynn would be OK with you leaving town before he's been paid?"

"Why do I care what he thinks? He can't do anything if I leave!"

"Maybe not. But trust me, there's satisfaction I can't begin to explain in proving them all wrong. Especially him." Stu grunted as he grabbed another wrench from the floor and set it back in his toolbox. "It's called the higher road and you're doing great. Giving up now would undermine all the progress you've made."

Tears burned Tess's eyes. She swallowed hard against them. She was tired, lonely, and angry. This line of thinking wasn't doing her any good.

Stu wrapped an arm around her and pulled her close against him. "I'm telling you the truth," he said. "And for the record, I think you should stick with Josh. He might be exactly what you need to get you out of this funk and convince you that you aren't the same girl anymore."

Tess gulped as 2 Corinthians 5:17 popped into her mind. In an effort to try to make it real again, she said softly, "Therefore if any man be in Christ, he is a new creature: old things are passed away; behold, all things are become new. "

"And you're doing that," he said. "I hope you believe it."

Tess wished she could. She'd believed it when she was with Josh but now, back home, it might have been a dream. "I need to get to work," she muttered. "I can't be late again or Derek will harass me–or worse, fire me."

"Before you go, call Josh," Stu said.

Tess closed the toolbox and lifted it as she followed her uncle from the apartment and out to his truck. "What for?" She'd spent nearly an hour the night before talking to him, and while it was wonderful, she'd sensed there was something he wanted to tell her but was holding back. It could only mean that he was reconsidering his intentions, and of course, she could hardly blame him.

"What for? For fun, for a smile," he said. "So, he can tell you how wonderful you are and you can giggle like a high school girl." Stu shuddered, making Tess smile as he continued. "I don't want to think what you two talk about. Tell him your plans for the bike this year." He tossed some supplies into the back of his truck. "Go on. You got an hour." He opened the door to his truck and glanced back at her. "I'll stop by the diner around six. Make sure you got a Reuben sandwich ready for me."

Tess nodded and went into her apartment. She glanced at her phone and sighed, not wanting to need Jed but realizing she truly did.

16

Consider it pure joy, my brothers and sisters, whenever you
face trials of many kinds, because you know that the testing
of your faith produces perseverance. Let perseverance finish
its work so that you may be mature and complete, not
lacking anything.
James 1:2-4

"Hey, Tornado. Miss me?" Josh asked, pleased that despite their long conversation the previous night, Tess was calling again.

"Ha. Ha." Something in her voice told Josh she wasn't calling for fun.

He closed the door to his office, against the prying ears of his students and the secretary. "What's wrong?" he asked. The long pause that followed told him that despite the miles between them he'd managed a bullseye. "Tess?" He heard a sniff and what sounded like Tess blowing her nose. "Hey..." Josh said gently. "Can I help?"

"No," she said. "I'm not even sure why I'm calling."

"Maybe because you like me?" Josh teased.

Tess laughed weakly. "Nope." She paused. "Ok, maybe a little."

"Good. That's how much I like you too."

Tess exhaled, indicating her defeat. "I'm burned out. I've been working my tail off for the last few weeks and I guess I realized how hopeless this all is."

Josh sat at his desk, accepting her point and yet confused at the same time. "What's hopeless?"

"You and me. Getting out of town. Convincing anyone I'm different," she said. "I guess I called to tell you that we should probably stop calling each other. I don't want to drag you down. You need to focus on your job and I have a lot of debt to work on. I can't even be a good, fake girlfriend in another state."

Against his better judgment, Josh laughed. "I'm sorry," he said. "I didn't mean to laugh but...well, I won't stop calling you."

"You will if I change my number."

"Tess."

"You think I'm kidding?"

Josh sighed, wishing they could talk in person. "Talking to you is the highlight of my day. I love it. You will win and I'll be there cheering you on, you hear me?"

She sniffed.

Josh imagined her nodding as she wiped her nose. "Don't give up," he whispered. "I'm on your side. I always pick a winner."

Tess groaned. "No, you don't. You used to be a Brown's fan."

Josh laughed until his sides hurt. "It was one summer. And I'm reformed. I promise. I've been a Pittsburgh's fan for years."

"OK. I guess I can still be your fake girlfriend."

The sound of her light chuckling filled Josh with pride. He'd done that. He'd made Tess smile. "That's my favorite girl," he said.

"I..."

"You OK?" Josh asked gently.

"If I'm really your girl, Jed…I think I'll be fine."

Josh smiled. "Good," he said. "Because you are. Listen, there's something I want to ask you." Josh leaned back in his chair as he waited what seemed like an eternity.

"Yeah?" she finally asked, her voice shaky. "What is it?"

"Well, I was thinking about what you said about everyone in town thinking you hadn't changed, or at least not believing in you and I wondered if you might think about…I don't know. Addressing that in a public way. Maybe if you talked to your pastor about being baptized. Maybe they'd accept you, and believe you're serious."

Tess didn't speak for several moments.

Josh wondered if she'd heard him. "Tess?" he asked quietly. "What do you think?"

"I think you've been talking to Uncle Stu," she snapped.

Josh laughed. "No, I don't make a practice of talking to your uncle about you," he said. "Why? Did he mention it?"

"Maybe." Her voice held bitter tone.

Josh tried not to let that discourage him. He plunged on. "You always said he was smart," he said gently.

"Even smart men make mistakes."

"Hey, it's just an idea. But maybe you should consider it. It might take something like that, something dramatic, for the naysayers to believe you mean it."

"You don't get it, Jed."

Josh glanced at the clock, aware that he had a meeting in less than twenty minutes. He didn't care.

"Tell me. I want to be sympathetic. But baptism is a public confession of your faith. You aren't ashamed of your relationship with Christ, are you?"

"Of course not. It has nothing to do with that, and everything to do with the judgmental people in the congregation." She paused. "I sneak into the back of the service alone—or if I'm lucky with Morgan—maybe get out before I'm forced to talk to anyone..." her voice drifted off as she laughed wryly. "I can't even get anyone outside my family to shake my hand during the greeting time."

Josh's hopes sank. "Just because it won't be easy doesn't mean it won't be worth it. Look, Tornado, I'm happy to answer any questions about it, and I'll be praying for you. But you shouldn't move ahead until you're ready even though I think you are."

Tess snorted. "I'm going to work."

Josh smiled as her defiant attitude returned. "Better?"

"Maybe."

Josh couldn't stop from laughing. "Oh, Tess. I miss you."

"I miss you too, Jed. Even if you do get on my nerves."

Josh laughed again. "Oh, it's taking a lot of effort right now not to hop on a plane, so I can be with you."

"Ditto."

"I better go," Josh said reluctantly. "We'll talk later, OK?"

"Sure."

Tess hung up before Josh could say anymore. He set his phone aside and leaned back in his chair as he closed his eyes.

~*~

"Here's to the end of double shifts!" Morgan cheered as she toasted Tess, clanking their milkshake glasses together.

Tess laughed, though her heart wasn't in it. In the few weeks she'd been working double shifts she'd managed to pay off some debt, even as the rest of her troubles appeared to be weights she'd never escape. "I'm so glad I get to sleep in tomorrow." She set her glass on the table. She reached for a fry and dragged it through a mountain of ketchup before popping it into her mouth. "I forgot what that's like."

Morgan nodded. She'd worked some of the overtime with Tess, though her responsibilities at home—taking care of two sickly parents—hadn't allowed her to do nearly as much time at Pine View. She lifted her burger but before taking a bite, said, "How on earth did you get out of the Saturday breakfast rush?"

Tess shrugged. "No clue. The only thing I can think is that Derek's too busy with his new best friend to notice me. He's not even tried to grab my rear end in the last week. It's been like a vacation."

"I can imagine." Morgan laughed but suddenly grew serious. "Hey, I ran into Stu over at Flynn's pharmacy. He..." she glanced around the restaurant before continuing. "...I mean, it might not be anything, but he was with a woman and when I walked over to say hello I was sure I saw them holding hands. He's not dating anyone is he?"

Tess tried to mask her shock. Her uncle was a handsome man when he made an effort to clean himself up—but he preferred work, which drove him away from most women. He'd told Tess many times that he didn't need the drama a woman would bring to his life. And judging by the way he rarely got along with his sister-in-law, Tess took him at his word. That she'd never heard of him dating, mention a girlfriend, or show any interest whatever in the opposite sex convinced Tess completely that her uncle was a loner. It never occurred to her that he could have a life outside of his work and taking care of her.

Tess forced a laugh before responding to her friend. "You're working too much," she said. "Uncle Stu hasn't ever dated that I can think of. I don't think it's possible."

Morgan raised an eyebrow and shrugged. "I'm only telling you what I saw."

"I'll ask him but I can already predict his answer, 'I can't help it if the ladies love me. I can't get rid of them,' and then he'll change the subject." Tess reached for her milkshake and took a long drink before continuing. "Besides, don't you think he'd tell me?"

Morgan squirmed. "Well, you have been a little…I mean, you've had enough on your plate for a while now. And then with the Josh situation, maybe he didn't want to bring it up."

Again, Tess laughed. Between work and daily calls, and sometimes hourly texts from Josh, she was pretty busy. She hadn't even been able to get to church in a few weeks. But surely Stu would tell her something as important as his having found a girlfriend.

Someone approached her. Thinking it was the waitress, she glanced up with a smile that quickly faded.

Justin.

"Scoot over," he demanded.

Tess moved to the end of the bench to keep him from sitting down. "Go away," she said before taking a bite of her sandwich.

Justin shoved Tess, forcing her to the side so he could sit. "I only want to talk."

"I could get a restraining order."

Justin laughed and nudged her.

Tess dropped her sandwich back into the basket with her fries, her appetite gone.

"You like me too much," he said.

Morgan cleared her throat and glared across the table at Justin with great distaste. While she and Tess were friendly in high school, Morgan wasn't intimately familiar with the side of her friend's dark path that came later. Morgan was a good girl. Good grades, perfect attendance, and kindness that oozed from her pores. To find she was sitting across from a convicted drug dealer was probably enough to make her lose her appetite too.

Tess met her friend's eyes, trying to communicate the apology she wanted to speak but couldn't.

"You should go," Morgan said.

Justin turned to meet the redhead's green eyes. He smiled, reaching across the table with all the smoothness of a snake. He touched Morgan's hand gently before she yanked it away from him, nearly knocking over the ketchup bottle in the process. Justin laughed. "Easy, babe. I won't bite. Well, unless you want me to."

Tess turned to him. "What do you want? Is there a reason you keep turning up where I am?"

"Easy!" Justin exclaimed. "I gave you enough time

to cool off. I wanted to rekindle our friendship or maybe more if you're up for it."

Tess nodded toward the door. "Get out of here," she said.

"And what if I wanted to go to church with you, Sister Theresa?"

Tess met his eyes for a brief moment, wondering what he was up to. "The doors of the church are open to everyone. It would do you some good actually."

Again, he burst into laughter. "Yeah," he gasped. "I'll call you when I'm serious."

"Please don't," Morgan said. "I don't think she wants you here."

Justin adjusted the thick gold watch around his wrist, making sure both women saw and noted its value, before he leaned back in the seat, his long legs stretching out next to the booth. "It's a wonder I waste my time. Aren't Christians supposed to be so kind and loving and hate the sin, not the sinner?"

"That works when the sinner wants to repent," Tess said. "Well, we were about finished here, so if you'll excuse us…" she tried to nudge him aside but he refused to budge.

He might be a drug dealer, but he was too smart to actually do the drugs himself. Instead he was the picture of health. Slimy, dirty, drug-money health, but health nonetheless.

"Not so fast, sweets," Justin glanced down at her and brushed a wisp of hair from her eyes. "I miss you. I don't understand why we should let all this religion stuff come between us."

"Don't touch me!" Tess tried to retreat to the other side of the booth but there wasn't any room left and she was pressed against the wall. "It's not the religion.

You're a drug dealer and I don't want any part of that. I'm cleaning things up. Can't you leave me be?"

Justin reached out and grabbed Tess's arm so tightly she blinked back the stars that popped before her eyes. She grunted and tried to break free, but he held firm, smiling as he tightened his grip. "I'd appreciate it if you wouldn't say that so loud."

"Everyone already knows," Morgan said. "Get out of here."

Justin ignored her and kept his eyes trained on Tess. "I want your bike."

If Tess was shocked to run into him again, this was worse. No one touched her motorcycle. No one.

"What?" she asked. "Why?"

"I need to get out of town. Lay low for a bit," he said. "Can't exactly take my car. Cops will find me in a second."

"It's in storage," Tess said, glad when he released her arm. "And I need to check the engine before it's ready for the road this year."

Justin gritted his teeth. "Give me the keys."

"Go away." Tess glanced up.

Morgan's face was ashen. She was completely focused on something going on over Tess's shoulder.

Justin slid out of the booth, towering over the women as he placed his hands on the table. "You wouldn't even own that bike without me."

Tess turned her attention from Morgan's face to Justin's. She glared at him. "What?! I bought it!"

Justin laughed. "OK, if you think you could afford a piece like that for what you paid…" He stood to his full height and reached out to touch Tess's cheek. "You go on ahead."

Tess stared across the table.

Morgan gulped. "Um...." She began, her gaze now focused behind Justin's shoulder.

Tess turned.

Joshua Thorne was approaching their table.

~*~

On the way to Maple Ridge, Josh had plenty of time to ponder his relationship with Tess. He wasn't able to talk to her as much as he'd wanted in the last two weeks, and he was certain that surprising her would show how much she meant to him. The anticipation of being with her again was enough to nearly drive him mad.

As soon as the sign for his old hometown was in view, Josh rolled his neck and sat up straighter, the fatigue of the long trip suddenly gone. He was intent on finding Tess immediately, so instead of wasting time, he stopped by the home of the one person he was certain would know exactly where she was. Stu immediately told Josh where to find her, and if the smile Tess's uncle wore was any indication, Josh made the right choice in electing to surprise the woman he was daily becoming convinced would soon be his wife.

As Josh approached the table it was apparent something was amiss.

The man standing over Tess touched her several times while she tried to shrink away.

Josh drew a deep breath. He needed to stay calm, and yet he was nearly overcome with a desire to rip the man to shreds. Was this what she'd been trying to tell him so many times? Josh didn't have time to act.

The man took a step back and walked away.

Maybe it was best to let him go. Josh wasn't looking for a fight on his first night back in town. And from the looks of the guy, that's all a confrontation would bring.

The man left the restaurant out a side door.

Josh took the opportunity to surprise the woman who'd consumed his world for weeks. He stepped up to the table and smiled. "Surprise!" he said, bringing his arm from behind his back to reveal a bouquet of flowers. He held them out to her and met her eyes. "How's it going, Tornado?"

Tess stared at him in complete shock.

Morgan's horrified face melted into a smile as she recovered. "Josh! Wow! What are you doing here?"

Dumbstruck, Tess slowly took the flowers and moved over so he could sit.

Josh smiled at her, curious at the strange expression on her face, but so overcome with the relief of being with her again, he chose not to ask. "I came to surprise you," he said, wondering when the restaurant became so hot. He swallowed, praying he'd imagined the fear that washed over Tess's face. He continued, "… and to tell you that I'm being interviewed for a position at your church." He paused. "I didn't tell you until it was sure, and since we weren't able to talk much lately, I figured it might be nice to…" his voice drifted off as he scanned her face again. "Um… why are you looking at me like that?"

Morgan stifled a laugh. "I think she's speechless…" She tossed some bills on the table. "I'll catch up with you later, Tess. He can give you a ride home." She stood and touched Josh's arm. "Welcome back, Josh."

Josh nodded and slipped from the seat beside Tess to the one across from her. He smiled as he reached over and took her hand, relieved to be in her presence again. "I hoped you'd be happier that I'm here," he said, wondering if he'd made a huge mistake. He took a deep breath, trying to quiet his racing pulse.

Tess shook her head, glancing around the restaurant in a panic. "Did you tell anyone you were looking for me?" she asked, keeping her head low.

Josh laughed. "No." He paused. "Well, I told Stu. I wasn't sure where to find you."

Tess groaned. "We need to get out of here." She grabbed his hand and started to tug him from the booth but released him quickly. "Oh!" she yanked some money from her pocket, tossed it onto the table and grabbed Josh's hand again. "Let's go!"

17

*For ye were sometimes darkness, but now are ye light in the
Lord: walk as children of light.*
Ephesians 5:8

"Slow down!" Josh exclaimed, giving Tess's hand a firm pull in an attempt to stop her.

She plowed through the parking lot, pausing only when she realized she wasn't sure where she was going. "Which car's yours?" she demanded.

Josh glanced around, still shocked by the strength in Tess's small frame as she tugged on his arm yet again. He reluctantly pointed to his green compact rental. "That one."

Tess glanced around again and tried tugging him toward it but he refused to move.

"Tess." His voice was calm but invited no protest.

She stopped and anxiously gestured for him to move. "I need to get out of here," she pleaded.

Josh could scarcely mask his annoyance any longer. "What is the matter with you?" he demanded. He'd wanted her to jump into his arms, thrilled to be with him, not go tearing across a parking lot as she tried to escape the reality of his presence. "This isn't exactly how I imagined this would go," he muttered, hating that his voice sounded so whiny.

Tess stopped and dropped the flowers against her leg with a slapping sound. "Do you want to ruin your chance for this job before you even walk in the door for the interview?" she asked. "If anyone catches you with me, you can count your chances as gone, Jed. And you better not even mention my name either…"

Josh threw his hands into the air in frustration. "Oh, come on!"

Tess put her hands on her hips. "Did you notice the guy talking to me when you came into the restaurant?" she asked.

Josh wished he could say he missed seeing the man—he wanted to pretend that it never happened at all, but he nodded, his stomach clenching.

Tess raised an eyebrow. "He's my ex-boyfriend. A drug dealer I can't shake no matter how hard I try. Any other questions?"

Josh shook his head as his mouth went dry. Tess nodded and again nudged him toward the car, grabbing his hand and yanking the keys from him to open it. "Now, let's get out of here before something bad happens."

~*~

Tess tried to sit as low in the seat as possible as Josh drove toward her apartment. She hadn't been sure where to tell him to go. Every place she could think of held the potential for trouble.

"Don't do that," he said with a grimace, nudging her to sit up. "You really make it hard for a guy to be romantic."

She bit her nails. "I didn't ask you to come. And I tried to warn you." She paused. "This was a mistake. It wasn't fair to let you think…"

Josh stopped the car abruptly at a stop sign and pulled a U-turn to head back for town right as they'd been about to escape the possibility of being spotted. Tess gasped. "What are you doing?" Her stomach flipped.

The tires squealed as Josh slammed on the brakes at a light. He glanced in her direction. "What I'm doing is taking you for a cup of coffee so that I can prove to you how ridiculous you're being," he spat. "I'll not go into hiding because this town is full of idiots. I'll skip the job if need be, and…"

Tess snorted. "And what? We'll spend the rest of our lives texting and talking on the phone? Good plan, Jed. That's always been a dream of mine. Talk about romantic!"

"Come on." His voice softened. "I missed you, Tess."

"Yeah? Well, I missed you too," Tess snapped, as she folded her arms angrily over her chest. This was the man Tess remembered. He wasn't quick-tempered, but he did tend to speak his mind. He'd put Tess in her place many times when they were younger, and she'd pulled yet another prank in an effort to get his attention. It was a wonder he still spoke to her.

"Jed," she pleaded. "You just got here. You don't understand." It seemed so unfair that even as things were slowly righting themselves in Tess's life, Josh should do something so stupid as to surprise her with a visit. If only he'd told her he was coming, she could have considered how she'd handle it. Now she was barely on auto-pilot, praying her reputation wouldn't ruin his life.

"No, I don't think *you* understand." Josh

continued driving until he reached the diner. He pulled into the lot and parked as Tess's stomach rolled. "We are going in there to get a cup of coffee and a piece of pie like two civilized adults out for some conversation. And you'll find that this situation you think you're in is nothing but a figment of your overactive imagination." Josh jumped from the car, slammed the driver's door to emphasize his point, and yanked Tess's door open in a swift gesture. He held out his hand to her and drew a long deep breath as he winked. "A tornado goes where it pleases, right? Come on. Show me what a rebel you really are. Go on a date with me."

A wave of nausea hit Tess and she prayed the little she'd managed to eat for dinner would not find its way to the floor of Josh's rental car. "I wish you'd take me seriously," she begged.

Josh leaned into the door, still holding his hand out for her. "I'm only here through Monday morning. Do you want to spend that time arguing over whether or not the town thinks you're a pariah?"

Tess finally took his hand and let Josh help her from the car. He slammed the door as she turned to him and spoke. "I don't want to argue with you. It's the truth, Jed. And, unfortunately, you're about to view it firsthand." She took a step toward the doors of the diner.

"Now you're delusional," Josh muttered.

Tess snorted as he held out his arm for her. She shook her head. "There's no way I'm touching you. You'll become a leper," she said and yanked the door open. "Fine, Jed. Let's get this over with."

~*~

Josh entered the diner behind Tess, his confidence waning the minute he noticed the way people glanced at her and immediately turned to one another to whisper. He wanted to say it was his imagination, but he feared Tess spoke truth. His resolve wavered, if only for a brief moment.

Tess slid into a booth and sank low, covering her face with the menu as a waitress appeared.

"I'm Dee and I'll be your server tonight. Can I get you....? Hey! What are you doing here?" Dee snapped her gum and winked appreciatively in Josh's direction before turning back to Tess. She gestured toward him as she spoke. "Why on earth would you bring a guy like that into a place like this?"

Tess groaned quietly but forced a smile.

Josh folded his hands on top of the table. "I forgot you work here," he said. "Well...I guess she can recommend the best pie, can't she?"

Dee winked at Josh. "What can I get you to drink, hon?"

"I would love a cup of coffee. Black, thanks."

Dee nodded and turned her attention to Tess, who was still sitting low in her seat.

"Me, too," she said. "Thanks, Dee."

"Sure thing." Dee turned and headed back to the waitress's station.

Josh turned his smile back to Tess. "Well imagine that! No one asked us to leave."

Tess rolled her eyes. "Give it time."

Josh grinned, wishing she was as relieved to see him as he was her. The relaxed, joking, fun Tess he'd met in Florida was replaced by a wary, nervous, frightened woman Josh didn't recognize. He reached across the table and tapped her hand. "Hey," he said with a smile. "What did you think would happen, Tess?"

She snorted. "Not this."

Josh continued leaning toward her. "Well, I wasn't spending the rest of my life calling and texting you. I figured there'd be a point when we actually lived in the same town, went on dates like normal people. I like you, Tess," he said. "I wouldn't have started this if…"

"Starting this at all was a mistake!" Tess exclaimed. "If you'd listened to me…" she glanced up.

Derek headed in their direction, carrying the coffee Dee got for them. "Well…" Derek set the mugs down and smiled at Tess, and then Josh.

Josh smiled back, only registering at the last moment that his date was doing her best to avoid the man's gaze.

"I'm Derek Patterson, the manager. Tess's boss."

Josh smiled and extended his hand to the man. As they shook hands, he wondered if he was encroaching on the other man's territory. Dismissing the notion, he sat back in the seat. "Josh Thorne. Tess and I go way back," he said.

Derek nodded, smiling in an unsettling way. "Yeah. She's like that with a lot of guys around here."

Josh straightened in his seat as the meaning behind the man's words registered. "Excuse me?" he asked, noticing Tess's horrified face. "I think you owe her an apology."

Derek burst into a fit of laughter. "Yeah, right." He walked away.

Dee approached and pretended to wipe the table.

"Sorry. He insisted on coming over." She stood straight up and smiled. "Now, what can I get for you?"

~*~

Now that Josh had gotten a glimpse of what her life was like he didn't seem bothered enough to run away. It appeared as if he wasn't planning to go anywhere. He was taking his time with each bite of pie while smiling across the table at her.

Tess ate her pie quickly, hoping they could leave as soon as she finished. "Don't you need to meet with someone or something?" Tess asked in exasperation. "I mean, about your job?"

Josh took a drink of coffee and waited while Dee refilled it before he answered. "Thanks," he said with a smile.

She nodded and left.

He turned his attention back to Tess. "I've got a meeting tomorrow morning but I'm free until then." He smiled and pointed at her with his fork. "You're not getting rid of me."

Tess sighed heavily and slumped back into her seat. "Why not?"

"I already told you why not," he said and scraped the last piece of pie from his plate. "This banana cream was delicious."

"Jed." Tess wondered how to make him understand. But Josh wasn't interested in entertaining her protest.

"So," he continued as if she hadn't said his name. "Tomorrow I've got the interview, followed by lunch with the pastors and their wives, after that I meet with the board..." Josh pulled his phone out and went through the schedule. He groaned. "I don't think I'm really free until about eight o'clock. How's that for you?"

Tess shrugged. "I work late. I'm not even sure I can get to church on Sunday."

Josh appeared to be disappointed by her answer. "Oh," he said. "I was hoping you'd be there for my sermon."

Tess finally looked at Josh. It was such a relief to find him sitting across from her. She wanted to jump into his arms and hug him, but she held herself back for both their sakes. Now that Derek caught them together, it was only a matter of time before everyone else in town was privy to the relationship as well. "I can't," she whispered. "I...I'm ruining this for you. My plan is to get out of here by the end of the year if possible...so, I understand you want to put down roots, but I may be gone soon."

"Hey." Josh reached across the table and took her hand in his. "I do want to put down roots, but you are not ruining anything. Promise. But, if you leave, I'm not sure what the point of my putting down roots in Maple Ridge would be."

Tess couldn't miss the meaning of his words. "But..."

Josh smiled as he took his hand back and ran fingers through his hair. "Yeah. Maybe I'm crazy. But I think home is where you are, Tornado. So how about we give this the time it deserves, and you stop worrying?" Josh held her gaze. "OK?"

Tess nodded reluctantly.

Josh's smile widened, and his dimples sank deeper

into his cheeks, making her warm all over.

Derek stood at the counter watching them.

Her stomach sank. "I promise I won't say 'I told you so'. I mean, when I'm right."

"What if I said you shouldn't say it at all?" Josh continued smiling.

Tess, for a moment, forgot what she'd been so concerned about.

~*~

"I'm sorry it's late," Josh said as he slammed the door on Tess's side of the car. He relished the sight of her. She was slowly returning to the comfortable, confident Tess he'd witnessed a few weeks earlier. As they'd drawn closer to her apartment, and gotten further from town, Josh noted that the walls around her were falling brick by brick. "It's good to be with you again," he whispered.

Tess reached for the door to her apartment. "You too," she said with a smile as she widened the door. "You want to come in?"

"I...probably shouldn't," he said carefully. "Hey, didn't you lock your door when you left?"

Tess leaned in the doorway and shook her head with a laugh. "No one wants my stuff," she said. "Besides I'm so far out of town...no one comes out here without a reason."

Josh nodded, certain he was being ridiculous. Still, he couldn't stop himself from saying, "OK...be careful. I hate the idea that something might happen."

Tess laughed.

Relief washed over him and Josh noticed the tension in his neck and arms begin to ease. He reached up and touched her cheek. Tess closed her eyes and Josh's heart constricted. He cleared his throat as his hand slowly dropped to his side. "I, um, should probably go."

Tess smiled as she opened her eyes. "Yeah." She paused. "They'll love you tomorrow."

"I hope so. I wouldn't want to bother putting on the suit if it wasn't really important."

Tess laughed again.

Josh couldn't resist. He leaned down and kissed her softly. "I'll call you tomorrow and let you know how it goes."

"OK. I'll be praying."

Josh stepped away from her, reluctant to leave but certain he'd be in trouble if he didn't. "Thanks." Josh got into his car. He smiled at her one last time, memorizing the way she waved as she stood in the doorway. "Soon," he muttered. "I won't be telling you good night at the door, Tess."

~*~

The ringing telephone ripped Tess from a dream about Josh. With a groan she reached beside her bed and grabbed it, pressing it to her ear, not caring to mask her irritation at having her one day to sleep in destroyed by the fact that she'd forgotten to turn her phone off. "Hello?"

"Hey, T, it's Brody."

"What the heck?" she muttered in annoyance.

"Sorry—I didn't mean to wake you," her brother's voice was apologetic.

"Don't worry about it," she grumbled.

"Oh, uh, well, I was on my way to pick up some papers I left at the office this morning and I was sure I spotted Josh coming out of the convenience store. Is he back in town?"

The words dragged Tess to the moment, reminding her that the night before they'd been together—along with her undesirable old friend. "Why did you call me and not him?" Tess asked.

"Well…"

Tess glanced at the clock and realized she should already be up, even if she did have the day off from the diner. "It was him. He's interviewing for a position at North Street church," she said with a yawn. "I saw him for a few minutes last night." She deliberately left out the rest of the story. That was enough for her brother to chew on.

"Hmm. So, it's getting serious?"

"He wants to put down roots—the church called to interview him. I don't think that has a whole lot to do with me, bro."

Brody laughed, making Tess's nerves bristle. "Sure, it doesn't. How long is he in town?"

"Monday, I think."

"OK—well if you two kids want to stop by, Stell said she's making pierogis tomorrow after church."

"Oh, I'm working, but you could text Josh…or call him. I'm sure he'd love to meet Stell." Tess paused. "Hey, Brody?"

"Yeah?"

"Is Uncle Stu dating someone?"

Brody laughed. "What? Are you serious? He'd

never…"

"Yeah. That's what I thought. I'll talk to you later."
Tess hung up the phone and flopped back into the bed,
yanking the sheets over her head, certain she'd not be
going to sleep again.

18

*Have not I commanded thee? Be strong and of a good
courage; be not afraid, neither be thou dismayed:
for the Lord thy God is with thee whithersoever thou goest.*
Joshua 1:9

Josh sat down at the head of the table as Dave
instructed him. The man was shorter than Josh
expected, and thicker. He'd been the first to greet Josh
that day and immediately the men hit it off. Where
Josh was uncertain and nervous, Dave inspired ease
and confidence.

Before Josh could even begin to wonder if the
elders or staff would be disappointed to find he was
not his father, Dave assured him that there were no
doubts about his path and that the interview was
largely a formality. Short of a red flag, the church
board would likely offer Josh a position thanks to his
stellar references and his own achievements and
education.

Despite this reassurance, Josh's confidence slipped
as he glanced around the table. The church was big,
but it was also growing, a testament to those gathered
around the table and their hard work. The many
pastors and key members of the support staff helped
everything go smoothly with the large congregation.
Finally, Josh rested his gaze on his predecessor: John
Williamson.

All the confidence Josh built in himself over the first part of the day dissolved as he looked on this giant of the faith. He'd been a pillar of the Maple Ridge community for nearly forty years. He'd been the pastor when Josh and his family came to take over for a time when John was too ill with cancer to lead the church himself. They'd stayed on as Paul Thorne filled different gaps in the church for several years after from youth to adult ministry. That Josh now might be the one to replace Pastor Williamson was overwhelming.

Before Josh could allow himself to melt under the pressure, John winked at him and reassured him with a smile. "Welcome, Josh. We can't begin to tell you what a pleasure it is that you're with us."

Josh smiled back and did his best to catch the eye of every person around the table. "It's an honor to be here," he said honestly. "I told Dave that I've always considered Maple Ridge the only home I've ever really had. It's the only place I lived for an extended time. I've always wanted to get back here and put down roots."

Dave shuffled some papers and began passing things around the table. "I already sent out attachments of these, but I like hard copies too, so I made some for everyone." He shuffled more papers and passed them again. "These include Josh's resume, references, and so on."

As the papers were passed around the table, Dave turned to Josh and nodded. "While those are going around, why don't you go ahead and give us a quick rundown of things—your education, why you chose to focus in church ministry, anything you think might be important to our conversation."

Josh laughed. "Well, that's a tall order but I'll do

my best. And if there are any questions for me…"

Dave nodded, and Josh drew a deep breath. "All right. Let's get started."

~*~

A short time later, Josh was certain he was exactly where he was supposed to be. The camaraderie among the pastors was evident and already Josh laughed so hard he was nearly in tears. He liked these people. The only matter that remained was his sermon on Sunday.

"Well, we've kept you trapped here long enough," the adult ministry pastor, Mark Davidson, said as the meeting came to an end. "I'll catch you later for dinner…" he stood and extended his hand and the men shook on it.

Josh smiled. "It was nice meeting you. I'm excited to have more time for fellowship later."

More conversation was made briefly until all that remained in the room were John, Dave, and Josh.

"Well," the elderly patriarch struggled to stand, leaning heavily on his cane as he did. "I'm starving. Let's get to it."

Josh smiled. The only reason John finally decided it was time to retire was that his wife recently passed, and he wanted to live closer to his children who moved to the southern states years ago. They'd convinced him that the climate would do him good—at nearly eighty years old, he'd finally agreed.

The men left the church together and Dave drove them to an Italian restaurant. They were seated quickly, and their orders were taken.

Josh sat back and was beginning to enjoy the warm atmosphere when his cell phone vibrated in his pocket. Because Dave and John were talking between themselves, Josh stole a glance down at his phone and noticed he'd gotten a text from Tess. It read: *I've been praying. Hope all is going well.* Josh smiled as he closed the text and stuffed the phone back into his pocket.

The other men were smiling at him.

"Anything important?" Dave asked.

Josh fiddled with his napkin. "Oh, no, just a friend wishing me well today. She said she was praying for me."

John smiled confidently. "My wife always was my best friend—from the time I met her," he said.

Josh quickly shook his head. "Oh, no, she's not my wife...I mean, I'm not yet married."

"Well, there's time," John said.

Dave reached for his glass of water. "I understand you lived here for a few years, Josh. Any chance you get to catch up with any friends if you move back? I mean did you stay in touch with anyone from the area?"

Josh smiled. "Actually, I grew up next door to the Carson family and was very close with Brody. We lost touch when we went to different colleges, but recently I reconnected with his sister, Tess, when she came down with your church group to help our church rebuild our youth center." Josh swore he caught the men exchanging a glance but the moment was gone before he could be sure.

The waitress arrived to take their order, ending any chance for Josh to ask about what he feared he'd seen.

Dave cleared his throat. "Well, we hope you'll

invite your friends to Sunday's service," Dave said. "Always good for more of the community to be involved in our worship of the Lord."

Josh nodded. "I hope they can make it." He smiled. "Shall I say the blessing?"

~*~

A short time later the men were back to the church for more meetings and further conversation.

John kept Josh company as he waited for the elders' board to convene. As they sat alone in the church's conference room, John glanced at Josh before speaking. "I'm sure you noticed that there's a problem surrounding your friend," he said.

Josh swallowed hard. "My friend?"

"Theresa Carson earned a reputation around here not long ago...and she's got an enemy on our own church board. Now, I wouldn't condemn anyone..."

The sweat began to bead on Josh's forehead. He fought the urge to take a swipe at it, opting instead to fuss with the cuff link on his right sleeve.

"...but Harrison Flynn has a strong dislike for that young lady—with some justification, of course. She did deface his building multiple times with various profanities."

Josh swallowed again. So here was the problem Tess feared. He said a quick prayer before answering, asking God to speak through him.

"Yes...well, Tess has been making many efforts to clean up her act," he said. "I wouldn't defend her actions, of course, but," he paused, hoping he didn't sound desperate. "I've known Tess since she was a little girl and she's always been…" he paused. "What I mean is, she's working hard to turn things around. I have faith in her."

John smiled and nodded. "Of course." He patted Josh's hand. "I would simply encourage you to be careful with whom you choose to associate yourself. If I've learned one thing over the years, it's that the people of the community expect to trust their pastor for guidance and strength. You need to take that responsibility seriously."

Josh forced a smile, not sure what he was agreeing to with this discussion, yet he nodded anyway. "Indeed, sir. Indeed."

John struggled to stand and hobble toward the door. "Until tomorrow, son." The man left.

Josh wondered if perhaps Tess wouldn't be able to say 'I told you so' soon.

~*~

By the end of the long day Josh was exhausted and confused. He'd loved everything about the church and the pastors. He'd even met a few of the families and was completely at peace with his increasing desire to take the position should it be offered to him. It was only when Tess came into the conversation that things got messy. And it only got worse when the elders questioned him at length as to why he wasn't yet married.

One board member tried encouraging him, saying, "Time to get your priorities in order," while another was more direct, "You're thirty-one? Whoa. I had two kids and another on the way already at your age."

Josh tried not to be annoyed or dejected, but it was clear there was much room for growth in the adult and singles ministries. He wondered if the rest of the singles in the church were at all frustrated by the pressure and scriptural misunderstanding among the elders.

Josh trudged out of the restaurant where he'd just finished eating dinner with some families from the church. He'd texted Tess a few times but she was busy and couldn't respond to him. He truly needed to talk to her. Josh got into his rental car. The dash clock read eight-fifteen. Tess wouldn't be off work for hours. He yanked at his tie before sending her a text.

I'm done. When can I see you?

He started the car and backed out.

The phone chimed.

I'll be home in about an hour. Meet me there?

Josh sent back a happy face. He dropped his phone and headed for the hotel to get a quick shower and change clothes.

~*~

"You invited him to your apartment?" Morgan's face was incredulous. She handed Tess a vacuum. "Now, don't you look at me like that! You aren't doing anything wrong but there are other people who don't trust that yet."

Tess sighed heavily. "What else can I do? I don't want him to go out with me in public either." She pushed the vacuum toward the movie room. The group had watched a classic film and there was popcorn all over the floor. Since the movie was her idea, she was required to clean it up.

"It's a sticky situation," Morgan agreed. "But if you want him to move here...he has to get the job first, right?"

"That's just it. Do I want him to move here?" Tess stopped in the doorway. "You still aren't telling me what to do."

Morgan laughed and shook her head. "Well how should I know what to do?!"

Tess unwound the vacuum cord and plugged it into the wall. "Helpful. Really..." she muttered.

"Sorry." Morgan shrugged. "I gotta go get the laundry from Esther Jenkins' room before Ashley-Marie reminds me again. Let me know what happens."

Tess waved her off and positioned the vacuum to start cleaning.

A man walked toward the room.

Praying it wasn't Josh, she leaned out the door. "Uncle Stu," she called.

Most of the residents went back to their rooms for the night, so the lobby and main floor were nearly vacant. While Stu sometimes dropped by, it was unusual for him to come in so late.

He walked toward her, one hand stuffed into his jeans pockets. "What are you doing, Mouthy?"

"Same old, same old," Tess muttered. "You?"

Stu shrugged. "I was on my way home and..."

Tess suddenly remembered Morgan's question about Stu dating and she gave her uncle a quick once over, intent on finding anything about him that was different. He was dressed normally but he smelled like cologne instead of grease, his hair was clean, and he'd shaved. He rarely shaved.

Tess squinted and leaned close, inhaling again to be sure. "Why do you smell good?" she asked warily.

Stu took a step back and shrugged. "Finish what you're doing."

"Oh, no..." Tess said as she plugged in the vacuum. "Morgan said she saw you at Flynn's the other day holding some woman's hand. Are you dating someone?"

He gave nothing away. "Are you?" he asked. "Your boyfriend stopped by yesterday. Did he find you?"

"Don't change the subject."

Her uncle held up his hands and sighed. "OK. You got me. I am dating someone."

"Humph." Tess tried to mask the sting of his admission by starting the vacuum and taking her time with the entire room in an effort to clear her mind.

Stu sat off to one side while she finished her work.

"Why are you still here? Traitor." Tess unplugged the vacuum and began winding the cord back into place.

Stu's brow wrinkled in confusion. "Why am I a traitor?"

"You didn't tell me." Tess couldn't mask the hurt in her voice. "Everything's changing, except the things that I really need to change. But you can't leave me like Brody did," she said weakly. "Not when I still need you. I don't have anyone else left." Tess was shocked at the tears that burned her eyes.

Stu stood and wrapped her in his arms. "Hey. Do you think there'll ever be a time when you don't need me for something?" he asked. "No matter what happens for either of us, I'll be here."

Something in his voice made Tess look him in the eye. He smiled, and she couldn't help but do the same. "Who is she?" she asked with a sniff.

Stu's eyes lit up. "She's a secretary for one of the landscaping companies I work with. We get along and she doesn't mind me being me."

Tess grabbed the vacuum.

"Actually, that's why I stopped by," Stu continued. "I mean, besides to harass you about Josh."

Tess glanced up at him.

"I want you to meet Marlene. Maybe I could take my girls to church or dinner or something."

Tess still didn't like it but she needed to give the poor woman a chance. If Stu liked Marlene, she was special. Tess forced a smile. "OK. Just say when."

19

Humble yourselves, therefore, under the mighty hand of God
so that at the proper time he may exalt you,
casting all your anxieties on him, because he cares for you.
1 Peter 5:6-7

Josh parked his car outside Tess's door and drew a deep breath. Her truck was nearby and her apartment lights were on. He stifled a yawn and got out, anxious to tell her about his day.

He walked toward her apartment.

Tess came outside and ushered him backward. "We can't stay here," she said anxiously. "People find out you came into my apartment and spent anything over ten minutes and it will be all over town I'm having your baby."

Head spinning, Josh tried to smile. He glanced around. "No one's here, Tornado."

Tess groaned as she shoved him at his car. "Don't be stupid. They're everywhere."

Josh allowed her to jostle him toward the car until he put his hands up in defense. He opened the door and she got in. "I'm not sure my hotel room is a good choice either, considering."

Tess laughed despite the intensity on her face. "No." She buckled her seat belt. "I got the perfect place. I hope you brought a jacket. It might get chilly."

Confused, Josh started the car.

~*~

Ten minutes later, Josh was navigating terrain that barely registered as a path.

Tess's demeanor softened the farther they got from the town's lights. She kept her gaze trained on a distant spot in front of them. "You better kill the lights and park back here," she said.

"How are we supposed to see anything?" he asked.

She yanked a flashlight from her purse. "Call me prepared," she said.

Curious, Josh turned off the car. "All right, Tornado. What are you up to?"

"You'll see."

Josh took Tess's hand as they walked along a narrow path that was riddled with branches, leaves, and debris of all sort. "Where are we going?" he asked.

"You mean you don't remember?" she asked, offended. "Geez, we used to spend a lot of time here."

In the dark it was nearly impossible to tell, so Josh took her at her word. But when he looked ahead to a small clearing he caught sight of a tree that was as familiar to him as his own childhood home once was. With a smile he dropped Tess's hand and hurried forward, his eyes up above them. "It's still here?" he exclaimed, glancing back at her. The tree house was a staple of his childhood fun with the Carson kids. Josh couldn't believe he'd forgotten about it until that moment.

Tess laughed, nodding. "Wanna go up?"

"Think it can hold?"

She pretended to check him over carefully, even going around him once, squinting. "I'm not sure. You've put on some weight and..."

"Stop!" Josh laughed as his gaze travelled up the old tree house. He, Brody, Tess, and of course, Stan and Stu, spent a great deal of time crafting the structure, and in the years that followed they'd maintained it, and played there nearly every day.

"Go on. It's been a long time for you," she said. She held the flashlight out to him.

Josh took it and lifted his big frame up the tiny pegs that led inside.

Once his eyes adjusted he was able to take in the posters, toys, and other odds and ends that were still mostly intact—even the small makeshift seats were there. This was the reason he wanted a place to call home. The value of a tree house was too high to name. The bonds of his first friendships, the roots of what he considered his first home were established in this place, the tree made by God, the makeshift shelter made by the hands of his friends and himself.

Tess crawled inside the tree house. She stood, smiling. "Pretty great, huh?" she asked as she sat. "We can talk here, and no one will care."

Josh sat next to her. "This is great. But I think you need to understand that I'm not OK with this as a solution. We shouldn't hide. We aren't doing anything wrong."

Tess laughed. "Aren't we? Don't tell me no one has commented yet."

Josh didn't want to lie but admitting to the truth was dangerous too.

"Right." She sighed and stood, pacing the small space. "Well, how did it go today?"

"It went well, I think. Will you be in church tomorrow morning?"

Tess shook her head. "If they see me there..."

Josh started to protest. "I wanted you to say different. But I get it...even if I don't want to."

Tess smiled down at him and reached out to touch his face. "It doesn't mean I'm not praying for you...or that I don't want you here or in my life."

Josh closed his eyes, taking her hand in his. "I know." He waited for a moment before smiling at her. "Did you think any more about getting baptized?"

It was clear Tess wanted to say something, but she stayed quiet.

Josh didn't want to push her, so he waited.

"I'm still working on it," she managed to say. "Morgan thinks it's a good idea, so does Uncle Stu...but God knows who I am. I shouldn't have to rehash my sins in front of a town that already gossiped them to death anyway, right?"

Josh squeezed her hand. "It isn't about you," he said gently. "It's about Him."

For a long moment they held hands silently.

Tess squeezed his hand, smiling before she released it. "We should go. You'll want to review your notes for the sermon and get a good night's sleep."

Josh nodded as he stood. "Tess."

She turned to him before setting her foot on the top step. Josh smiled. "I'm pretty sure the job is mine, barring any major screw-ups tomorrow. I guess we'll need to think what that means for us." He swallowed hard. "I mean before this goes any further. There is an 'us' isn't there?"

Tess grimaced. "There shouldn't be. For your sake."

"That's not what I asked."

Tess sighed. "I've been handling this town on my own but I don't want to lead you on. I want out of here. I don't want to hide in a tree house, Jed. I want to date someone openly and it not be the subject of scrutiny or gossip. I need to be with a man who can be proud to be with me. I don't think that's too much to expect." She drew a deep breath, "So if you really think you need to stay here…"

"I think I do. I mean, that's the answer I keep coming up with."

Tess nodded. "Well, maybe this should be it. Our last…whatever this is."

Josh smiled. "Date?"

She laughed wryly. "Sure. Date."

Puzzled, Josh wondered out loud. "I'm not sure why God would make two seemingly-opposed things so much an obvious answer to prayer," he said, his eyebrows knitting together. He regarded Tess cautiously. "Let's pray."

Tess sat, and Josh did the same. He held her hand tightly as he spoke the words that burned all the way to his core when he realized his courtship wouldn't be at all what he wanted or hoped it would be.

"Dear Lord, we come before You now in confusion. Please, in Your name, make things clear to us both so that we might live to serve You through our relationship if that is Your intention for us. Help us to understand and accept Your will and to abide it. In Your name, Amen."

Josh raised his head and met Tess's eyes. Under the light of the moon that filtered through the windows of the tree house, he noticed the tears sparkling as they rolled down her cheeks. Josh gently wiped them away with his thumb, desperate to bear her pain for her, but unsure how to do so. He hated that his spirit was still so heavy despite his constant prayers. "Can I ask you something?" he asked softly.

Tess shrugged, waiting.

"Why Harrison's place?"

Tess turned away.

"Come on…" Josh's voice trailed off. He didn't want to beg, but it made no sense to him why there would be animosity between Tess and the elderly man whose family had owned the town's pharmacy for generations.

"I can't defend myself," Tess said.

"I'm not asking you to."

Tess's shoulders sagged as she spoke. "I was home, at my lowest point, and alone… His wife worked with my mom for a while and she'd tell mom all about how her granddaughter was the softball captain after I graduated, then she went to college on a full scholarship." Bitterness crept into her voice. "She got hurt too, but of course she didn't make the choices I was making. Of course not. She never pitied herself or made bad decisions."

Josh took her hand and squeezed it reassuringly. "I'm sorry."

Tess shrugged half-heartedly. "I finally hit my limit. They'd get Mom angry. And suddenly I was alone. No more school, no direction, no Brody. Even Stu and Dad were off working. So, I'd get riled up. It was a perfect storm." She paused. "And once I got started it felt impossible to stop with the pranks and vandalism. It was as if I couldn't help myself. At least then someone paid attention again."

"But you've apologized," Josh said, trying as

much to convince Tess as himself. "And you've made amends. You two might never be friends, but Tess, you can't worry about him."

Tess snorted. "Except that he also has the power to crush you too. I can't have that on my conscience with everything else."

Josh shook his head, hoping she'd believe him. "I can handle it." He kissed her hand softly. "We can handle it together. Because I still believe we're supposed to move ahead. Together."

She nodded but said nothing.

With little left to say, Josh stood and pulled her with him. There was nothing else to do but take her home.

~*~

Tess woke the next morning and rolled over with a groan. Her cell phone had been vibrating for nearly an hour but she'd managed to ignore it several times and fall back asleep. There was no ignoring it now. She sighed and picked it up, scrolling to find three texts from Josh.

The first read: *Hoping you changed your mind. It would help to see a friendly face*

The second read: *blue tie or red?*

The third: *Whatever comes today, I'll still be praying for you—and us.*

Tess smiled. She wanted to believe him. That the people's opinion of her didn't matter, and that nothing would impact his chances for a job. Deep down she knew better. Surely Harrison Flynn would be in the congregation this morning and if he caught her in his church... She couldn't go.

The phone buzzed again, this time with a phone call.

She sighed heavily, pressing it to her ear. "Yeah?"

"Hey, Mouthy, want me to pick you up for church?"

"I don't think so," Tess said as she sat up. "Besides, I work later and..."

"Not until, what, three?"

Tess bristled, wishing he wasn't so on top of things. "So?"

"So, I'm bringing Marlene. I want you to meet her. I'll pick you up at eight-thirty."

Tess groaned but didn't respond because he'd already hung up. And that was how Uncle Stu worked—how he'd gotten her to behave and focus. He hadn't given her a choice.

With a heavy sigh, Tess rolled from her bed and went to get dressed, wondering if she owned a pair of glasses and a mustache.

~*~

Josh hardly slept all night. He finally got out of bed around five o'clock in the morning, made a cup of coffee and sat reading his Bible and praying, unsettled by what he understood to be true but as yet could find no way to fathom. He was in love with Tess Carson and she was in love with him. But everything appeared to be against them. What Josh still couldn't understand was why. He struggled through his mixed-up thoughts.

His father texted him: *God is good. Praying you're in His will today.*

And a short time later, his sister Caroline also texted him: *Hoping to catch up with you today. Good luck!*

Josh smiled. If he moved he could form a relationship with his sister who lived only forty-five minutes away from the church. And he could be an uncle—a real one—to her three children. Tess wasn't the only reason he wanted this job. Josh went to his knees and prayed from the bottom of his soul for an answer—a clear answer.

~*~

"We're set," Dave said as he stepped back into the green room behind the main stage of the sanctuary.

Josh nodded with a smile as he glanced at John who was sitting beside him.

Dave went back to the stage and the music began.

It was energetic and motivating and Josh was certain he could get used to worship being that way every Sunday.

"He's good," John said. "But he's too young for me. You all are." He struggled to his feet and smiled. "It's a packed house today. They're all curious."

Josh laughed and squelched the nervousness that pricked his confidence. "I figured it would be."

John smiled and closed his eyes. "Lord, You've carried and blessed this church in ways I can't even begin to say. I pray in this moment that Your guidance will continue to pour forth over this church, its people, and those who most want to serve You in the ministry. Be with Josh this morning, Lord. Let him feel Your presence and know Your will. In Your name I pray. Amen."

Josh smiled as he opened his eyes. "Thank you."

John nodded as the song came to an end. He motioned for Josh to follow him. "Let's go worship the Lord together," he said with a wink and a smile.

~*~

Despite wanting to wallow in her misery, Tess got ready for church in record time. She was confident in her favorite green dress, and her hair did exactly what she'd wanted it to. She exchanged numerous texts with Josh who, she was certain, was nervous about the sermon. Though she said she'd pray for him, she didn't tell him she was on her way.

Stu's car tires crunched across the gravelly driveway outside.

She jumped from the couch, grabbed her purse and ran outside.

Her uncle stepped out of the car to greet her.

Tess nearly gasped.

Gone were the usual jeans and button-down shirt he wore to church, replaced by dress pants and a sport coat.

She wasn't sure she'd ever seen him dressed like that.

"Not a word, Mouthy," Stu said as he caught his niece trying to stifle a giggle.

"I wouldn't dream of it."

A woman opened the passenger door and stepped out, her long blond hair trailing behind her like a veil. Stu's girlfriend was beautiful. While she was only a few years younger than him, this woman was not under any delusions about her age. She was dressed conservatively in a long skirt and light blue top that made her eyes appear to be a deeper shade. She was smiling and reaching for Tess even before she'd completely gotten out of the car.

Tess liked her already.

"Oh, Tess. It's so good to finally meet you," Marlene said as she hugged her.

"It's nice to meet you too," Tess said.

Marlene stepped back and regarded Tess before turning to Stu who was beaming at them both. "You really are a man," Marlene said as she shook her head. "You said she was pretty but my goodness, Stu, she's beautiful. Stunning!"

Tess tried to hide behind her long hair as Stu shook his head. "She takes after her uncle."

Marlene laughed and turned back to Tess. "He sure is proud of you. And in case you were wondering, he wouldn't let me meet you until we'd gone out for a while. Said you were too important to him. He didn't want you think he was...messing around."

Tess's hope swelled. It was a matter of pride that Stu remained single as he'd impressed on her the importance of taking relationships seriously. She'd always imagined that he loved his work and that was why he never married. But now, watching him as he helped Marlene back into the car, Tess was sure there was more to it. He wanted a woman he could love and take care of, not one who was only in a relationship for fun. She smiled at her uncle as he opened the back door for her. "You mess this up and I will hurt you," she whispered. "That woman is awesome."

Stu smiled and kissed her forehead. "So is this one."

~*~

In no time at all the contentment Tess glimpsed briefly slipped away in favor of familiar anxiety. She groaned inwardly as she followed Stu and Marlene to the front of the church where Brody and Stell were reserving seats in the third row. She'd always hidden in the back rows, staying clear of the judgmental eyes of the congregation. That her brother would force her to the front was just mean.

Stell smiled as Tess flopped into the seat beside her. "So," she whispered. "What do you think of Marlene?"

Tess glanced down the row where Marlene showed she was capable of making the usually somber Karen Carson smile. Tess glanced back at Stell and shook her head. "If he doesn't marry her, I think I might."

Stell laughed. "I think Pastor Thorne might say something about that. Can you come after church for pierogis?"

Tess shook her head. For Josh's sake, she wanted to begin increasing the distance between them. "I shouldn't. I need to be at Pine View later."

"Really?" Stell sounded disappointed. "Josh is coming…"

Tess laughed. "Tempting, but probably more

reason for me to go to work."

The music minister walked onto the stage and the music began to play loudly. "Please stand with us," he said. "As we worship the Lord together."

Tess stood and let the music wash over her, refreshing her and renewing her resolve—if only for a few short moments.

When the song ended, the elderly pastor, John Williamson, stepped onto the stage with Josh close behind him. "Welcome," Pastor Williamson said as the congregation was seated, and the worship team left the stage. "We're pleased to welcome a delightful pastor here today to share God's word with you." He gestured.

Josh stepped forward, smiling at the congregation.

Tess gripped her hands tightly in her lap as she drew a deep breath. What was she doing? It was one thing to hide in a tree house and talk to Josh, or spend time with him states away, but this...? Even as she watched him standing there confidently in front of the congregation in his best suit—he'd gone with the red tie at Tess's urging—Tess was certain she needed to put a stop to their relationship before it got any further out of control. He was good, trustworthy, and moral. She wasn't worthy of a man like him.

"I've known Joshua Thorne since he was a boy," Pastor Williamson continued.

Tess forced her gaze away from Josh and back to the pastor's words.

"His father, Paul, pastored our church and worked with us years ago." Pictures of Josh as a child and growing up, in various mission experiences and work flashed on the screen.

Tess was horrified that there was one of she,

Brody, and Josh as kids. Was he insane? Why would he put her up there in such a public way? She sank down into her seat as the pastor continued speaking. Tess took a moment to steal a glance around the sanctuary and found all of the women's eyes trained hungrily on Josh. But, of course. He was a single, incredibly handsome, Christian man. Every unmarried woman in the right age bracket—and even some of those who were out of that range—would want a chance. And they all deserved it.

"I'm certain you will appreciate Josh's message for us this morning."

The congregation applauded as Josh stepped forward to the podium.

Tess hadn't listened to anything Pastor Williamson said.

Stell nudged her with a grin.

Tess did her best to smile back. She wished she'd gone to work early. Dealing with Ashley-Marie would be much more pleasant than dealing with her personal life.

20

I have chosen the way of faithfulness;
I have set my heart on your laws.
Psalms 119:30

Josh regarded the congregation and wondered what he'd gotten himself into. The sanctuary was filled to almost standing room only and it struck him that the church hadn't had a new pastor since his father took over for a time all those years ago. His presence there was exciting, sure, but it gave him pause that it appeared they'd stopped the search with him. Surely, he wasn't the best candidate? Was he? The congregation waited patiently as Josh set his Bible and notes on the podium. He smiled and said, "Good morning. I'm humbled by the kind words Pastor Williamson shared about me this morning. I'll do my best not to disappoint you. It's certainly an honor to be here." Josh drew a breath and tried not to notice that despite her protests, Tess had come to support him.

His heart beat wildly as his insides danced. She was so beautiful. He prayed he could show half the courage she did. He wasn't worthy of a woman like her. Josh cleared his throat and turned his attention to the sermon. "I want to share with you a message of hope this morning. A message that I pray will inspire you to understand that God's plan for you does not include hopelessness and despair, but rather a hope and peace that—as we know but rarely acknowledge—surpasses all human understanding." He opened his Bible to the first tab and looked again at his flock. "Before we begin, let us pray for His wisdom and blessing." Josh bowed his head and drew a deep breath, silently praying for God's word to speak through him as the congregation waited for his words to begin.

~*~

As the service ended Tess trained her gaze on the floor to avoid the many stares aimed in her direction.

One woman nearby smiled and touched her arm as she leaned in to whisper, "Don't give them any mind, honey. You belong here. Come sit with me anytime." She chuckled. "I'm always in the same seat." She gave Tess a reassuring pat on the arm. "My name's Sara."

Tess tried to smile but was too shocked at the woman's kindness. She nodded in Sara's direction as she walked away with her group. No one ever spoke to Tess like that since she'd started attending services. For a brief moment, she was able to hold her head a little higher.

"Oh, how nice! Caroline came," Karen said as the family moved toward the exit.

Josh's sister and a man who was likely her husband, had cornered the pastor shortly after the service ended. The couple, along with small twin boys and an older girl, were a few rows from her.

Before Tess could turn away, Josh looked directly

at her and smiled as if he'd known all along that she was there. Tess smiled back, and Josh waved her over. With a heavy sigh she tried to go the other way, but Brody caught her arm and shook his head. "Your boyfriend wants you," he said as he practically dragged her over, flanked by the rest of the family.

"Oh, my! Is this Theresa Carson?" Caroline reached out and hugged Tess happily. "You sure grew up. I think you were about ten or twelve years old the last time I saw you." Caroline was stunning, with short, trendy blonde hair and all the accessories befitting the wife of a successful attorney.

"You look great too, Caroline," Tess said. "I, uh, better go."

Josh reached out and grabbed her arm, shaking his head as he did. "Oh, no, you don't," he said softly before turning back to Caroline. "I'll call as soon as I hear anything. Thanks for coming. It means a lot to me."

Tess was certain his sister was aware Josh was still holding onto the 'little' neighbor's arm.

Caroline hugged Josh again. "You made us proud today, little brother."

Josh nodded as he crouched down to pick up the twin boys in his arms.

In an instant Tess imagined he was holding their children, and just as quickly, the image was gone. Her heart quaked with the daydream of what could be. It stayed firm in her heart even as she prayed that God take this desire from her. It was too painful thinking of all the things she didn't deserve and would never get. She was too weak.

"Uncle Josh will be back soon, OK?" he said to the boys. "And we'll get some ice cream...maybe go to the zoo…" He crouched back down so he could talk to the girl too. "Would you like that, Bella?"

She nodded with a smile and wrapped her arms around Josh's neck.

He set the boys down. "I'll miss you kiddos. Be good, all right?"

As Caroline and her family left the sanctuary, Tess realized her whole family was still standing nearby. They congratulated Josh on his sermon and began to disperse toward the exits.

"You'll be over at one?" Stell asked, taking hold of Brody's arm.

He smiled down at her. "You sure you can make enough to feed that oaf?" he asked.

Stell playfully smacked him as she laughed.

Josh chuckled and nodded. "I'll be there. Thanks for the invitation."

Tess smiled and started after Uncle Stu. "I got a ride with Stu."

A few people remained in the sanctuary. Most were watching her and Josh, as if there would be some kind of show.

"Wait," Josh said. "Will you be at Brody's?"

"I…I'm not sure yet." She smiled. "Great sermon. For once you knocked it out of the park."

Josh contemplated her words and the pointed reference to his few homeruns from high school baseball. "That's cold, Tornado."

Tess shrugged and hurried after Uncle Stu. Unfortunately, she didn't catch him.

Harrison Flynn caught her. "Ms. Carson."

Tess closed her eyes with a quick prayer for patience before turning to him. She plastered a smile on her face. "Hello, Mr. Flynn."

He cleared his throat and glared down his nose at her. "I believe I told you once not to mock the Lord. Showing up here today, throwing yourself at our new pastor..." he cleared his throat, dismissing her. "You'd be wise to find another church for your shenanigans. We won't tolerate this here."

Shocked, Tess gaped at him but said nothing.

Harrison nodded. "We need a new pastor and Mr. Thorne was the perfect candidate until ten minutes ago when I caught him cavorting with the likes of you. Don't ruin this for him. He has the chance of a lifetime and to throw it away on a teenage fling would be ludicrous."

Unable to stop herself, Tess spat, "Neither of us are teenagers." Oh, how she wished she could keep her mouth closed!

Harrison raised his eyebrows. "It is within your power to act like an adult."

Against her judgment and all of Uncle Stu's advice, Tess drew a deep breath and challenged him. "So, your church's reputation is worth more than my salvation? Is that what you're saying?"

Harrison shook his head. His voice remained calm, but something in his eyes told her he would never change his mind. "What I'm saying is that your reputation has not yet been disproved and attaching yourself to an upstanding man like Pastor Thorne will only serve to drag him down, not build you up faster in my, or this community's, eyes." Harrison straightened to his full height and cleared his throat again. "I'm saying that if you do not cease this conquest, you will find he is not likely to be hired here. The reputation of this institution has been established over many long years of continued service to this community—it would only take a moment for you to dismantle that altogether."

Tess's mouth went dry. "Are you threatening me?" she whispered. Tears stung her eyes. "What will it take for you to believe I'm reformed?"

Harrison stared down at her as if he intended to answer in a way that might not have been appropriate in church.

Uncle Stu came to stand beside his niece, placing a firm hand on her shoulder as he said, "I was wondering where you went." He extended a hand to Harrison and waited as the man reluctantly shook it. "Harrison."

"Stu." Harrison finally acknowledged him.

The men sized each other up.

"I trust Tess is on time with her payments?"

Harrison grunted and nodded reluctantly.

Stu reassured Tess with a side-hug.

Harrison continued glaring at her.

"Very good," Stu said. "Come on, young lady. Let's get you fed and back to work again." He smiled, nodding in Tess's direction. "She's come a long way, don't you think?" Without waiting for a reply, he guided Tess toward the church doors and outside.

The cool breeze did little to wash the angry heat from Tess's face.

~*~

"No." Tess started for her bedroom, but Stu stopped her with one word.

"Change."

Tess turned slowly and glanced from Stu to Marlene. Despite her protests, they'd followed her into her apartment and refused to leave until she changed clothes and went with them to lunch. "You don't get it." She'd spent the entire ride home blinking back tears of shame. She'd cried enough over the last few years so that there shouldn't be a tear left in her body, but Harrison managed to bring the worst darkness in her back to the light.

Marlene met Stu's eyes for a long moment and they appeared to understand what the other was thinking without a word being spoken.

He nodded and gestured toward his niece.

With a soft smile, Marlene went to Tess and took her by the arm. "Let's talk."

Tess reluctantly allowed the older woman to guide her into the bedroom where she closed the door and said, "Josh is only here a short time. Hiding yourself because one man who doesn't at all comprehend Christianity is giving you a hard time means you're letting that man win—which means you are completely ineffective for God. He can't use you if you don't believe that He can. Understand?"

Tess stared at the woman.

Marlene went to the closet during the lecture, opened it, and yanked out a cute shirt. She inspected it before offering it to Tess. "This one's nice," she said. "It will bring out your eyes." She handed Tess the top and sat on the bed as if the conversation was over.

"Where in the world did Uncle Stu find you?" Tess asked incredulously.

Marlene laughed. "It's more like I found him. I'd all but given up—finally embraced my life as a single woman. I was sure I could be happy working and being a good aunt to my nieces and nephews." She paused, thinking, a look of pure joy washing over her face. "But he walked into the office one day and I was stunned. Dumbstruck. He was exactly the man God told me I'd meet one day."

"I'm guessing it was a day he bothered to shave?" Tess asked.

"I honestly don't think it was," Marlene said, meeting Tess's eyes. "It was his directness, his confidence, and above all that he was clearly a man of integrity. I don't meet anyone like that often at my age." She paused. "It all sounds stupid when you say it out loud."

Tess shrugged. "Not too stupid," she said softly. "I was six-years-old when I met Josh. He said hello and I said, 'I'm going to marry you,' and I spent the next seven years chasing him."

The women laughed together.

Tess began to rummage through her jeans until she came up with her favorite pair.

"So why let him get away now?" Marlene's blue eyes challenged.

Tess sank down onto the bed next to her and sighed. "Because we aren't kids anymore and I'm not.... Every woman in that congregation today was staring at him as if he was the prize at the state fair. I'm not exactly the best of the best. Josh deserves better."

Marlene snorted. She stood and yanked Tess to her feet. "Now you listen to me." She gazed deep into Tess's eyes. "He didn't even glance at anyone else. I watched him. His eyes never left you because you are exactly the woman he needs. And he's the one who gets the privilege of being with you—not the other way around." She adjusted Tess's hair and smiled again.

"Get dressed. If there's one thing I understand about your uncle, he's got no patience when there's food involved." Marlene left her.

Alone, Tess got dressed, and more importantly, she thought over Marlene's words, Harrison's actions, and Josh's sermon.

~*~

"That guy is a piece of work, I'm telling you," Brody said as he handed Josh a cup of lemonade.

Josh sipped the cool drink, still reeling from the time he'd spent trying to deflect Harrison Flynn's concerns about his 'questionable relationship' with Tess. It was no small task. "He..." Josh held his hands out in defeat as he tried to calm down. "He hates her and wants to make her life miserable. So much for redemption and grace."

Brody regarded his friend before he spoke. "Well, Tess did make it her mission in life to terrorize the poor man."

"And she made amends," Josh said incredulously. "She's got two jobs to pay him back and she's doing whatever she can to show she's changed."

Brody glanced up as a car pulled to a stop in front of the house. "Uncle Stu's here," he said, tapping Josh on the leg. "Listen, you don't need to convince me— she's doing great. I get it, but I'm not sure we'll ever forget what she was and what she did, and we're her family. Flynn has no reason to let it go."

"Besides the proclamation of his faith, you mean." Josh was relieved to be in his friend's living room, able to say what he wanted without fear of judgment. He hadn't been this angry in a long time. And now, he was questioning whether he should take the job with the church at all. "She has asked his forgiveness and as a Christian he should be offering that freely, along with support to keep attending church. Ugh!"

Brody stood to open the door and laughed. "Man. It's like an alternate universe. Stu has a girlfriend, you're as in love with Tess as she used to be with you..." He paused to shake his head. "I can hardly take it." He opened the door. "Marlene!" he said and gave her a hug. "Hey, Uncle Stu." He accepted a bag of fresh-baked bread with a smile. "Stell's in the kitchen if you wanted to..."

"Sure, honey." Marlene took the bread with her and headed in that direction. "Your mom said they were visiting with Vi, but they might stop over later."

Brody nodded as Stu sat across from Josh.

"Survive the first day all right?" he asked.

Josh nodded, not wanting to alarm Tess's uncle with his anger. "Where's Tess? I mean... is she, uh, coming?"

Stu smiled. "We dropped her off, so she could change. You know Mouthy. Says she isn't coming but she'll be here. Likes a free meal."

Josh managed to smile.

"Hope she brings a pie," Brody said as he sank down into a plush arm chair. "Otherwise I'll ask her to leave."

The door swung open and Tess entered, balancing boxes that contained four pies. "Who's leaving?" she asked as she kicked off her shoes near the door.

Josh jumped to his feet and went to her. "Let me."

Tess laughed. "I got it all the way in here, didn't

I?" she asked.

He took two boxes and started for the kitchen.

"You drop that, and I will ask you to leave," Brody said as Josh disappeared. He glanced at Tess. "What'd you bring?"

"One blueberry, two apple, and a banana cream."

"Mmmm," Uncle Stu said. "When did you find time to do that?"

Josh came back into the room.

"Couldn't sleep last night."

Josh caught her eye.

Tess turned away quickly, her face flushed.

Brody rolled his eyes. "OK, Stell says we need to get in there because it's ready."

~*~

A short time later lunch was finished, and Josh sat back in his seat, filled, and yet itching to get Tess alone so they could talk. Sitting across from her for the entire meal was as close to torture as he'd ever been. And the more he contemplated what he'd witnessed earlier in the day, the more convinced he was that there must be a way around the naysayers that would still allow him to preach and date Tess too. But so far, he was coming up empty. It was possible that his original plan to not date anyone might actually make the most sense after all.

"What time did you say you need to get to Pastor John's?" Brody asked.

Josh glanced at his watch. "Oh, they're not expecting me until three or later," he said. "I've pretty much met with everyone—this last meeting is a formality, I think."

Tess drew in a deep breath as she glanced around the table. "I actually should get going." She glanced at Stell and smiled. "Thanks for having me. It was nice catching up with everyone." She stood and pushed in her chair.

Josh stood too. "Would you mind if I came too? I would…" He cleared his throat as the silence around the table stretched to a breaking point. "Um, I'd like to talk to you about something."

Tess shrugged as she turned to go.

Brody took his sister's turned back as an invitation to hit Josh in the arm as hard as he could.

Josh groaned but barely gave a passing acknowledgement to his friend as he hit him back before going after Tess. "Hey…" he said as she paused to slip her shoes on. "I need to be at the airport at seven tomorrow. I wasn't sure if I'd get to see you."

Tess took her purse from a hook by the door. She finally peered up at Josh and smiled. "Your sermon was awesome, Jed." Her voice was filled with a fondness that encouraged him, but even as he sensed hope, she continued. "But I don't think this…" Tess motioned between them. "Is a good idea. Harrison can make things hard and I can't fight anymore." Tess pushed the door open and went outside.

Although Josh heard the words he refused to believe them. He followed her to the truck, not caring that the dining room window faced them and the Carson family was watching him pathetically following Tess. "I got some fight left in me," he said, hope tingeing his voice. "Lean this way."

Tess shook her head as she opened the door to her

truck. "I can't do that to you," she said. "I'll find another church."

Josh leaned against the door, his body blocking her from getting in. "Come on," he said gently. "Am I losing you already? Right when I found you?"

"Maybe you are," she said, forcing a smile as she nudged by him, got in, and closed the door. "Have a safe trip home, Josh."

His ears burned. For the first time since he could remember she didn't call him 'Jed.' He'd never hated his given name until that moment.

21

*But they that wait upon the LORD shall renew [their]
strength; they shall mount up with wings as eagles; they
shall run, and not be weary; and they shall walk, and not
faint.*
Isaiah 40:31

Tess shoved a cart full of dirty bed sheets toward the laundry elevator, grateful her shift was nearly at its end. She'd worked from the moment she'd arrived—cleaning, assisting, organizing, and cleaning some more, and now her feet were sore, her hands and back were tired, and she was completely unfocused on what she was supposed to be doing because her mind kept wandering back to Josh.

The dopey expression on his face when he'd followed her out to the truck said he'd expected the conversation to play in his favor. Now he was probably confused and angry with her. But there was no other way.

"Theresa."

Tess stopped, wondering why Ashley-Marie never went home. She turned and leaned against the heavy cart.

Her boss walked on those awful stiletto heels until she got close enough to talk. Ashley-Marie leaned over Tess, nostrils flaring. "Why didn't you tell me Josh was in town? Honestly, are you still in grade school? Do you think we're in competition for him?" She paused, smiling. "Oh. Wait. You probably do think there's a chance now that you're, well, you." She waved her hand in dismissal. "You never did understand him…not as I did."

Tess stepped backward, pushing the cart with her rear end. "I should get the laundry done."

"Oh, no, you don't." Ashley-Marie waved her hand to stop her. "What's he doing here?"

It was pointless to play dumb—she'd get away much sooner if she told the truth. "He's being interviewed for the job at North Street Church."

"What?" The administrator who usually controlled her features appeared confused. "Why would he…?" She burst into a fit of laughter. "Oh, he's a pastor. I forgot. Well, now, I guess you really don't stand a chance, do you?" She walked away, the echoes of her snorting vibrating down the next hallway.

Tess continued on her way and finished the laundry before punching out for the day. Getting home would be a relief. Josh would be gone the next day, and she'd already made up her mind to ignore his texts and calls. It was the right thing to do for his sake and hers. And she intended to get even more resumes out across the country as soon as possible.

~*~

The parking lot outside Tess's apartment was barren, as usual, save for the few cars that belonged to the residents there. She pulled her truck into the usual spot right outside her door and hopped out, rolling her neck from side to side in an effort to eliminate the kinks. Something was out of place. Tess looked around again.

The door to the shed across the parking lot had been pried open and there was a crowbar nearby.

With a shudder, Tess moved closer and stared into the darkness. Nothing else seemed amiss. She wondered if she should call the police but immediately dismissed the idea. They didn't like her and wouldn't be in a hurry to come to her aid. She inhaled deeply, hoping for the resolve she needed as she moved toward the shed.

Uncle Stu kept the lawnmower and other supplies in there, but the shed was also where she hid her motorcycle during the winter months since she didn't own a proper garage to keep it in.

"Please let me be imagining things," Tess whispered to herself as she got close enough to confirm that the shed had, in fact, been broken into.

And her beloved motorcycle was gone.

~*~

Josh sat in his hotel room staring at the wall. He'd spent a good amount of time after he'd left John's home pacing the floor, running through numerous scenarios, and yet he'd come up with no real answers. He was still convinced he was supposed to be with Tess.

But John Williamson was clear that the congregation would love a pastor who was married...if only to the 'right kind of girl'.

Josh understood what that meant, but he'd pressed about repentant sinners and transformed lives.

"It all takes time. I'd advise any man in a position such as you're hoping to take on to be very careful." John smiled as he spoke.

The conversation was unsettling everything Josh had been confident of a short time ago.

"But there's something I like about Carson girl," John continued. "I can't quite put my finger on it, but I think she can do great things for the church. Only I'm not yet sure if it would be hurtful to you as a new pastor to tie yourself to a woman of her reputation right now."

Josh paced the floor again, certain he wouldn't sleep if he didn't talk to Tess again. It was already after eleven, but she'd be home. Without waiting another second, he grabbed his jacket and headed for her apartment.

~*~

Josh turned his car into the parking lot.

Tess was standing outside staring at a small shed. She appeared to be horrified.

Josh nearly forgot to set the parking brake before hopping out and slamming the car door.

She didn't even glance his way.

"Hey." Josh jogged over to her and to see what she was staring at. "Everything OK?" He peered around her into a garden shed that was full of tools and lawn care items.

Tess glanced up. "No. Everything is not OK," she

said, seemingly not surprised he was there.

Josh grew serious. "What's going on?"

Tess smacked Josh hard in the chest, nearly causing him to lose his balance. "My motorcycle was in there!" she shrieked. "And now it's gone!"

The reality of the situation sank in and Josh pulled his cell phone from his pocket. "What? I'll call the police."

Tess continued staring at the empty space, as if willing the motorcycle to reappear. "Don't bother," she muttered. "They won't rush out here for me. And even if they do, I'm sure it will somehow end up being my fault this happened."

"Tess," Josh began, aware she wasn't listening to him even as he wondered if this wasn't another sign for him to stop his pursuit of a relationship with her.

"Uncle Stu is on his way." Tess sat heavily on the curb. "I already know who took it anyway and until he wants to bring it back, it's gone."

Josh sat beside her. "But who would do that?"

"Remember that ex-boyfriend?"

Josh nodded. Was he still talking to the woman who moments before he'd been thinking he would marry?

Tess glanced at him and nodded. "Yeah. Him."

"Well, we should still call the police," he said simply.

"You really should get out of here. You don't want to get wrapped up in this. If Flynn finds out..."

Stu's car rolled into the parking lot.

With a quick glance at Tess who continued to appear to be dazed, Josh stood and moved closer to where Stu parked.

The man was out of the car in seconds, his gaze

trained on Tess.

"I think she's in shock," Josh said.

Stu closed the car door. "Figures."

"I only got here a few minutes ago. She didn't want me to call the police."

Stu nodded. "Still thinks they're all out to get her." He glanced in Tess's direction. "I already called them anyway." He patted Josh on the back. "Take her inside and I'll handle the police. I'll get you if we need her for anything."

Josh nodded and went to Tess. He extended a hand to her and said, "Come on, Tornado. Let's go inside."

Without protest, Tess lifted one weary hand and allowed Josh to tug her to her feet. He led her into the apartment and closed the door.

A police car turned into the lot.

~*~

Tess sank heavily into the couch as it registered that Josh was supposed to be at his hotel. It was after eleven o'clock, the police were outside her door, and the prospective pastor of the biggest church in her town was sitting in her living room. In anyone else's life it might have been funny, but considering her situation, humor was the last thing on Tess's mind. "What are you doing here?" she asked as Josh hustled around the kitchen making coffee.

He tossed her a grin that made her flush. She cursed his dimples even as he spoke.

"Would you believe I hoped I'd come over here

and sweep you off your feet before I went home? Maybe change your mind about me?"

Tess grunted. "I actually do believe that. Funny you're still here."

"I don't think it's funny at all," he said as he opened a cabinet and pulled two mugs out. "How am I doing so far?" He winked at her. "Still think I'm adorable?"

Tess released a dreamy sigh and hated herself. He was adorable as he poked around her kitchen, making himself right at home.

Josh laughed. "That's my girl." He filled two mugs and brought them into the living room. "So tell me about your bike. You said before you were going to paint it. Did you get to that yet?"

Tess shook her head. "I was thinking red. I wanted it to stand out."

Josh groaned. "Red? Yuck."

Shocked, Tess looked at him. "Yuck? What are you? Five? Besides, red will look awesome."

Josh snorted. "Black is the only way to go. Stealthy. Like mine."

Tess rolled her eyes as she accepted the mug of coffee from him. "I'll stick to red. Thanks." She relished the warmth on her cold hands and even more Josh's sweetness for comforting her when she was upset.

"I'll still ride with you if it's red," he promised.

"You're a saint," Tess muttered as he sat across from her.

The door opened, and Stu entered, followed by a police officer Tess hadn't met before. She was surprised, but thankful for small favors.

"Officer Dixon wants to ask you some questions," Stu said.

Tess nodded.

The officer stood near the doorway with a notepad in hand. "Did you touch anything when you found the shed like that?"

Tess didn't answer immediately.

He raised his head. "Ma'am? Did you touch anything?"

Tess shook her head. "No, sir, I didn't."

"Any idea what they wanted?"

"All that's in there are lawn tools and…" Stu began.

"My motorcycle," Tess finished.

"I told them that," Stu said as he leaned in the doorway.

She nodded as she set her mug down. "Justin Trapp threatened me when I wouldn't loan him the bike the other day. He said he'd take it."

The officer stared at her. The name alone was enough to make anything else Tess said suspect. "You're too nice a girl to be mixed up with a guy like that."

Stu glared at the man. "My niece has been in some trouble. But that's all far in the past, I can assure you— this is her pastor, Joshua Thorne."

Josh stood and shook the man's hand. "Nice to meet you, Officer Dixon."

"Were you here when she got home?"

Josh sat back down. "No sir, I got here immediately after."

The officer nodded and began a series of questions that made Tess's head spin. She'd been on the other side of the questions before—guilty and well aware that her trouble was only beginning. Never before had she been on the side of the questions that meant the police were trying to help. It was still a little too much to believe.

~*~

A short time later the officer finished, promising to do what he could to locate Tess's motorcycle as quickly as possible.

Stu thanked the man and escorted him out. "Get some rest, kid," he said, and gave Tess a hug. He gestured for Josh to follow him to the door. "Make sure she's calmed down before you leave. And that she locks the door for a change. You can drop her at my place if need be and I'll get her to work in the morning."

Josh turned to Tess.

She was staring across the room as if her heart was broken.

He sat. "You all right, Tornado?"

Tess laughed wryly. "It was just a money pit anyway...and I still have the truck."

"It was insured, right?"

"I could only afford collision."

Josh grimaced.

Tess offered a weak smile. "It's all right."

"The police will find it."

"Wrecked? Scrapped for parts and left at a junkyard?" Tess stood. "Go back to your hotel. You shouldn't lose sleep too."

Josh followed her into the kitchen. "I want you to make me a deal."

Tess groaned. "Yeah? What kind of deal?" She

took the coffee mugs to the sink and began washing them.

Josh grabbed a dish towel and dried. "Well, you're so nervous about us…and maybe I see a little as to why that is now, but I still don't think we should call this off. There's something between us, Tess."

"Mmm-hmm," Tess hummed doubtfully. "So what's the deal?"

Josh exhaled nervously, wracking his brain for how to say it and not sound as if he was trying to weasel his way out of being with her. He wouldn't do that. Would he? "I just hoped there would be a way for us to figure this out. Perhaps we can just see each other quietly. We don't owe anyone anything. We don't have to make dating—if I get the job and move here, that is—more than it is before things are serious. Right?"

Tess looked at him, her eyes full of disappointment. She forced a smile and nodded. "Yeah. Sure. So we agree to date in secret?"

Josh squirmed. It sounded awful when she said the words aloud. "That's not exactly what I meant."

"No," Tess's face brightened. "It's a fine idea. No one gets hurt and we figure things out. It's great." But her voice wasn't at all convincing.

"Tess…"

She laughed as she shut the water off and dried her hands. "You're getting the job," she said. "And if you purposely associate with me when you move here, in secret or in the open, don't you think that's asking for trouble?"

Josh tossed the dishtowel away and followed Tess to the living room. He took her hands and gazed into her eyes. "I wasn't asking for this. I wasn't searching for you. I'm just trying to figure it out and find a way to get you on board. With me."

"And what about all the people in this town who know what kind of a woman I am?"

"What kind of a woman you were," Josh corrected.

"Ha. They'd say it's the same thing."

"They'd be wrong."

Tess sighed. "Jed."

Josh pursed his lips and raised one eyebrow.

"What?" Tess asked warily.

"Now that you're back to calling me Jed I figure I've got a better chance at winning this argument." He winked playfully, hoping his dimples were doing their job.

"Cocky, aren't you?"

"You always said I was."

Tess groaned.

"So, what do you think?" Josh asked.

Tess folded her arms over her chest in annoyance. "That you're delusional?"

"Try again. You called me that already."

Tess thought for a long moment. "If you get the job, we'll...date quietly."

Josh scooted closer to her and put his arm around her. "How long will you need to hide until you're comfortable with us?"

Tess leaned into him for a brief moment before moving away. "I don't know."

Josh sighed heavily before nodding. "All right. I think I can live with that. For now." He paused. "Are you sure you're OK?"

Tess considered his question. "I don't have a choice, do I?"

Josh smiled and kissed her. "Not as long as I'm here you don't. I promise to make sure you're OK from now on."

~*~

Tess wanted to hate how safe and loved Josh made her feel. She didn't deserve it. But even in the face of a complete meltdown over the loss of her motorcycle, she couldn't help but be overwhelmed by his care for her. And the fear that their association would ruin his life. Sadly, she now was certain he felt it too.

His 'deal' made that clear enough, and a little part of Tess was disappointed to find he wasn't as sure of overcoming everything that stood in their way as he'd once seemed. She now wondered if he loved her enough to follow through on his promises. But deep down, Tess didn't want to know; so rather than ask, she changed the subject. "Ashley-Marie was upset with me for not telling her you were in town. She figured I was trying to keep you to myself."

Josh smiled broadly and leaned back against the couch cushions. "Yeah? How is Ashley-Marie?"

Tess rolled her eyes. "Annoying. Mean. Still mad about the garden hose."

Josh laughed. "Maybe I should give her a call." He nudged Tess. "We could all go out and catch up on old times."

Tess studied her nails as he spoke, refusing to take the bait. "We had different old times since she's as old as you are."

Josh burst out laughing. "That's true, but I wouldn't remind her of that if I were you," he said, shuddering. He smiled as he looked into her eyes. "So, are you trying to keep me to yourself?"

Tess snorted as she looked away. "No. I tried unloading you on her but even she wouldn't take you. I'm doing you a favor letting you hang out with me. No one else wants you."

Josh laughed as he stood, tugging Tess with him. "I figured as much." He hugged her and stepped back. "I hate to go. I'm not sure when," he swallowed. "Or if I'll be back."

Tess shrugged as if it didn't matter. "Well, as long as I'm still paying off debts, I'll be here."

Josh kissed her and stepped away so he could grab his jacket. "Call me when they find your bike. I'll talk you into painting it black."

Tess groaned and followed him to the door where he stopped.

"You don't think he'll come back here tonight, do you?" he asked, worried. "I could sleep on the couch if you don't think you're safe. Or Stu said I can drop you off at his place."

Tess laughed openly. She'd never let Josh put his reputation in jeopardy no matter the chances of Justin coming back. Thankfully, she didn't think he would, so saying, "Bad idea," was easy enough for her to manage.

"But what if he comes back and tries something else? What if he gets violent?" Josh's forehead wrinkled in his worry.

"Violence was never his thing—at least with me. If he needed to send a message he'd get someone else to do it. And I don't see what purpose that would serve in this case. He already has what he wants."

Josh nodded reluctantly. "OK. Lock the door when I go. Stu's orders. And mine."

Tess smiled. "I'll be all right."

"Lock it anyway." Josh kissed her quickly and opened the door. "Goodbye...for now."

Tess nodded. "For now."

22

What shall we then say to these things?
If God be for us, who can be against us?
Romans 8:31

The next morning Tess drove to the diner to work the breakfast rush. Since the weather was finally warming and she had a little time without double shifts, she'd planned on working on her bike. But now she wasn't sure if or when that would happen. Against her best judgment she'd even tried calling the last number she knew for Justin but it was disconnected. Figured.

"Carson! Order up!"

Tess hustled behind the counter and grabbed a tray. She loaded it with plates for the businessmen seated in her section and made her way to deliver the food. As she set it on the table she smiled, "How's everything look?" she asked.

One of the men smiled and nodded. "It's wonderful, thanks."

"Great. I'll be back in a few minutes with refills." Tess rushed behind the counter again and stood waiting for the coffee to finish brewing.

"Hey." Derek leaned against the counter. "What's going on with you?"

Tess watched the coffee slowly dripping into the carafe, wishing it would go faster. "What do you mean?"

"Justin was in here yesterday asking about you."

Tess glared. "Yeah? Well, I'm pretty sure he stole my motorcycle so if he told you anything, maybe you could help me out by telling the police."

Derek laughed and shook his head. "And admit I talk to that guy? No way. I don't want to lose my job. My dad would kill me!"

Tess laughed. "Sure. But you party with him..." She reached for the pot but Derek stopped her cold.

"Listen, he's..." he paused, looking around before he turned back to Tess. "He really is bad news. I don't trust him. You watch yourself."

A warning from Derek was strange since he wasn't exactly a pillar of the community himself. Tess smiled, appreciating his effort. "Thanks. I'll, uh, keep that in mind." She grabbed the coffee and went back to work, grateful to be busy.

A short time later, Tess hustled home, changed clothes and went to Pine View for an afternoon and evening full of whatever Ashley-Marie wanted of her. As she drove toward her second job, her cell phone rang. "Hello?" She pulled neatly into a parking space and set the brake.

"Tornado?"

As usual, Tess's stomach flopped and her cheeks flushed. She cringed in response to her traitorous body. "Hey...you home?"

"Walking through the airport."

"And you're calling me already?"

"I'm a sucker, what can I say?" Josh asked with a laugh.

"Well make it fast, sucker. I need to go—I'm sitting in the parking lot at Pine View now. I start work in five minutes."

"Any word on the bike?"

One of the staff members was helping Mr. Bowman, an eighty-three-year-old former professional athlete turned physical education teacher, into his daughter's car for their weekly trip to the mall.

Tess smiled. Even though she worked on her resume already and made plans to get more copies printed and sent out that evening, she was beginning to realize she actually would miss the people she served at Pine View. "No. I doubt I'll hear anything. Justin won't be found until he wants to be. And my bike is pretty easy to hide."

"Well, call me if anything changes."

"I will."

"Um, I actually called because I...hold on a sec." There was some jostling and Josh talked to someone else before breathing heavily into the phone. "Sorry. I was getting my car..." He paused. "Anyway, I called because the board gave the go-ahead on hiring me. I can start as soon as I get things settled here."

Tess's stomach clenched. She forced a smile and hoped it carried into her voice when she said, "Wow. That fast? That's great."

Josh laughed. "You're not very convincing."

"Really? I tried so hard."

He laughed again. "Keep working at it and maybe you'll improve. Hey, I was thinking about everything, and our 'deal'. I don't want to hide with you. I'm sorry I ever said that, Tess. It's insulting. I don't feel that way. The only way I want us to be together is out in the open. And if it doesn't work, it doesn't."

Tess's mouth went dry as she tried to respond.

"But I don't want to make this hard for you or

bully you into something you don't want." Josh's voice trailed off but he didn't need to finish the sentence.

Tess understood that he now had time to think things through without her presence clouding his decision. He'd witnessed the way the town treated her, and their opinion of Tess Carson was clear despite their claims to be a 'church-going community'. That she expected it would be coming didn't lessen the pain. And of course, Tess was also aware that it was her chance to escape before she got hurt.

Images of Josh as a kid, leaning against the doorway at the front of her house as he waited for Brody to get ready to go to a game—or when he was older, the way he would try to act as if he didn't enjoy her attention—and again when he was leaning over helping her hold up the framing for the walls in the youth center. It all crashed together and made her dizzy. Tess loved him and she always would. She released a deep breath and said the last thing she wanted to. "I want the best for you, Jed."

Josh was silent for so long that Tess wondered if he'd hung up. Finally, he whispered, "You know I don't agree with this? And neither do my dimples."

Tess nodded though he couldn't see her. Tears filled her eyes. "Yeah." She wondered if there was any way to make it easier. "It's not about you. This isn't your fault."

"That doesn't make it yours either," Josh paused. "I just hope that one day you'll forgive yourself, Tornado. And stop caring so much what everyone else is thinking." He cleared his throat. "They shouldn't get a vote in how you live."

Tess shrugged, with a quick glance at the clock. "I need to go."

Josh groaned. "We need more time for this conversation."

"I don't think we do. Goodbye, Josh. And congratulations." Tess sighed. "I'm sorry." Her voice cracked.

"Me, too. So, I'll call you later?" He paused and gave an uncomfortable laugh. "Or...maybe I shouldn't?"

"Yeah."

"Tornado...?"

"Yeah?"

"I..." the silence dragged on for a long moment.

Tess tried to imagine what more he wanted to say.

Finally, he sighed. "Never mind."

"OK. Bye, Jed," Tess whispered.

The relationship was over before it began.

~*~

Tess spent the next week and a half printing resumes and sending them. She omitted this fact, and nearly everything else about her personal life, from any conversation with Uncle Stu, until one day he said, "I heard Josh got the job at the church—surprised you didn't tell me."

They were eating dinner at one of their favorite Mexican places after having hardly talked to one another for several days. Tess took a drink of water to avoid answering him. Finally, she said, "Yeah. He called."

Stu grunted. "I expected a billboard."

Tess wished they could talk about anything else.

Josh was always on her mind and she was ready to move on. If only she could. "I...we decided it was for the best if we stay friends. I..." She squirmed in her seat. "I've been sending out resumes."

Stu opened his mouth.

Tess quickly raised a hand to stop him. "I paid mom and dad, Brody is nearly done, and I'm so close to being done with Harrison I can taste it. I'm not staying forever. I can't. I won't."

Stu put down his fork and dug into his pocket. A moment later he came up with a box he laid on the table. "Open it. I want your opinion."

Tess opened the box and found a diamond ring inside. She gasped. "No."

He smiled and nodded. "I'm asking her next weekend," he said. "I figured we're already sure, so why wait?"

Tess stared at the beautiful ring, closed the box, and handed it back to him. She smiled, hating that life insisted on changing in ways she couldn't control. "Right. Why not?"

"So, why not with you and Josh?" He stuffed the ring back into his pocket.

Her stomach twisted with envy that was overpowering and unfair. Stu waited a long time, and she didn't begrudge him happiness. And yet she'd been through so much she wondered if it would ever be her turn.

"He called me the other day," Stu said. "Asked if I could give him a job doing construction. Said he was thinking the pastor thing might not be for him."

Tess shoved her plate away, nauseated that Josh would consider giving up his career to be with her. She tried for several long moments to calm her racing mind.

"I told him that wasn't the answer." He shrugged as he went back to eating. "He already knew that. I guess he was grasping at anything that might give you a different perspective and maybe trust him."

"I...trust him. It's everyone else..." Tess took a drink and closed her eyes. "I don't want to talk about this anymore."

Stu sighed. "Fine. How's work? How's your grandma?"

"Losing stuff, getting frustrated," Tess said quietly, her mind still on Josh. "It's hard enough to watch when it's someone you're working with, but it's really painful when it's your own grandmother. I'm glad I can be there to take care of her."

"But you're willing to leave."

"Don't do the guilt trip," Tess said with a moan.

Stu shrugged. "Your parents won't be happy."

"When are they ever happy with me?" Tess muttered, her appetite gone. She sat back in her seat and regarded her uncle. He was the same man he'd always been, only now he radiated a happiness Tess never noticed was missing. "How will you propose?"

Stu wiped his mouth with a napkin. "I figured I'd give her the ring and ask her. No need to muck it up with a bunch of stupid frills."

"Ugh! No! Really?" Tess shook her head. "She will be so disappointed! I mean she's what? Almost fifty and hasn't ever been married? Do you really think that a simple 'Hey.'" She paused, grunting like a man as she lowered her voice. "'Why don't we get married?' will really be enough? Any woman on earth would want more."

Stu looked at her with a twinkle in his eye.

"Really? And what do you suggest?"

"Something more than that."

"Do tell."

"Well…" Tess sighed. "It needs to be special. It's the start of your life together. Of your commitment to each other. Throwing a ring at her will be a huge disappointment. Even if it is one monster ring."

"All right. I'll think about that."

Tess forced a smile. "You'd better. She's a special lady."

Stu held his niece's gaze for a long moment before he said, "So are you, Tess. Josh believes it. It's time you do too."

But Tess could only turn away with a sigh, wondering if she'd gotten any calls about her resumes. If Uncle Stu didn't need her anymore, there was even less reason to stay.

~*~

"Well, I didn't think you were coming by today."

Tess stepped into Gram's apartment and peeked around, distraught that the place was out of sorts and not in the usual pristine condition she was accustomed to finding it.

Gram turned to Tess and waved her hands frantically. "I never got any candy for the trick-or-treaters," she complained. "Did you bring some, Karen?"

Tess shook her head. "No. I…forgot."

Gram came closer and put a hand on her cheek. "Honestly, what did you do to your hair?"

As usual, Tess yanked her hair into a messy bun, giving little care for how she appeared. It was a distinct difference from her mother's always-polished appearance. Besides, her mother's hair was blonde. "Oh, I didn't take the time to fix it today," Tess muttered as she looked around. "Um, Gram?"

Vi's empty blue eyes tore at Tess's soul.

"What's going on here?" Tess asked. "Did you lose something?"

"Hmm?" Vi smiled and suddenly she was back in the room. "Oh, goodness, Tess, when did you get here?"

Tess smiled at her grandmother and helped her sit. "Right now. Why's it so messy?" she asked as she started to pick up and put away the clothes strewn about the floor.

Gram watched her for a moment, confused.

Tess bit her lip against the tears coming on. She could not cry in front of her grandmother. She would be strong.

"I was trying to find something," Gram put one hand to her silver hair. "I…" she gave a weak laugh. "Only I'm not sure what."

Tess worked on cleaning the room. "Well, I forget things a lot of the time too, Gram."

Gram didn't respond.

Tess glanced in her direction. Her heart dropped at the expression on her grandmother's face.

She was frightened.

Tess dropped a sweater on the bed and went to sit with her. "Hey." She took Gram's hands in her own and smiled. "I'm here and…Mom and Dad and Brody and Stell…we won't let you forget." Tess kissed her grandmother's cheek and smiled. "I love you, Gram."

She continued holding her hands as she sat back, thinking. "How about I bring my softball scrapbooks over? We could go through them and laugh at all of your crazy hairstyles over the years."

"Humph." Gram straightened with a smile. "I was the height of fashion. Still am."

"Of course."

Vi met Tess's eyes. "Honey. I worry about you. I don't want you to be alone."

Tess patted her grandmother's hand and tried to put on a brave smile. "I'm not alone, Gram."

Gram smiled and nodded. "Maybe. But you are putting a wall around yourself no one will bother trying to get over if you don't knock it down." She smiled. "That nice pastor you told me about deserves a chance. Oh...that Thorne boy." Her eyes twinkled again. "I always liked him."

Tess laughed. "You and me both."

"Well, I want you to give him a call. And definitely make sure he stops by to say hello." Gram stood, suddenly back to herself again. "Come on, Gretchen said there would be hot chocolate and cookies in the lobby today."

Tess smiled and stood. "All right, Gram. Let's go."

23

I will praise thee, O Lord, with my whole heart;
I will shew forth all thy marvelous works. I will be glad and
rejoice in thee: I will sing praise to thy name,
O thou most High.
Psalm 9:1-2

Weeks later Josh arrived back in Maple Ridge, half-afraid of calling Tess even if she'd consumed him completely since their last conversation. He'd started and deleted more texts than he could recall in that time, but he refused to change her ringtone, hoping to hear it again when she changed her mind.

If she did.

And although Josh already told her he'd been offered the job, he struggled with how or if he should tell her of his impending arrival. The longer he withheld, the harder it became to say anything. So, he chickened out. He told his parents, his sister, and his mom's elderly Aunt Millie, with whom he'd be staying until he could find a permanent place. She'd offered her tiny basement while he searched for an apartment. After Josh unloaded some things at Aunt Millie's, he headed to Dave's for dinner.

"Well, how was the trip?" Dave's wife, Alison, asked as she refilled his coffee cup. She was now six and a half months pregnant and sat heavily in the chair next to her husband.

Josh took a sip of coffee and smiled. "It was great. No problems at all."

Dave raised an eyebrow. "And everything's good here? No run-ins with Harrison Flynn, our resident critic?"

Josh laughed and shook his head. "Haven't seen him yet, but Aunt Millie did say he stopped by to check if I was around, so I'm sure it's only a matter of time before I get the packet of information on who would be appropriate for me to date, where I'm allowed to eat, when I can speak on which subjects..."

Dave laughed and gestured to him with his coffee cup. "You think you're kidding, but there's a lot of truth in that statement."

Josh groaned.

"Be nice," Alison said with a kind smile. "He means well, I think."

"My wife, ever the diplomat," Dave said, grinning.

"Oh..." Alison shook her head. "I would be careful. At least starting out. For some reason people listen to him, even if I'm not sure why. I guess he can be convincing."

Josh nodded as he sipped his coffee. "I would assume the pastoral staff was on board with hiring me, right? There isn't any dissention there?"

Dave shook his head. "None that I'm aware of. Everyone was thrilled with your sermon—not to mention your education and missionary history. I don't think there's anything to worry about."

Josh's chest tightened. "So you..." He wasn't even sure he could say it. "I should keep my nose clean and getting involved with Tess is out of the question."

Dave set his coffee cup aside as he exchanged a glance with Alison.

She rose from the table and went into the kitchen without a word.

Josh wondered if he'd said something wrong.

"Sorry..." Dave said after a long pause. "But I think Tess is the kind of person you want to lead to Christ, but when they finally commit, after all that's happened, you wonder if it's real or only a matter of time." He met Josh's eyes. "I guess that sounds awful. I'm only giving you my honest opinion."

"I was close with her and her brother growing up. When she came down a few months ago on a mission trip, I didn't know about her history. All I saw was a girl in love with God who was funny and comfortable for me to be around. Maybe I got nostalgic..." He shook his head. "It wouldn't still be on my mind all the time if that's all it was though—would it?" He sighed. "I've never been in love, I guess, so it's all so hard to understand."

Dave took a sip of coffee before answering. "The church isn't interested in supervising your romantic life. I mean, I'm not anyway."

Alison entered the room with a tray of cookies. She set it on the table and refilled their mugs. "I've talked to Tess a few times. When she first started coming to church with her uncle. She was scared of everyone and she never really even talked to me for a while.

"I used to see her outside the pharmacy smoking, or in town causing trouble, hanging out with all the, well, people you don't want dating your daughter...I guess she remembered that too and seeing me at church was a little embarrassing for her." Alison's smile was genuine. "I can't find a reason to pay attention to any of it. Let your personal life be yours. You aren't doing anything wrong or inappropriate being interested in Tess or anyone else."

"I don't think she'll be convinced. I mean, I think we called it all off," Josh said. "And even if I could change things between us, there's the congregation to consider."

Alison smiled. "She will be convinced if she's in the same emotional space that you are. I tried to get her to talk to the ladies group about her trip to your church in Florida but when I finally got hold of her she said she didn't think she was qualified for that." She paused. "I think she needs a good old-fashioned dose of confidence." Alison placed a comforting hand on Josh's arm for a moment and they shared a smile.

"Have you talked to her since you've gotten back?" Dave asked.

"No." Josh blinked. "Based on our last conversation, I wasn't sure she'd want that."

Dave laughed. "Unless you're planning on hiding yourself under a rock, she'll find out you've come back eventually. I'm sure she'd rather hear it from you."

Josh groaned. His friend was right. He only hoped he could get to her before someone else did.

~*~

"Theresa." The name sounded like a threat when it escaped Ashley-Marie's mouth.

Tess turned from her job of making up bags of craft supplies for the next day's afternoon activity.

Her boss teetered on heels so high it appeared as if she was trying to give the Empire State Building a run for its money.

"Yes, boss?" Tess went back to her job, turning her back on the woman.

Ashley-Marie cleared her throat. "I'm wondering if you've talked to Josh."

Tess's phone hadn't buzzed with a message from the pastor in a long time. She drew a breath and kept working, hoping her focus on her job was enough to send the woman away. "Not recently."

"Well…a friend said he was over at the Gormans' today. I figured if anyone heard anything about him coming back it would be you. Well, I mean if you two are still talking."

Tess refused to take the obvious bait. She kept working on the bags and said nothing.

"OK. In that case, I'll call him to catch up. There's no reason…"

"Go ahead," Tess said, cutting the woman off, and hopefully, the pain festering inside her.

"What was that?"

"I said…" Tess finally turned around. "Call him."

Ashley-Marie didn't bother to mask her shock. "Really?"

Tess swallowed and turned back to her work. "Yeah. Why shouldn't you catch up?" Tess paused. "Hey—I'm applying for some nursing positions so I'm not sure I'll even be around here much longer. I'll try to give you two weeks' notice if I can if anything comes up."

Ashley-Marie gasped. "Really?" she asked in annoyance.

Tess nodded as she finished the last bag and tied it closed before tossing it into a large box. She stood and lifted the box to move it aside. "Yep. Really. I want to go check on my grandmother before I punch out. Did you need anything else?"

The shock on her boss's face was priceless.

Tess smiled and patted her arm. "Put your mouth back with the rest of your face. And don't worry. I got rid of the garden hose years ago. Your hair's safe. Go get 'im."

~*~

Tess arrived home late, but she was thankful she planned ahead that morning to put dinner in the crock pot. It would be enough for another day's eating and she was always glad to save herself the time, and the calories, from eating too much on the run. But as she turned into the parking lot near her apartment, something was clearly very wrong.

Josh's van was parked in front of her door and he was pacing in front of it with his hands stuffed into his pockets.

As Tess pulled into a parking space near him, she got out of the truck, slamming the door.

Josh jumped as he turned toward her. He smiled awkwardly.

Tess was sure she caught a faint blush on his cheeks in the fading daylight.

"Hey," he whispered.

Tess wondered how she was supposed to feel about his return to her life, and now her home, too. Her resolve to stay strong dissolved as she met Josh's eyes.

He smiled again.

Those dimples.

She cleared her throat. "Ashley-Marie said you were back."

"Oh? Yeah. I was thinking about leaving you a note."

Tess nodded.

"I wanted to surprise you— but then I wondered if that was a good idea." He walked over to where she stood but seemed at a loss what to do next.

"It is a surprise," Tess said, side-stepping so she could get to her door.

Josh stared at her but didn't move.

"Welcome home." Tess opened the door and turned to him. "Is there something else?"

He shrugged.

Tess's cell phone rang. She yanked it out of her pocket. The police station. Curious, she pressed the phone to her ear and held up a finger asking Josh to wait a moment. "Hello?"

"Is this Theresa Carson?"

"Yes."

"Theresa, this is Tim Winters from the Maple Ridge police. We've recovered your motorcycle if you'd like to come down and pick it up. We got the suspect in custody."

"I bet you do," Tess muttered. "Sure. I'll be right over. Thanks." She hung up the phone and stuffed it back into her pocket before turning to Josh. "Any chance you'd want to take me to the police station?"

~*~

Moments later Josh was driving toward the police

station working hard to squelch the butterflies in his stomach. Being in an enclosed space with Tess was making his previous resolve to stay clear of her and a possible relationship questionable at best. And what was worse, he couldn't figure out why she wasn't talking. He cast a sideways glance at her before focusing back on the road. "So, they found it?"

Tess nodded but her gaze remained focused on some distant point ahead of the car. "Yep." She chewed on a hangnail. "Pull over anywhere. I'll walk the rest of the way."

Josh turned a corner and continued driving. "What? No." His jaw tightened as, for the first time in a long time, he got angry.

The situation was unfair to both of them, and since they'd done nothing wrong he wasn't even sure anymore why they were struggling. With a heavy sigh, he steered his van into the parking lot and set the brake.

Tess escaped, slamming the door behind her. She stormed into the station.

Josh willed himself to calm down. With a deep breath, he got out and followed her inside.

Tess stood at the main desk facing a tall officer who was so thin he appeared to be sickly. The man glared down his nose.

Tess seemed desperate to hold her ground. "Why would I want to help the man who stole from me?" she demanded.

The officer shrugged as he squinted at the computer in front of him. "No idea. It says here that I should ask if you want to post his bail."

Tess gaped at the man. "Of course I don't want to post his bail!" Her gaze darted around the station.

"Where's my bike? Is it destroyed? Please say it isn't destroyed."

"Didn't seem destroyed to me," the officer said with a sigh. "I didn't see even one scratch." He handed her a set of keys. "One of the guys caught this...Justin..." Before he could finish the sentence, he groaned. "Oh..." He gave Tess a once-over. "I almost didn't recognize you without the short skirts and make-up."

Josh sensed the tension.

Tess stepped backwards, grazing his chest. She glanced behind her, glaring as she stepped away from him. "Go home," she said through gritted teeth.

"No." Josh gritted his teeth back at her. "What if your bike isn't drivable? I'm not leaving you here alone."

The officer now took a moment to turn his attention to Josh. His smile held a note of condescension. "My son used to date this one..." he gestured toward Tess. "I'd advise you..."

"I'm her pastor," Josh said firmly.

The man's mouth snapped closed for a moment before it broke into a grin. "Pastor, huh?" He didn't bother to mask his amusement as he turned to Tess. "You sure you don't want to talk to the guy who stole your bike? He does have a right to a visitor even if..."

"Oh, I'll see him."

The officer gestured to another man. "Take them back to the Trapp kid," he said.

"He doesn't need to come..." Tess began.

Josh was already following her down the hallway.

She rolled her eyes and turned so he couldn't see her face.

Josh didn't care. He wasn't about to let her go in

there alone. Was he marking his territory? Maybe. Regardless he wanted her to understand that he was with her.

"Hey, gorgeous!" Justin stood and went closer to the bars that separated him from the outside world.

Tess kept her distance, glaring up at him angrily. "You're lucky you're in here," she snapped. "What gives you the right to my bike?"

"I told you. It's sixty-five percent mine. I got the majority share."

Tess grunted in her anger. "I did not ask you to help me buy the bike. That you did it only shows how stupid you are. The thing is in my name, I pay the insurance."

Justin rolled his eyes and appeared to no longer be listening to her protests as he scanned Josh. He nodded at him. "Who're you?" Without waiting for a response, he raised one eyebrow at Tess. "Fresh meat?"

"I'm her pastor," Josh said calmly. "Joshua Thorne."

Justin burst into a fit of laughter. "Her pastor?"

Tess started to walk away but stopped cold when Justin said, calmly, "I'll come back for it again, Tess."

Tess slowly turned and walked back. "Why?"

Justin grinned. "Like you need to ask." He reached through the bars and touched her hair.

Tess stepped backward to escape him.

But he wasn't finished. "I'd hate to tell the good…" he stifled a chuckle. "…pastor, or anyone else about all the things you did. I mean, I don't want to ruin the little fantasy world you've created, but if I don't have a choice I will. It's hardly fair for you to lie to the good people of this town."

"Stop!" Tess stood for a long moment, her hands

on her temples.

Horrified, Josh wanted to reach out to her but he held back, astounded that her family watched her sink to the depths of associating with people like Justin. She needed to work through this and stand up for herself, so Josh waited while she continued.

"I want to start over without all this hanging over me. What will make you stop?" she pleaded.

He shrugged. "I put two grand out for it."

Tess nearly choked. "Two grand!?"

Justin smiled triumphantly. "Come on, Tess, I always thought you hid your brain in that pretty head." He glanced at Josh for a brief moment but quickly turned his attention back to Tess. "Don't act like you don't got it. All you do is work. You ought to be rolling in money."

"I'm trying to pay off all my debts..." Tess shook her head desperately, the panic radiating from her.

Josh swallowed hard against the desire to rescue her.

"I only have a few hundred in the bank right now. And it's all spoken for between the loans and my bills..." She paused, thinking. "You can keep the bike. I'll sign the registration over."

Josh could tell how painful the words were to say.

Justin laughed again. "I need the money, brainiac."

"So, sell it," Tess said, defeated. "I don't care."

Josh cleared his throat and before he could think it through he spoke. "If I give you the money will you leave her alone?" He wasn't sure where the words came from.

Both Tess and Justin looked at Josh in shock.

"What did you say?" Justin asked.

Tess went to Josh and met his eyes, her own pleading with him. "No," she whispered, gripping his coat sleeves with her hands. "Don't be stupid."

"I'll take it," Justin said.

Josh gently urged Tess aside as he stepped closer to the bars. "I want your word. I give you this money and you stop bothering her. The bike's hers now. You touch it again and we'll have a problem."

Justin grinned with a nod. "Oh, you got my word."

"You two will need to wrap it up," the officer said, stepping back into view.

Josh nodded and reached out to take Tess's arm.

Justin watched them. "Don't let her get her claws into you," he said. "Friendly advice, one man to another."

Josh ignored him as Tess allowed him to turn her toward the door.

"Hey! You two posting my bail?" Justin called.

"No," Josh said.

"Well how can I be sure I'll get my money?"

"You have my word. I'll get it to you as soon as I can."

Justin pointed at Josh. "You better or you'll be sorry. Ask her. You don't want a warning."

24

The Lord is my light and my salvation; whom shall I fear?
The Lord is the strength of my life; of whom shall I be afraid?
Psalm 27: 1

Tess walked out of the police station toward her motorcycle, still in shock at what was happening.

And why was Josh still trailing after her? She said nothing as she checked her beloved bike over, wondering if he was crazy or in shock himself. That must be it. He was now realizing that her warnings were valid, and he was trying to figure a graceful way to bow out of pursuing a relationship with her.

"Is it OK?" Josh asked, squatting next to her.

Tess nodded as she stood to increase the distance between them. But he followed, watching as she yanked her helmet from the back of the bike. "You can go now." Perhaps he needed her to be even more direct. "I'm fine. You aren't responsible for any of this."

"Hey."

Tess turned to him.

He was smiling. "It'll get better," he said with confidence.

Tess found it hard not to laugh. Instead, she snorted and threw one leg over the bike, relieved at the comfort of having it back in her care. She would take it to Stu's house where she could lock it safely in his garage. "You'd better get away from me, Jed," Tess said as she raised her helmet to put it on. "And don't you dare pay him. This isn't your problem." Tess started the bike and drove toward Uncle Stu's house. She didn't care that she'd left Josh standing alone in the parking lot looking as lost as she was. He needed to realize there were many women around who were much better-suited to him. Maybe Ashley-Marie would give him a call and order would be restored to the universe. Tess planned to print a hundred more resumes before she went to bed because it was now abundantly clear that she would never escape her sins.

~*~

"Mouthy." Stu's voice was even, as if he wasn't surprised to find his niece at his door again. He glanced toward the driveway and closed the door.

Tess flopped into a chair near the kitchen counter. If he noticed her bike he didn't mention it, instead waiting as he often did for the news to come out on its own. "Justin stole my motorcycle. I just got it back," she said, blinking back more annoying tears. "Can I lock it up here for now if you don't mind driving me home...?"

Stu nodded as he held out a piece of pizza to her.

She shook her head as he went back to eating what was clearly a late dinner-on-the-go. "Marlene will not like you eating that garbage," Tess muttered as she dropped her head into her hands, still in shock over her day. She groaned. "Josh, of all people, took me to the police station to pick it up and..."

"Glad to hear he's back," Stu said through a mouthful of pizza.

Tess sighed heavily, refusing to acknowledge her uncle's sentiment. "And the worst of it all is he let Justin blackmail him into paying two thousand dollars to leave me and the bike alone. Why would he do something like that?"

Stu grinned as he polished off his slice and grabbed a drink. He took a long swig before speaking. "I wonder."

Tess groaned.

"He called and asked if I could rent him an apartment," Stu said. "Of course, I told him that we just finished painting that one right above yours..." He took his plate to the sink and began washing it.

Tess stared at his back. Finally, she went to the door, angry. "You're the only person who wouldn't do this to me," she said. "I'm supposed to be living my own life now, Uncle Stu. I was doing a good job, wasn't I?"

Stu avoided eye contact. "What's your problem, Mouthy? I got an apartment for rent and he needs one. He'll make a good tenant."

Tess opened the door and stepped outside, aware she would be taking a chance if her motorcycle was back at the apartment with no protection.

Stu followed her and stood behind her, watching her stare indecisively at her bike. "I can take you home if you want to leave it," he said as she yanked her helmet off the seat.

"And listen to you lecture me all the way there? No thanks." Tess swung her leg over the chopper and sat heavily, willing the tears to go away. "I'm out of here."

Stu was beside her shaking his head. He gestured toward the open garage. "Put it in there and we'll lock it up. I'll take you home."

There was no point in arguing so she did as he said, yanking her helmet back off her head and forcing herself not to throw it against the garage wall once she got the bike inside.

Stu locked the doors and gestured for her to get into his truck, which was sitting in its usual spot outside the front door.

"I won't let Josh pay that fool a dime," Stu said as they got into the truck. "He got caught up in the moment, trying to protect you." He started the truck and drove down the road. "I'm showing him the place tomorrow since he said he can't stand staying at his aunt's house very long—can't say I blame him since I've seen that tiny basement."

Tess nodded but said nothing as the numbness washed over her. Life was going from bad to worse whether she wanted it to or not. With a heavy sigh, she said, "I'm done."

"You're...done? With what exactly?"

Tess watched the scenery pass by as her uncle drove toward her apartment. "With all of this," she muttered. "Josh. This town. Justin. I don't even care about my motorcycle anymore. I'm tempted to get on a bus and not look back."

Stu laughed. "Don't blame you. But hang in there. I imagine it's all about to get a lot more interesting."

Tess grunted, resigned to her fate. "That's what I'm afraid of."

~*~

Josh handed Stu a check for the deposit on the apartment and stuffed his checkbook back into his pocket. "So that's it? I can move in anytime?" he asked.

Stu handed the keys over. "It's all yours."

"Thanks. I'm glad this worked out." Josh didn't say what they were both thinking. It was beyond a bonus that he'd be living above Tess's apartment and so might now get the chance to wear down her defenses against him. How he'd do it he didn't know. Josh only knew he had to.

Stu laughed and nodded. "Well, you'll need some linens and towels and you'll be good to go."

Josh took in the small, tidy apartment and nodded. It was a step up from his last place and exactly what he imagined Stu would offer him. That Tess would be downstairs made him think he should offer Stu more money.

"Tess said you offered to pay Justin off."

The words made Josh wonder if he was part of a gangster's dirty deal. "It's not like that. He was giving her a hard time, saying he would tell everyone what she really was. She's fragile enough. She didn't need that." He paused for a long moment, hoping he could make it clear. "I'm certain Tess is different. Only I wonder whether she believes it. I wanted to help—I mean, make it go away."

Stu fussed with a handle on one of the cabinets. "It won't go away like that. And you probably bought yourself a boatload of trouble. Don't give that slime one cent. You can't trust him."

Josh swallowed and nodded. "But I gave him my word."

"You gave your word to a drug-dealing criminal.

Josh stuffed his hands into his pockets. "Sir?" he asked.

Stu laughed as he headed for the door of the apartment. Wordlessly he opened and closed the door.

Josh was stunned. And smiling.

~*~

"OK, ladies and gents, you said you want me to work you a little harder, so let's see what you're made of," Tess said with a smile. "Get those arms up! We're doing ten reps today. Let's do it!"

The class alternately groaned, laughed, and struggled through the set of exercises in the routine as Tess stood at the front of the room.

Ashley-Marie walked by several times as the class rolled on.

"Well...that was fun!" Gram smiled as she swiped her hand across her forehead.

Tess laughed.

Sarah and Gretchen joined them.

"Ladies, great job today."

"You sure do make it harder each time," Gretchen said with a chuckle. She was a round woman who didn't make much effort toward the exercise, choosing instead to clap along and laugh while everyone else did the work. She was a lot of fun to be around and Tess noticed she and Gram instantly connected. Sarah, on the other hand, was a reserved woman who'd been friends with Gram nearly their whole lives. That they were now neighbors in Pine View was a comfort to them all.

"I'm glad you enjoyed it," Tess said as she glanced at the door.

Ashley-Marie was, once again, peeking in.

Tess smiled at her grandmother. "I need to go, Gram. I'll stop by later." Tess hustled to the door, doom filling her. "Did you need something?" she asked.

At first, Ashley-Marie didn't say anything, but her lip curled in an unattractive snarl. "Josh is here for you. I said you were busy, but he said he'd wait," she glanced around before leaning confidentially close. "I'll not be shut out a second time."

Tess tapped the woman on the back. "No worries, Ash. I'll put in a good word for you."

Ashley-Marie glared. "Humph. He probably thinks he'll save your soul." She pointed toward the entrance. "He's by the piano."

Tess drew a deep breath and tried not to care that she wasn't wearing any make-up and barely bothered to yank a hairbrush through her hair that morning. She focused instead on hurrying toward the entry to get rid of Josh before anyone else spotted him waiting for her. Like Harrison on a random visit to check on his aunt. Because that would be the disaster Tess's life had come to be.

He was sitting comfortably talking with Mrs. Torrofsky, a former voice and piano teacher who now struggled with mobility and was unable to live on her own.

Tess was glad she was enjoying Josh's company.

He appeared to have no intention of moving as he

listened to her talk, his smile genuine as he nodded, urging her to continue her story.

Tess smiled as she got closer. "Um, hi, Pastor Thorne," she said formally. "Ashley-Marie said you were looking for me?"

Josh raised his head in her direction, his smile glowing. He nodded and gestured to a seat nearby. "I was. How are you, Tess?"

Mrs. Torrofsky winked at her with a smile.

Tess turned her attention back to Josh. She would not sit down with him. "I'm fine?" Her words came out like a question. "Maybe we could talk later?" she asked, willing him to go away. "I have work…"

"Sure. I didn't want to bother you," Josh smiled at Mrs. Torrofsky and reached out to shake her hand. "It was a pleasure," he said. "I hope we can talk again."

"I'll be looking forward to it," Mrs. Torrofsky said with a smile.

Josh stood and started walking with Tess. "Sorry about stopping by like this," he began. "But I was on this side of town anyway."

Tess stepped behind the counter to grab a pen. "Make it quick. I need to outline the activities for the week or Ashley-Marie will freak out."

"Can I take you to dinner tonight?" Josh asked. "There's something I want to talk to you about."

"I am not marrying you," Tess said as she grabbed the activities log from the previous week.

Josh laughed. "I hate to disappoint you but that wasn't it."

"Mmm?" Tess turned on the computer and started searching for the program she needed.

Josh leaned against the counter.

Ashley-Marie hovered nearby, pretending to be

busy but appearing more like a poor excuse for a spy.

"No," Josh stopped, clearing his throat. "I actually had a great idea for a ministry here that I wanted you to help with."

Tess stopped typing and stared at him. "You can't be serious."

"Oh, but I am," he said with a wink. "Six o'clock?"

"Can't. I work until seven-thirty."

"Great. I'll catch you at home at eight." He stepped back, his face brightening. "And I'll bring my dimples."

Before Tess could say anything, Josh was gone. She closed her eyes for a moment and went back to work.

~*~

Several hours later, Josh smiled at Tess across the table, shocked he'd managed to get her out of the apartment, into his car, and inside a public restaurant.

And she was wearing a dress. And make-up, too.

It was making him squirm. Part of him feared she was well aware of the effect she was having. He was too transparent.

"Well, Jed. Despite our previous agreement, you've gotten me here." She leaned her chin on her hand, causing her dark hair to fall over one shoulder. "What is this all about?"

Josh waited while the server set steaming plates on the table.

"Everything OK?" the waitress asked.

Josh and Tess both smiled and nodded.

"It looks wonderful," Tess said. "Thank you." She looked back on Josh. "Well?"

Josh took his time setting his napkin on his lap before answering. Something about her demeanor was throwing him off but he wasn't sure what it was. She wasn't distant but she wasn't warm either. He was certain that being direct was probably best. "I wondered if we could connect some of the residents at Pine View with some of the disadvantaged kids who come to our youth group. I started a similar thing in Florida and it was really great."

Tess cut into her chicken. "You aren't in youth ministry anymore, Jed."

"Old habits die hard." He relaxed. "I noticed how a lot of the kids have talents that their parents can't or don't encourage because they can't afford the lessons it would take to help them grow. Many of your Pine View residents are skilled in those areas, some of them probably used to teach or coach and can't anymore, at least on a regular basis. But Mrs. Torrofsky, for instance, she's still sharp as can be. Why shouldn't she give a voice or piano lesson to a kid who wants it? I think the benefits on both sides would be amazing."

Josh was certain of the fire in Tess's gaze that hadn't been there before. He tried not to smile as she masked the passion by turning her attention back to her plate.

"I'm not sure how much longer I'll be sticking around here. You should talk to Ashley-Marie." She took a bite of her dinner.

He cut his meat and tried not to sound presumptuous. "She'd think I had ulterior motives."

"She's not that bad."

Josh laughed vigorously. "Maybe not for someone

else. But she's not for me."

"Mmm, I can understand how a stunning piece of arm candy wouldn't be your type. Plus, she's a champion in high heels. Probably won a contest for it or something. I can't do that."

"Tess."

She looked up innocently. "I promised I'd put in a good word for her. Is it working?"

Josh laughed. "No. So, is this a yes to my question? You know the residents, Tornado. Maybe you and Morgan can help me, and the youth ministry team, make the connections."

"I can't speak for Morgan..." she said as she dug back into her dinner. "And you didn't need to bribe me with dinner to ask this question."

"Ulterior motives," Josh said, winking at her.

"I am not interested in any more of your cherry ice cream, Mister Thorne," Tess said firmly. "We've been over that."

Josh leaned forward confidentially. "I checked this place out before I brought you here. Would you believe they specialize in homemade cherry ice cream?"

"Stop."

"Nope. I don't have plans to stop anytime soon."

"But we agreed..."

"I reconsidered that decision. Sorry. I'm not leaving you alone or hiding anymore." But there was no apology in his voice.

~*~

By the time Josh turned his van into the

apartment's parking lot Tess all but forgot about her desire to keep him away from her heart. They'd talked and laughed, and she'd barely managed to avoid agreeing to his ridiculous plan. But somehow, she remained non-committal, reminding him of her intentions to leave town as soon as she could.

"Don't you dare get out," Josh said as he set the parking brake and yanked the keys from the ignition. He hopped out of the car and rushed to her side to open the door for her. He'd held doors all evening, taken her to a nice restaurant, and made her laugh. It had been a real date whether Tess wanted one or not.

As Josh tugged the temperamental door open and held his hand out to help her from the van, it occurred to Tess that he wanted her to get all the frills a relationship offered. He believed she deserved that. Reluctantly Tess took his hand and let him help her from the car as a deep emotion overtook her and a tear trailed down her cheek. He wasn't giving up on her and he continued to treat her with respect. Maybe she was worth it.

Josh held her hand as he shoved the van door closed and started for her apartment.

"I'll make sure the Pine View thing is OK with the board and get back to you," Josh said as he waited for her to open the door to her apartment.

Tess quickly swiped at her eyes as she nodded.

"Hey." Josh took her arm and stopped her from going inside. "Did I do something?"

Tess smiled, not sure how to explain. A lump grew in her throat. "It was fun," she managed to squeak out. "Thank you."

Josh's eyebrows knit together briefly before he smiled. "I had fun too. Thank you for coming."

"You didn't exactly give me a choice," she said with a slight laugh. "But I'm glad you didn't take no for an answer."

"Me, too." Josh regarded her nervously.

Tess was certain what he was thinking. She should spare him. "Well...thanks." Tess stepped inside the door and started to close it. "Good-bye..."

Josh put one hand on the door frame and the other on the door to hold it open. "Tess."

"Hmm?" she looked at him.

He smiled for a long time before he spoke. "You survived. We went out in public and we both survived." He stepped back. "Think about it."

Tess nodded and slowly closed the door, hoping he was right and the next day wouldn't bring any judgment on either of them.

25

It is of the Lord's mercies that we are not consumed, because his compassions fail not. They are new every morning: great is thy faithfulness.
Lamentations 3:22-23

Josh sighed heavily as he hung up the telephone. Stu contacted the police about Justin and they, in turn, called him to find out exactly what happened. Josh wondered if he should be worried that they'd advised him not to go out alone at night until they caught up with Justin, who, for the moment anyway, was again nowhere to be found.

"Josh?" Alison poked her head into the office.

Josh shoved the worries about Justin aside as he forced a smile. "Hey, come in," he said.

She widened the door and entered with a shy smile aimed at him. "Sorry, but I'm guessing Delia's out for an errand or lunch maybe. I dropped off Dave's lunch and figured I'd stop in and say hello."

"Sit. Please. Can I get you anything?"

"No." She smiled. "I wondered if you'd caught up with Tess."

Josh felt his cheeks warm with embarrassment. He met her eyes. "That transparent, am I?" he asked.

"A little." She laughed and then drew a deep breath. "I was hoping you could convince her to come to our Bible study. I hope you don't mind, I took a chance and talked to a few women who wouldn't flinch about having her there and they were very receptive. I hope this isn't overstepping my boundaries. I guess I hoped it might help you both. Maybe the more people get to know her the more they'll see this is a good thing."

Josh smiled at her kindness. "I'll do what I can. But there's no reason you shouldn't ask her yourself."

Alison smiled as she stood. "Tess is proud. It'll be hard to convince her that this isn't a handout. We want to walk beside her because we all struggle, but this isn't charity. Tell her that. I mean, I'll talk to her if you think it will help, but since I don't know her well, I thought you might be more convincing. I just wouldn't want her to lose all the ground she's made because of a few mean-spirited souls."

"Thanks. Really." Josh smiled.

Alison nodded and left the office.

He sighed heavily as he sat back in his seat, grateful he'd moved home, and frightened of what it really meant.

~*~

Weeks later, Tess stared at the computer screen, hardly believing she'd finally earned enough money to pay Harrison Flynn off for good. While it would leave her with barely twenty dollars in her account, it would only be two weeks until her next paychecks. The risk seemed worth it when she considered the freedom it would bring. She smiled as she yanked her checkbook from her purse and began to write the man's name for the last time. All of the overtime paid off. Before she could fill in the amount, there was a knock on the door that made her heart flutter. She glanced at the clock. It was time for Josh's visit. "Come on in!" she shouted.

The door opened, and Josh stepped inside, bearing two bags filled with food. "I went out on a limb and got burgers," he said as he kicked the door behind him.

"Sounds good."

Since Josh's return, they now maintained a consistent ritual of texting that usually ended in planning their dinner and evening coffee or a movie. Sometimes Josh cooked or brought food, and sometimes Tess did. But at Tess's insistence, the meals were almost solely eaten under her roof or his.

Despite the success of their one public date, Josh hadn't pushed that point. Yet.

Tess could see he hated sneaking around and wouldn't abide it much longer. Already he'd been disappointed to go alone to several group outings where it would have made sense for Tess to go along. Her excuses appeared to be grating on the good pastor's nerves. Tess shoved her checkbook aside and turned off the computer.

Josh was grabbing the plates, condiments, and even vinegar for her fries, without any prompting. "You want tea or water?" he asked as he set everything on the table.

She smiled. "Tea is good. Thanks. I made a pie."

Josh groaned as he got her drink and set it on the table. "Marry me now."

"Nope."

"Don't think I didn't notice you still forget to lock that door most of the time, Theresa Marie Carson."

"Ohhh, Theresa Marie," she repeated since he

rarely called her by her given name.

"I mean it. The police still don't know where Justin is. They told me the other day to not go out alone until they nab him again. Please lock your door." Josh captured her hand. "What if he shows up and I'm not around to protect you? I don't want anything to happen."

Tess dropped the fry back onto her plate as Josh held her gaze. She nodded stupidly as he leaned forward and kissed her. He didn't kiss her often and she understood it was to avoid the temptations it brought. He was still trying desperately to respect her and show her she was worth loving and being loved.

"I'm not sure how I'd handle it if he hurt you," Josh whispered, still holding her hand. He leaned forward and kissed her again.

Tess was glad she was sitting down.

"I tease you about marrying me, but I mean it. Someday, I hope you'll be my wife," he concluded seriously. "I'll protect you. Forever."

Tess swallowed hard. "Josh…"

Josh shook his head. "I'm only asking that you understand where this is heading. I can't turn it back now. Not after all the time we spend together, and what I know to be true about you."

Tess nodded slowly, her head swimming. "Oh. Right. Sure."

"Good. So lock that door. Did you finish today's chapter?"

Tess was grateful he changed the subject to the safety of the Bible study they'd been working on together. "Yep. I think this was the best one yet. What did you think?"

Josh groaned. "I hated it. The theology is good, but

the writing is terrible!"

Tess laughed. She really would marry him. If she could learn to believe in miracles.

~*~

"I'm not sure..." Marlene turned to one side followed by the other as she peered into the full-length mirror.

It was only the third dress but already Tess was bored. Planning a wedding was akin to torture. How Stell did it every day was beyond Tess. Looking at dresses made her want to poke out her eyes.

Stell gave Tess a gentle nudge and stood as she smiled at Marlene.

"I like the last one better. It flattered your figure and really accented your eyes," she said.

Tess tried not to groan, wondering why she couldn't be more 'girly' and enjoy this sort of thing. But her mind was stuck on the numerous phone interviews she'd been having day after day since hospitals began receiving her resume. The job offers were beginning to come in, some from as far away as Colorado and Arizona.

And Josh and Stu still had no idea.

"Tess?" Marlene appeared concerned as she tried to catch her eye. "What do you think?"

Tess shrugged. "I think you should listen to Stell, she's the expert. I'm not exactly into weddings."

Marlene laughed. "Bet you will be soon enough if that pastor has anything to say about it. We went to talk to him about our ceremony and he sure talked about you a lot."

Stell grinned.

Tess rolled her eyes. "I'll elope if I ever get married. I'm not wearing some goofy dress and veil. No offense."

Marlene pulled the dress out and let it flutter back down as she watched in the mirror. "Stu won't hear of you eloping."

Tess laughed and stood, fussing with the train on the dress to avoid the women's scrutiny. "I don't like this one," she said. "Wait…did you say Josh was doing the ceremony?"

"Of course, he is…get the top button, would you?" Marlene held her hair to the side as she waited for Tess to do as she'd asked. "We set the date…and we've been very happy at the church, so we figured we should do the service there and join officially."

Tess helped Marlene get back into the dressing room and closed the door.

"Here." The dress came flying over the top of the door.

Tess caught it.

Stell took it from her and began putting it back on the hanger. "You should try the first one again…unless you want to go to the other dress shop," Stell said.

"I'll try the other one again," Marlene said. "How about lunch? My treat!"

"That sounds good," Tess said. She'd managed to get the day off from both Pine View and the diner and she was hoping to stay busy all day. Going home to find Josh waiting for her was too much to think about. But going home to him was exactly what she wanted to do—especially since she hadn't yet told him about the job offers. After their conversation days before about the direction of their relationship, she was certain he wouldn't be receptive to her moving away when he'd only just gotten settled again in Maple Ridge.

"Hey. Your phone's ringing," Stell said, holding Tess's purse out to her.

Tess grabbed it and was surprised when the screen revealed it was Stu who was calling. "No, you can't steal your girlfriend," Tess said, not bothering with a kinder greeting.

"You need to get to the hospital, Mouthy. Now."

Tess's stomach dropped. "What? Why?" Images of Gram falling and getting hurt—or worse—flashed through Tess's mind.

Stu cleared his throat. "Josh got beat up pretty bad," he said. "Brody's with us. He found him."

Tess tried to speak. "What? I mean...I'll be right over," she said. She hung up and tossed the phone into her purse.

"Hey...what's going on?" Stell asked as the dressing room door opened and Marlene stepped out.

Tess blurted, "Josh is hurt. I'm going to the hospital." She ran out of the bridal boutique, intent on finding out what happened, the guilt of her past weighing heavy. The consequences would never leave her.

~*~

Josh lay in the hospital bed listening to the continuous beeping of the machines and hallway bustle around him, wondering how he'd managed to get into such a stupid predicament. He'd been sure Stu was right and that paying Justin wasn't a good decision, but since he hadn't heard from the drug-dealer, he was also unsure whether there was any merit to the deal or if he could dodge it.

So, as he'd left for a quick game of basketball with Brody that morning, he wasn't thinking at all about Justin or the money that wasn't in his account. He was thinking about his friend and a good game of basketball.

When he got to the basketball court, Josh wasn't surprised he'd arrived ahead of Brody. It gave him time to warm up and process the first weeks of being home. While Tess continued to press him to keep their evening meetings for dinner or coffee confined to her place or his, Josh was becoming uncomfortable, even antsy about hiding their relationship. He didn't like keeping his feelings a secret and he was sure the time was coming when he'd tell her so. For now, he was content to enjoy spending time with her, guiding her toward a deeper faith, and to reaffirm his conviction that marrying her was a certainty.

"Hey." Brody stepped into the hospital room. He'd been the one to find Josh, beaten and bloodied on the basketball court.

Through swollen eyes Josh could see his friend remained shaken by the experience. Josh tried to speak.

Brody silenced him with one hand. "Tess is on her way." He sat beside the bed.

Josh groaned.

Brody's eyes revealed his concern. "Do you need the doctor? They said they could give you something for the pain."

"No," Josh said, his voice low and strange. "She'll blame herself. But it's..." he flinched as he tried to sit up, failing. He fell back against the pillows and drew a deep breath. "It's not her fault."

Brody nodded but said nothing.

Maybe it wasn't the time to convince him. Josh wasn't sure how bad his injuries were, but he dreaded Tess hearing what happened. Already she'd resisted going out in public with him or getting involved in the Bible study at church despite his numerous protests and a personal call from Alison. This situation wouldn't serve to make her any more confident about her status in the community.

"The police got them," Stu said as he entered the hospital room. "This will put them away for a good long time..." He stood beside Brody and assessed Josh's injuries. "How are you doing?"

Josh tried to shrug, but his shoulder and arm were in a sling, tender from where he'd been shoved to the ground by two guys anyone would struggle to fight off. And he'd tried. He'd tried hard.

They'd beaten him until he couldn't struggle any longer, cursed him with words he'd never imagined could be aimed at him.

Justin stood by smoking, laughing occasionally, and finally stopping the men by saying, "All right. Enough. He gets the message. We'll stop by your place in a week. You better get the money or we won't be as nice." The tall, thin coward dropped his cigarette near Josh's face and said "Maybe next time you won't be so quick to give your word to someone you just met, Pastor." He spit the words at Josh so that the venom in them was unmistakable. "And I'd advise you to leave Tess alone too. No telling what kind of diseases she's carrying."

Stu tugged a chair next to Brody and sat. "Doctor

said you've got three broken ribs. Is there anyone else I should call? Your Aunt Millie? Someone from the church?"

Josh wanted to crawl under the covers and hide until his wounds were healed. He didn't want anyone at the church to find out what happened. Being connected with a guy like Justin Trapp when he'd hardly begun his job would be a disaster. He groaned again.

Stu and Brody exchanged a glance.

"Maybe we should get the doctor," Stu said.

Josh shook his head and drew a deep breath. "Call Dave Gorman."

Stu nodded and took the phone from the side table.

The door burst open and Tess walked in, her expression frantic. Her gaze met Josh's and he grew nauseated. She didn't need to say anything for him to understand he'd lost her forever.

~*~

Tess broke every speed and traffic law in her attempt to get to the hospital. She'd imagined the worst scenarios possible as she drove, cursing every bad thing she'd ever done to lead up to this. It was her fault Josh got hurt, her fault everyone hated her.

And as she stood near the doorway of Josh's hospital room, her brother and uncle staring at her in shock and disappointment, she was certain she'd soon accept the real consequences of her actions—losing her dreams right as she was about to grab them.

Tess cleared her throat, trying to force her gaze away from Josh's but finding it impossible.

Brody stood, shaking his head. "I'll be outside," he muttered.

Stu stood, cradling Josh's phone in his hand. "I'll, um, call your friend," he said, following Brody from the room.

Josh nodded, grimacing as he tried to smile at Tess. "Hey, Tornado."

Tess sank slowly into the chair beside his bed, blindly reaching to take his hand in hers as the tears began to fall. She willed them to stop but the effort was futile. She bowed her head and rested it beside his arm on the bed. "This is my fault," she whispered into the sheets.

"No..." Josh's voice was thick and strange as he tried to speak.

Tess raised her head and looked at him, not caring that there were still tears dripping down her cheeks, that the progress she'd made with her brother was now gone, that her own uncle—her biggest fan—would probably disown her. And that hurt almost as much as seeing Josh in a hospital bed.

Tess was certain of the deep disappointment she'd seen in Uncle Stu's eyes moments ago. And the way he failed to hug or comfort her now spoke as loudly as any megaphone or neon sign. Tess was sure Uncle Stu was finished. Maybe that was for the best. It was up to Tess to take care of things now.

"I did this." Tess gently untangled her fingers from Josh's and stood, pacing the floor. She avoided looking at him. He had a black eye, cuts on his chin, forehead and cheeks. His arm was in a sling and there was tape visible through his thin hospital gown where his ribs were broken.

And despite the smile he kept trying to plaster on his face, it was clear that he was in pain.

"I get that it's important for you to put down roots, to be in a place you can call home," Tess said as she gazed out the window. "You can't do that with all of my garbage hanging around." She turned.

He'd been watching her the whole time.

"No matter how many times I tell you to leave me alone, you won't do that…" she managed a smile even through the tears that began to subside. "And I guess part of me never wanted you to. I mean, I can't let you go either." She went back to him as she swiped in annoyance at her cheeks. "So, I'll do what I should have done all along, Jed. I'll stop being selfish." She drew a deep breath as she took his hand again. "I've been offered jobs out of state. I'll take one of them. It would be best for both of us. Now that I've paid everyone back, I'm free again."

Josh's face melted into a grimace.

Tess released his hand and stepped out of his grasp when he tried to reach for her. "No. I tried to tell you this so many times, but you wouldn't listen and I…now it's all caught up to me. It has to stop. I'll stop it. The only way to do that is to go away."

"Tor—" Josh struggled to make the words come.

Tess swallowed hard. He shouldn't be in that bed, beaten, and in pain.

He grimaced through the pain and tried to sit up taller, failing as he leaned back against the pillows. "You're a coward," he muttered. "You never meant to be with me. You're too scared to fight through this."

Tess stared at him, wondering if she'd missed something. "What?"

Josh closed his eyes and struggled before he continued in a voice devoid of emotion. "You won't go out in public with me, you won't go to a Bible study with women who..." he drew a breath and fought through the pain to continue. "...want you there. You won't even stand up in church and be baptized when you say you changed. You're no trouble-making rebel. You're no tornado. You're a coward."

Tess hated that the words hit her so hard. She blinked back tears as she drew a deep breath. She and Josh had not, as yet, disagreed on anything. That he would stand up to her was new, strange, and in her unbearable darkness, more painful than she expected. "Maybe I am," she said, fighting the tightness in her chest. "But I can't keep this up anymore. I really am sorry." She went to him one last time and pressed her hand against his face, her thumb lingering on a cut that was certain to turn to an ugly bruise in a matter of days. "You can say it was a robbery attempt. Your reputation won't be hurt and..."

Josh shifted his head away from her touch. Pain flicked across his face with the movement.

Tess understood the stabbing realization of what was happening. "Good-bye, Josh," she whispered. "I am sorry." Before she could change her mind, Tess fled.

26

But for that very reason I was shown mercy so that in me,
the worst of sinners, Christ Jesus might display his immense
patience as an example for those who would believe in him
and receive eternal life.
1 Timothy 1:16

Josh had known she'd blame herself. But what he hadn't known was how to handle it. And despite how much he loved her, he managed to do the one thing he swore he never would. He made everything even worse than it already was. The pain of his injuries paled next to the pain in his soul.

The door opened, and Stu entered the room quietly, placing Josh's phone back on the table beside the bed. "Brody went after her. But she may need some time to process this. Poor kid keeps getting hit from all sides."

Josh nodded but said nothing.

"Dave is on his way."

"Think she'll leave?" Josh managed.

Stu regarded him for a long time, his dark eyes betraying nothing of his feelings. "I hope not. But at this point, anything is possible. I'm not sure I've ever seen her like this."

A few moments later, the door opened and Brody entered, his face grim. Neither Josh nor Stu spoke as he fell into a seat, his head dropping into his hands.

Josh closed his eyes. He wished he'd resisted the urge to let his anger steal the chance to tell her he loved her. Now it might be too late.

Brody shook his head and angrily stood to pace the room. "I told her that this was what happens when you're friends with drug dealers. It happens when you decide that you're more important than anyone else in your life." Brody sighed. "I told her that a stripper gets this. I can't explain why I started to believe in her. I'm sorry, Josh."

"Hey." Stu's voice was stern. "Don't get caught on a view of your sister that isn't fair."

Brody laughed wryly. "She wasn't a stripper? Come on, Uncle Stu. We all remember what she did."

Josh was pained that this was what had become of Tess's life for far too long.

Stu placed a firm hand on his nephew's shoulder. "I took her out of there kicking and screaming, but she never removed one stitch of clothing for money." He paused. "Maybe you ought to think about what made her such a mess in the first place. It might make you a little more compassionate about how far she's come."

Josh wished he could say something that would change his friend's mind. Finally, he said, "Stu's right. This isn't her fault, Brody."

Brody snorted in disgust as he went to the window.

Stu sighed heavily.

The door opened and Dave entered quietly, his face showing his shock at Josh's condition. "Hey." He schooled his features into a sympathetic smile as he sat near the bed. "You all right?"

Josh did his best to nod. "Can you cover the service?" he asked.

Dave nodded. "Of, course." He glanced over Josh, assessing his condition. "What should I say?"

Josh sighed heavily. "The truth."

Both Stu and Brody looked at him, surprised.

"You might want to think about that..." Stu began.

Josh closed his eyes. "Tell them or the gossip will be worse. I'll be back next week if they still want me. If not, I'll figure it out."

Dave met Stu's gaze for a moment before turning his attention to Josh. "And Tess? Do I mention that or...I mean...?"

"She didn't do this."

Dave squirmed. "But people will talk."

Josh opened his eyes. "We can't control that. I got beat up by some lowlifes on a basketball court. I'm fine."

Reluctantly Dave nodded.

Josh closed his eyes.

The doctor entered. "All right, gentlemen, this room's becoming a circus with all the people in and out. Josh needs rest. You're welcome to come back later. One at a time."

Stu smiled at Josh. "Call if you need anything."

Josh nodded as the men left. The doctor checked him over quickly and followed suit, leaving Josh to his worries, wondering if he was losing his job along with his love.

~*~

Tess managed to avoid calls from Stu, Marlene, Brody, Stell, and her parents as she tossed her essentials into garbage bags, fearful one or all of her relatives would be knocking on her apartment door before she could escape. She wasn't sticking around any longer since clearly there was no point in it.

On the way to her apartment, she'd called the hospital in Pittsburgh that extended her most recent job offer and asked if it would be possible to start before the date they'd originally mentioned. Even though it was closer to home than any of the other positions, and so might be the easiest to find her, Tess was of the mind that it was also the one job where she'd be most difficult to find. Pittsburgh, after all, was barely an hour away. She'd be hidden in plain sight. And, if anything important happened, she would find out and be able to return quickly. But most importantly she'd be what she'd been longing for over the last few years—anonymous.

"We can't start you until Thursday, Tess," Nancy Cantini, the nurses' administrator said. "But in the meantime you're welcome to come and familiarize yourself with the hospital layout, the schedule, and you can also stop by to get all of the work forms completed."

"That sounds perfect. Hey, are you aware of any apartments for rent? Nothing fancy, but cheap, safe...or even someone searching for a roommate?"

"Well..." Nancy paused. "My brother-in-law owns a few units not far from the hospital. They're pretty small but it's a safe neighborhood and the price isn't bad. Not sure if he has anything open but you're welcome to check."

"Sounds perfect. Can you send me the address and his number? I'd like to set something up as soon as possible."

And suddenly, Tess was on her way to freedom.

~*~

Tess spent two days in an old hotel as she coordinated plans for the next step. She'd landed an apartment and would begin work soon. Everything was slipping into place more easily than she'd anticipated. Perhaps this was all God's plan. Maybe Uncle Stu was wrong all along and she was never supposed to stay in Maple Ridge. Regardless, there was a surprising peace even in the midst of the pain she bore daily.

Soon Tess was settled in a sparsely-furnished apartment she now called home. She didn't start her new job as an emergency room nurse for two more days, and she was anxious. Having worked almost non-stop for the last two years made Tess unable to sit still. She'd unpacked the garbage bags of clothes and shoes she'd tossed together before ditching town and she'd changed her bank account over to one closer to her new home.

And she'd avoided calls from Stu, Brody, Josh, and Morgan by leaving her phone off most of the time. Her parents, once again, gave up trying to get hold of her. The last message from her mother being, "Tess, we are not chasing you. You are an adult. You call when you're ready. We love you."

Tess snorted.

She stood and went to what she loosely-defined as her kitchen. It was so tiny she was glad she lived in the apartment alone, as two people in that room would be a fire code violation. She opened the cabinet and rooted around for a moment, giving up when she realized nothing in her meager rations would satisfy her. She sighed heavily as her phone rang.

Morgan.

Of those she'd willingly speak to, her friend was the only option. Although her heart leaped to her throat, Tess lifted the phone and pressed it to her ear. "Hey." To her own ears her voice sounded strained.

There was a long pause before Morgan's voice came over the line. "I didn't think you'd answer," she said softly.

Tess dropped back onto the couch. "What's up?"

"What's up? Geez, Tess. Where the heck did you go!?"

"Come on. I can't tell you or Stu will drag me home. I've already apologized to Josh, Flynn's paid off, and I start a new job in another day or so, and that will let me pay Stu back in a couple of months. I'm done."

"Oh, Tess..."

Tess cringed at the sound of her friend's voice. It was clear she was crying. "Hey," she began. "How's Pastor Thorne?"

Morgan sniffed. "Don't call him that," she said.

"It's his name."

"You're being stupid."

Tess snorted.

"You are, Theresa Carson. Do you think for one minute that anyone here who matters thinks you're guilty of causing what happened?!"

"Brody thinks it's my fault. He called me a stripper."

"He was upset." Morgan sighed. "Besides, Brody feels terrible. Have you even listened to the thousand messages everyone left for you?" she paused. "Listen, I understand how upsetting all of this was. But you're strong. You can't run away and act as if it doesn't matter. Your family, who has stood by you through all of the other stuff, is like everyone else. Running away makes you seem guilty of something when you aren't."

Tess sighed and shook her head. "I can't do it anymore, Morgan. I'm not coming back."

"I guessed as much."

"So, what then?"

"At least tell your family where you are," Morgan pleaded. "Please."

"I..." Tess thought of everyone. "I can't. The disappointment. It's too much. No one will change and when I saw Josh in that hospital bed, all beat up like that. I..." she paused. "Please tell me the church didn't let him go."

"No." Morgan spoke slowly. "He got out of the hospital the other day. I talked to um, Alison Gorman...? Anyway, she said he told the truth and the board isn't happy with him but after a severe finger-wagging he's all right. Harrison was steamed. He..."

Tess's ears perked up. "What? Did he do something?"

"Of course he did. He went to another church this week. Said he was finished with the game-playing going on at North Street and he wanted a church built on a stronger foundation. A few of the oldies followed but for the most part the congregation is the same. Supportive even."

"Good riddance," Tess muttered.

"Yeah, I guess." Morgan paused. "You should call Josh. He..." her voice dropped off for a moment. "I mean, maybe I shouldn't say because I'm not sure..."

Tess's stomach rolled. "What?"

"Well, Ashley-Marie was frazzled enough when she got your message that you quit. Said she never should have hired you. And she said that she was taking dinner over for him tonight. Seriously, Tess. You really think he wants to see her?"

"I don't have any idea who he wants to see," Tess said. "I gotta go. Tell everyone I'm OK."

"Tess."

"Morgan. Stop. This is for the best. For everyone."

"The wedding is in a few months. Stu said he might not go through with it if you aren't home."

Tess's eyes brimmed with tears. Maybe she was being selfish. She didn't want her uncle's happiness to hinge on her being found. "Don't let that happen, Morgie. Promise me."

"I can't promise that," Morgan replied. "Only you can make it happen."

Tess sighed heavily. "I'll be there for the wedding."

"Maybe you should call him."

"I can't. Take care, Morgan." Before she could change her mind, Tess hung up, swiping at the tears that started falling. Suddenly, she wished she could go home. Maybe she was a coward after all.

~*~

Tess worked for the next few weeks, still pondering her next move. During that time, she found a new church and joined a Bible study. She spoke to Morgan, still refusing to give any details about where she was living. But she'd discovered that Josh was better and his new ministry with Pine View was thriving. He'd even gotten Gram Vi on board to help teach some kids to cook.

The most exciting news came from Brody and Stell when they announced they were expecting their first baby.

A baby! Tess bit her lip, willing the tears to stay back. She would be an aunt. But she couldn't make herself dial the numbers that would bring her family back together.

She went to work at the end of the long week, anxious to enjoy the following day off when she could attend church and spend the rest of the afternoon re-stocking her barren kitchen cabinets full of munchies.

So, when she was near the end of her shift and heading for the nurse's station to log her final reports, she wasn't prepared for the sight of her parents sitting on the squeaky red chairs in the emergency room waiting area. They were clearly nervous, but that was nothing compared to what Tess was going through at the sight of them. She went to them on shaking legs. "Hey. Uh, what are you doing here?"

Her mother turned toward her, an expression of relief covering her face. She smiled even as it appeared she'd rather cry. "Theresa." She hurried toward her daughter and wrapped her in a hug that nearly took Tess's breath away.

"Mom?"

Tess's father wrapped his arms around them both. "Tess…"

Tess stepped away. "What…what are you doing here?" she asked, swallowing hard. "Gram's OK, right?"

Karen placed a hand on her daughter's shoulder. "Grandma's fine," she said. "We've been worried. I was afraid you wouldn't come back..."

Tess glanced around and caught another nurse's eye. "I...um, there's about forty-five more minutes on my shift. Do you mind if I meet you down in the cafeteria in a little bit?" she asked, not noticing that her co-worker had overheard the conversation and was now heading across the hall toward her.

"I can cover you. Janice is here, and it's been quiet. Go ahead. We can page you."

Tess nodded. "OK, thanks, Jackie. Um, these are my parents. Karen and Stan Carson."

Jackie nodded and shook their hands. "Nice to meet you both. I need to get over to check on that girl in exam one. Excuse me."

Tess turned to her parents. "We can get some coffee or something," she said awkwardly.

Stan nodded, and he and his wife followed their wayward daughter to the hospital cafeteria.

27

But the Lord said unto Samuel, Look not on his countenance,
or on the height of his stature; because I have refused him:
for the Lord seeth not as man seeth; for man looketh at the
outward appearance, but the Lord looketh on the heart.
1 Samuel 16:7

A short time later the family was seated in a booth in the cafeteria.

"We weren't very good at forgiving you," her father began. "Even when it was obvious how hard you were working, we kept holding onto the past. That wasn't fair."

Tess wondered if she'd heard correctly. Neither of her parents had ever been quick to admit their failings. For them to find her and make the effort to apologize was no small gesture. She drew a breath.

Her mother spoke. "We talked to Josh for a long time the other day and I realized I never understood how to relate to you. It was easier for me to focus on everything else, even myself, instead of trying to get to know you better. I'm sorry."

Tess nodded and pinched her leg under the table to be certain this wasn't a strange dream. Apparently, it was quite real. She searched for the right words but all she came up with was, "How did you find me?"

Stan exchanged a glance with his wife. "Stu was driving me nuts and Marlene started in on your mother, but the trouble was they both made sense. We played a part in this too. A bigger one than we wanted to admit." He toyed with his coffee mug for a moment before continuing. "So, I hired a guy. Didn't take him long. We..." he cleared his throat before continuing. "We were hoping that if you heard us say we believe in you, maybe you'd come home. Maybe you wouldn't care so much about anyone else's opinion. They don't matter, Tess. And you aren't alone. Not anymore."

Hope fluttered deep inside Tess's soul. She'd expected Stu to come for her—maybe even Josh—but she was wanted, finally forgiven, and her parents hadn't let her go as easily as they always did before. She managed a small smile.

"Will you come home?" Karen asked.

Tess wished it were that simple. But the idea of showing back up in Maple Ridge like nothing happened was enough to make her skin crawl. She shook her head, fearful of what so many of the people in town would think if she did something so brazen. "I couldn't."

"Justin's in jail. He won't be back."

"That's great." Tess said with a sigh. "I'm glad Josh is safe. I feel awful about what happened."

"It wasn't your fault."

Tess wanted to believe it, but her emotions were too raw.

Stan glanced at his watch. "We need to get going," he said. "We promised Gram we'd be there tonight but we couldn't wait to talk to you."

The group stood and waited awkwardly, unsure how to end the impromptu meeting.

"I'm glad you came," Tess said. "It means a lot to me. Really." She paused, thinking. "So, I guess you'll tell everyone where I am?"

Her parents exchanged a glance and let the question hang for some time before her dad met her gaze. "Not if you don't want us to. If you aren't ready."

Tess drew a deep breath. "Can I think about it?"

Her mom nodded and pulled Tess into a hug that melted years of tension between them. When they separated, her dad pulled her close and kissed the top of her head.

"Maybe you should come for Sunday dinner."

"I…" Tess met her father's eyes. "Maybe."

He nodded. "We eat at the same time every week. You're welcome to join us. Brody and Stell will be there and we can always ask Josh too, if you like."

Tess nodded. She badly wanted to go but not even a month had passed since she left. It might be too soon to think things could be different, even with her deepening faith and the understanding that she should let go of the control she'd held to—thinking that what everyone thought of her mattered so much more than the woman she'd actually become. Now that she was beginning to accept that, all else was secondary. "Maybe soon," Tess said.

Her mom nodded, reluctant to leave. "Can I call you?"

"Sure," Tess said with a smile. "I'd like that."

~*~

It was two weeks before Tess could convince herself to call Uncle Stu. She'd spoken to her parents a few times since their visit and with each conversation she was aware it was getting easier to forgive herself, and them too, for the roles they'd all played in their relationship. It helped that she'd also opened up to her Bible study group about some of her history and she'd found their candor refreshing. All of the women struggled with things they'd buried from their pasts—even things they continued to struggle with—and most were still dealing with some of the ramifications of their choices. The important thing was that they were growing, healing, and trusting God.

Tess was learning she could do the same. And yet it wasn't without some difficulty that she finally called her uncle.

"Mouthy." He said it fondly but with a firmness that was as it had always been. He expected an explanation.

Tess exhaled slowly. "Hey, Uncle Stu."

"You OK?"

"Yeah. I'm doing really well." Tess wished the sound of his voice didn't bring tears to her eyes. She ached with a need to be with him again.

"Running away wasn't part of our agreement."

"I'm sorry." Tess's voice caught on the apology as she sat heavily on her bed, wishing she'd worked through the conversation before dialing his number. "Things changed so fast. I guess I was afraid if I hung around it would get worse—for me and for Josh. I don't care what happens to me anymore. But it wasn't fair to do that to him."

"You can be sure that running away doesn't fix what's broken."

"And what did staying do?" Tess searched for words. "I'm sorry. You did so much for me and I kept trying not to disappoint you but I guess that's all I can do."

"You didn't disappoint me. Not even once, kid."
Stu paused.

Tess let his sincere words wash over her. Her
healing could begin now.

"You're in Pittsburgh?" he continued.

Tess couldn't find a reason to stay hidden any
longer so she said, "Yeah..."

"Leave it to you to be right under our noses."

"How do you think I left so fast?"

Stu grunted. "I already knew where you went. I
could have gotten to you a half hour after you left,
thanks to Mitch. But I figured you might need some
time." Mitch Hanson was a detective with the police
force in a nearby town. He and Stu went to high school
together and he often helped Stu when it came to
finding Tess.

"Figures," Tess said with a groan. "You two
always conspired against me."

"I'd call it keeping you safe," Stu said. "I miss you,
Mouthy."

The tenderness in his voice warmed her. Tears
sprang to Tess's eyes as she tried to speak. "It was hard
not talking, Uncle Stu," she said, her voice cracking on
his name. "I missed you. No one here to harass."

"Your apartment's still open. There's an annoying
neighbor upstairs but you could come home. Maybe
for Sunday dinner at least?"

It was one thing to talk to her family on the phone.
It would be another to have everyone in the same
place, ready for battle. "I'm thinking about it," she
said.

"Maybe if you call your brother it will be easier."

"I'm not sure a call would be enough." Tess

paused. "I should go."

"Mouthy."

Tess waited for Stu to continue.

"Will you come to the wedding?"

Although Tess knew Josh would do the service, she could only answer one way. "Of course."

"There's a baptism service coming up," Stu continued. "You give any more thought to starting over?"

Tess forgot the push Josh and Stu made for her to be baptized. The idea now wasn't nearly as painful as it had once been. She sighed. "That would be pretty bold."

Stu laughed. "Like that niece I used to have," he said. "Think about it."

Tess smiled. "I will," she said. And she meant it.

~*~

Josh tried to catch his breath after sinking another shot against Brody.

"Time out..." Brody groaned as he grabbed a towel and wiped his face. "What is with you?"

Josh shrugged. "I needed to get out some stress."

Brody sat heavily on a bench nearby and drank deeply from his water bottle before speaking. "You need to let my sister go...or get her back, for heaven's sake. This in-between stuff is probably killing you both."

Josh turned to his friend, wishing the words didn't make his blood boil. He drew a deep breath. "I don't think she was mine to let go."

Brody snorted before drinking again. He tossed his bottle aside before speaking. "My parents found her, and Stu said she finally called him yesterday. She's in Pittsburgh."

Josh's heart skipped a beat. "What?" She was that close this whole time? Leave it to Tess to pull that on everyone.

"That's what she told Stu." Brody shrugged. "Probably wouldn't be too hard to find her. I mean, how many hospitals are there?"

"Oh, come on. That doesn't even make sense. Why would I...?" Josh didn't bother to finish his sentence. He shook his head instead and sat as Brody stood.

"If you could be honest with yourself for a second, you'd admit there isn't a choice," Brody said. He wiped his face again before continuing. "I've texted her a bunch of times. I've left messages. She knows where I stand. She can call me or text when she's ready. Have you even reached out to her? Or are you hiding behind your ridiculous need to be liked by everyone in this town?"

"What?" Josh practically leaped to his feet, ready to fight.

But Brody was ready too. He shoved Josh, causing him to stumble backward. "You're as bad as I am!" he exclaimed. "Only I said what I was thinking and you tried to pretend it wasn't happening—or that it didn't matter. But it did, and she knew it, Josh. She saw right through you. You were thinking a pastor can't really date someone like her—with such a public past."

Josh reeled from his friend's words. "I never said that!" he shrieked. "I told her over and over again it wasn't like that. I begged her to go out with me, Brody. *She* said no." Josh sighed, his shoulders sagging in defeat. "We came to an impasse. I didn't know what to do."

Brody shook his head. "Maybe show her that it doesn't matter. I mean, is the job more important, or is she? I'm not saying there's a right answer—you worked hard and waited a long time to get back here. It's OK if that's your choice. But make it clear. Don't leave her wondering where she really stands or try to have it both ways if that's not possible."

Josh wished Brody wasn't so insightful or willing to speak the truth. He was already overwhelmed with all the ways he'd messed things up and his friend's words weren't bringing any solace. "Exactly what should I do?" Josh asked. He suddenly felt as if he was drowning. Again, he tried to think what he should have said or done. His last words to her had been a feeble attempt to shock her. Apparently, it worked. Josh slowly sank to the bench, letting his head fall to his hands. "I called her a coward," he muttered. "Those are the last words I said to her. That's what she believes I think."

Brody glanced at Josh and sat heavily with a sigh. "Stell and I have our problems too, man. That doesn't mean an apology wouldn't go a long way." He cleared his throat. "If you love her, you gotta make this right."

Josh nodded. "I'll sure try."

Brody reached out his hand and pulled Josh to his feet.

The men slowly began to gather their things.

It would take a miracle to make things right again.

~*~

Two weeks later Tess sat outside her parents' house, quietly watching as Brody handed Stell two trays from the trunk of the car.

Although she was frightened to face everything, and finally put the past behind her, Tess understood that it was time to be an adult and make an effort to right the situation she played her own part in creating. Blaming the world for everything wasn't fair or accurate. And, the power of her Bible study friends praying for her was unbelievable. Tess was convinced she'd never known such peace even as she wondered how this first meeting with her family would go.

Stell went into the house.

Brody stayed where he was, watching Tess.

She hoped the courage would manifest itself so she could go to him. Finally, it did. With a deep sigh and a silent prayer, she opened the door and got out of her truck, approaching her brother as if he might take a swing at her.

But he seemed scared too. He leaned against the back end of the car, his arms folded over his chest for a moment, and in the next they were open to her.

Tess swallowed the lump in her throat as she went face first into his chest, the tears already flowing.

"I'm sorry," he whispered as he hugged her. "It was so wrong to say those things."

Tess sniffed, unable to speak as the tears continued flowing down her cheeks and into the fabric of Brody's shirt. She was clueless that her family was watching them from the window of the house until Brody whispered, "We can go inside, T. I'm sure everyone's dying to talk to you."

She nodded but kept her face buried in his shirt. "I'm sorry I embarrassed you. I'm sorry for all I did," she murmured. "I'm an awful sister."

"No." Brody held her arms firmly and he nudged her back a step so she would stop avoiding his eyes. He held her gaze for a long moment before speaking. "You don't owe us more apologies. Here and now we go forward as a family." He exhaled. "You needed us to pray for you and all we did was worry about our hurts over things you couldn't undo. Things that were already in the past. Well, I'm over them." He smiled and wiped her cheeks free of tears. "You're going to be an aunt near Christmas."

Tess sniffed and nodded. "Yeah. That's so great."

Brody nodded. "You can help that little guy or girl learn about being a Carson. Maybe teach the kid how to pitch. Make him—or her—root for all the Pittsburgh before Josh screws them up by talking about the Cleveland." He gestured toward the house. "Come on."

Tess allowed him to lead her toward the house, aware that she'd finally, after so incredibly long, come home for good.

~*~

Tess swallowed hard as she went out onto the back porch where Stu and Marlene were drinking tea after dinner. During the meal, the family did its best to talk through things and all appeared to be forgiven. Of course, Tess needed to spend a little more time one on one with her uncle, assuring him that her transformation was finally complete. The woman she'd kept hidden and struggled to avoid for years was home. She accepted that she was herself again, and no matter what anyone else believed, everything happened at just the right time.

Marlene smiled at Tess and stood, giving her a hug. "Hey, honey," she said. "I'll check on your mom in case she needs help clearing things. Excuse me."

Tess nodded, grateful that the woman understood that she needed her uncle to herself. She sniffed back the threatening tears as the door closed. "I like Marlene a lot," Tess said softly. "Probably even better than I like you."

Stu smiled. "Feeling's mutual, kid."

"Uncle Stu, I..." Tess swallowed.

Stu wrapped his arms around her. "We're all good. And I love you, Mouthy," he whispered.

"I love you too," she said and stepped back, still overcome by how the day was going. "I talked to my Bible study group about everything, and I thought about what you, and Josh, told me. I've been reading my Bible—a lot. It's as if I finally got it. I shouldn't be ashamed. I needed God to get me straight, but I don't need to keep beating myself up that I wasn't perfect. None of us are. It's not as though He rated my sin on a grander scale because it was public. It just—was. And that's why I needed Him." She laughed wryly. "I still do."

Stu nodded. "That's how it goes. We don't stop needing Him." He sat and gestured for Tess to do the same. "I'm so proud of you."

"I'm not sure I deserve that."

"Probably not." Stu gazed out at the field behind the house. "You deal with that Thorne in your side yet?"

Tess smiled, shaking her head. "Not yet, I wanted

to talk to you about that. I'm not sure how to go about it."

Uncle Stu set his tea on the table and nodded. "OK."

Tess sat beside him slowly and drew a deep breath. It was time to take her life back.

28

Who can find a virtuous woman?
For her price is far above rubies.
Proverbs 31:10

Josh emerged from his office, still thinking about his conversation with Brody weeks earlier. He'd sent a few texts to Tess, but she'd not responded though he could see she'd read them. Since Josh was already convinced he'd ruined the chance of having a relationship with her, he didn't think he should pursue the matter any further. Still, he wondered if he should ask Stu what hospital Tess was working at and...he shook his head as he headed down the steps toward the first floor of the church. He could think about Tess later. Right now there was a baptism service to do. His first at his new church.

"Hey," Dave's voice made Josh jump. He'd been so lost in his daydream he never realized he wasn't alone. He forced a smile. "What's up?" he asked.

Dave laughed and handed him a towel. "Alison said you might want an extra towel."

Josh's eyebrows knit together in confusion, but he tucked the extra towel under his arm and nodded. "Thanks."

"You bet. I checked everything. I think we're ready."

Josh nodded and followed his friend into the

sanctuary. He prayed silently for focus and wisdom, and for God's words and love to reach those who weren't ready yet for the commitment of baptism. His mind strayed to Tess again. He shook his head and prayed quickly that she'd see and accept the love all around her.

~*~

Tess squirmed as she peered through the small window into the sanctuary as yet another member of the congregation went forward for baptism. Josh wasn't aware she was watching, and she knew it was too important of a service for him to be distracted by her presence.

But seeing him in that baptismal pool, and listening to the people give their brief testimonies and making their promises to follow Christ, made Tess's legs shake. She glanced toward the row where her family was seated.

Stu turn to glance in her direction. He winked.

She winked back. Someone came behind her and she stepped back, hoping she wasn't in the way.

Dave Gorman smiled at her. "You ready?"

Tess shrugged, fearing the ramifications of the bold statement she'd been preparing to make for weeks. "I think so."

He gestured for her to follow him. "He's clueless," he said as they approached the doors that were closer to Josh. "Wait here and let me talk to him a second. I'll give you the sign and you can come on in."

"Are you sure this is OK? I don't want to…"

Dave smiled. "Trust me. No one will turn away a woman who wants to stand up and say she's following Christ." He paused as Josh helped the last person from the pool. "Wait here. I'll be right back."

Tess stepped out of sight as Dave opened the door and hustled back inside so he could tell Josh there was one more baptism to go.

~*~

"I want to encourage you to pray for each of those who took this public step of faith today and..." Josh's voice drifted off as he noticed Dave approaching from the side door.

Dave smiled confidently at the congregation and held up a finger, asking them to give him a moment with the pastor.

Josh waited as Dave covered the microphone with one hand so he could lean close and whisper, "There's one more..."

"No...Mrs. Wilson was the last one and I can't..." he stammered, hating to be put in such a position as the congregation sat expectantly watching him. He glanced back at his friend, wondering if he'd forgotten the protocol. The precedent had always been for the senior pastor to meet with each person who'd asked to participate in the baptism service. Josh had done so and listened to their stories in advance so as to be certain of their commitment to their faith. He couldn't let someone slip in at the last minute without being certain of their understanding of this important step in their faith.

But something in Dave's smile stopped him. "I talked to her myself," he assured Josh. "Alison did too. Numerous times. Trust me. We followed through. There's not a thing to worry about."

"Why didn't she come to me?"

Dave shook his head. "Work commitments. Come on, let's not keep everyone waiting."

Reluctantly Josh nodded, wondering if this type of chaos was a normal occurrence at the church. He made a mental note to bring it up at the staff meeting to ensure such a thing didn't happen again. He didn't like being put on the spot in front of his congregation.

Dave took his hand way from the microphone and gestured to the side door. He cleared his throat.

"It, um, Pastor Dave has asked me to baptize one more member of our congregation," Josh said unsurely as the door opened.

Tess entered and set her towel aside.

Josh reached back to hold onto the side of the pool so he didn't fall. He swallowed hard as she confidently got into the pool, seeming so much like the woman he'd met in Florida. The one he'd fallen in love with.

She winked before smiling at him. "It was your turn for a surprise," she whispered.

Josh nodded dumbly.

Tess nodded toward the seats that were nearly filled with people. "Maybe you should address your congregation there, pastor."

Josh returned to the moment and cleared his throat as he leaned toward the microphone again. "Uh, yes," he muttered, forcing his gaze to the crowd even as he looked back at Tess. Her hair was in a simple ponytail, but it was her sparkling brown eyes that continued to capture his attention. She wasn't afraid anymore. Josh's hopes soared as he said, "Do you want to share your story with us, Tess?"

Tess nodded. "My parents always brought me to church so I definitely knew about God my whole life, but when things were good I didn't think I really needed Him. So...a lot of people already know this but when I was in college I hurt my shoulder so bad that I couldn't play softball anymore," she paused to release a deep breath.

Josh took the opportunity to show her he was proud of her. He gently touched her back and waited while she collected herself.

She smiled at him briefly and continued. "Softball was my life. So, I guess I thought I was invincible when I could still play." She smiled at many of the people who'd shunned her only a short time ago. "I expected to always play softball and be told how great I was. When that was taken away from me, I was completely lost. And I looked for support and comfort in all the wrong places.

"I made a lot of mistakes and hurt a lot of people." She swallowed, blinking back tears, eventually giving over to them. She continued even as they spilled down her cheeks. "But during that time, all those low moments, my family never gave up on me. They were praying all along. But it was...it was my Uncle Stu who showed me Christ's love and told me about salvation. Real salvation. And grace I didn't deserve then or now. I'd heard about it before so it wasn't new...but somehow it was the right moment and I asked Jesus into my life. And I am never, ever letting Him go."

The congregation applauded.

The entire Carson family was crying.

Josh smiled and repositioned himself so that he

could get one arm around Tess.

She nudged him with her elbow and whispered, "You drop me, and I'll never let you forget it, butterfingers…"

Josh tried not to laugh but a chuckle escaped before he was able to get control. He cleared his throat. "No way," he whispered. "Cross your arms over your chest…" He leaned close to the microphone. "Having professed your faith in Jesus Christ to forgive your sins, I ask you Theresa Carson, do you renounce Satan and all of his works?"

"I do."

"And do you intend to follow Christ and His teachings, following him as your Lord and Savior, all the days of your life?"

"Absolutely."

Josh didn't mask the joy that seeped into his voice. "On your profession of faith, I now baptize you in the name of the Father, the Son, and the Holy Ghost." Josh lowered her quickly into the water and back up to find the smile on her face more than he could stand. He choked back the emotion. "Congratulations…" he said softly as the congregation erupted in applause.

Tess smiled.

Josh turned away, drawing a deep breath in an effort to regain his composure. He exhaled slowly and leaned close to the microphone.

Tess gently squeezed his hand under the water before she slipped past him and accepted Dave's help from the pool.

"Well," Josh said with a smile as he did his best to keep his eyes on his congregation instead of following Tess when she ducked out of the sanctuary, a towel wrapped around her shoulders. He lifted his eyebrows as he focused on Brody, Stu, and the rest of the Carson clan. "If there are no other surprises, I would say that concludes our baptism service this evening." The congregation chuckled as he waited a moment before saying,

"Let's pray together for all those who made this important commitment to the Lord tonight."

~*~

Tess changed her clothes in the women's restroom, tossing the jeans and long-sleeved T-shirt she'd been wearing moments before into a bag. She quickly toweled her hair dry and fluffed it in a weak effort to make herself more presentable. She smiled at her reflection in the bathroom mirror for a brief moment and realized instantly that her hair or lack of make-up didn't matter to Josh. For the first time in her life, a man was interested in her heart, not her face or her body. His care for her centered on the person she'd become, not the temporary, superficial beauty that would fade in the years ahead.

But before Tess could begin to think of pursuing a relationship with him again, there were a lot of things they needed to say to one another. She tossed the bag of wet clothes over her arm and yanked the bathroom door open, intent on finding her family, but instead she found herself face-to-face with Harrison Flynn.

He stepped back, meeting her eyes with an expression that was a departure from his usual scowl.

With a firm resolve to do exactly as she'd promised, Tess smiled and nodded at him. "Hello, Mr.

Flynn."

Harrison nodded curtly. "Ms. Carson."

Tess kept staring at him, unsure what she should say.

He exhaled slowly. "I didn't think you were sincere until now. But your testimony tells me different. My apologies. I do intend to keep you in my prayers." He cleared his throat. "Well, I'd say your family is interested in finding you. Have a good night." And with that he was gone.

Tess was sure it took no small amount of courage and pain for him to approach her after the many times he'd condemned her.

Miracles were beginning to happen.

Tess leaned against the wall for support as a weight lifted from her shoulders. Already she was sure she was forgiven and new, but this was more than she could have prayed for. Harrison Flynn had been everything a good villain could be—mean, unforgiving, and angry at everything Tess did to try to make things right. That he could finally forgive her meant a lot. But before she could think too long, her mother and Marlene rounded the corner and squealed.

"You did great!" her mom said, reaching out to give her daughter a hug.

"Sorry I made you wait. I was soaked."

Marlene hugged her next. "We're all so proud of you."

"Someone is waiting for you," her Mom said, leaning toward Tess conspiratorially. "Why don't you catch up with him? Bring him over for dessert and coffee?"

Tess swallowed nervously. "Oh. I'm not so sure, Mom."

Marlene put one arm around Tess's shoulder as she guided her toward the large area outside the sanctuary. "And you never will be unless you talk to him."

Her mom fussed with Tess's hair for a moment.

Brody came over and playfully messed it up again. "Nicely done, sis," he said, pulling her into a hug.

Stell was waiting to hug her next followed by her dad.

Uncle Stu held onto her a long time and whispered, "That's the girl I remember," he said. "I'm glad she finally decided it was time to show up." He grunted. "You always were late for everything."

Tess stepped back and smiled. "Yeah, but it might be perfect timing this time."

"So, do I get a turn?" Josh's deep voice made Tess's stomach dance and she turned to him, wondering what would be appropriate. She wanted to throw herself into his arms and hold on for dear life. But there was still too much that needed to be said, so she smiled shyly.

He stepped forward and hugged her. "I'm proud of you," he whispered.

Tess swallowed hard against the years of emotions such a statement brought.

Her mom patted Tess lightly on the back as she said, "We're picking up Gram and will head over to the house for some pie. If you'd like to join us in an hour or so…"

Tess could barely pull her gaze away from Josh long enough to acknowledge her mother with a smile. She held out her bag of wet clothes. "Could you take these?"

Karen nodded as she took the clothes.

Before the family walked away, Stu gave Josh a look of warning that only a fool could have missed.

Tess stifled a chuckle as Josh nodded, looking petrified of the smaller man.

The Carson family exited the church.

Tess glanced at Josh. He smiled at her so goofily she couldn't stop herself from hitting his left arm in an effort to wake him up. "Knock it off, Jed," she muttered. "Or you'll…"

Josh laughed as he rubbed his arm. "I'll what?" he asked, gesturing toward the sanctuary. "I was stopped by about ten of the little old ladies who asked when I'll get it together and ask that 'fine young woman' to marry me." He laughed and leaned close to whisper. "I'm having a hard time convincing myself that right now isn't the perfect time."

Tess's toes tingled.

Josh unleashed his deep dimples. But then he shook his head. "Don't worry, I won't." He sobered and folded his arms over his chest. "You deserve better. Besides, it's too obvious."

"Jed…" Tess glanced around, trying to ignore that there were still a few members of the congregation milling about. "I think we need to talk."

"Yes. We do." He nodded toward Dave who jogged over quickly.

"What's up?" he asked.

Josh smiled. "I need to…"

Dave smiled at Tess and gave her a quick one-armed hug. "Go on. I can handle whatever's left here."

Josh released a deep breath and gave his friend a quick hug before smiling back down at Tess. "All right, Tornado. Let's go for a ride."

~*~

A few minutes later Tess was hanging on behind Josh as he drove over the streets. She wondered for only a moment where he was going, but then smiled.

They were on their way to one of the most precious spots from their childhood. The tree house.

Josh parked at the edge of the trees that led to the deeper woods and hopped off the bike, helping Tess do the same. They took off their helmets and he said, "I didn't bring you here because I wanted to hide you. I just hoped we could be alone for a few minutes. I have a lot to say."

Tess nodded. "It's OK. I do too."

Josh shyly reached for her hand and she gave it to him, the warmth of his palm reassuring her that he was really there beside her and that, despite the privacy of their setting, they no longer needed to hide. She could hardly suppress the smile that kept coming to her lips as they walked to their tree and stopped at the bottom.

Josh gestured for her to go first. He followed behind, lifting himself inside and leaning against the wall with a sigh. He simply looked at her for a long moment.

Tess squirmed.

"You scared me, Tornado," he said softly. "I was afraid I'd lost you."

Tess nodded, regretting her fears and lack of trust. So much had gotten in the way of her happiness, much of it her own fault. "I'm sorry," she whispered. "I felt so terrible for what happened that I couldn't...I guess I couldn't stay."

Josh met her eyes. "I get it. And I didn't mean to

hurt you when I said you were a coward. I wanted to rattle you enough that you'd fight. I should have seen you were too tired to keep going anymore for me or anyone else. I should have been there to help and support you. I'm so sorry," he said sincerely. "I should have believed that things were as you said. I didn't want to think people could be like that. And I wanted to fix it."

Tess shrugged. "I wasn't upset with you." She let her gaze again meet Josh's, the warm blush of his complete attention making her nervous and silly, as if she was still only a kid looking at a boy she'd convinced herself she'd one day marry instead of the man who actually intended to date her.

"The worst of this whole thing though is that I was scared, Tess. I think a little part of me did worry what everyone thought." He shook his head vehemently and pushed away from the wall where he paced the small space like a caged animal.

Tess waited as he worked out his emotions, saying nothing but understanding his frustration.

Josh finally stopped in front of her and looked into her eyes. "I said it didn't matter—and it didn't—but that's not what I showed you by my actions. I'm sorry that I didn't come after you. I was wrong."

Tess shook her head. "No. I needed that time, Jed. I needed to figure things out on my own. I knew you were thinking about me. I knew you were praying. That was enough."

Josh nodded but he didn't appear to be convinced.

Tess drew a deep breath. "I'm sorry I didn't trust you, that I wasn't confident in us."

Josh reached out a hand to her.

Tess took it, grateful when he squeezed tightly.

"I don't want to play games, Tornado." He held her gaze for a long moment.

"I don't either, Jed."

Josh laughed awkwardly and pulled away, his eyebrows knitting together as he stuffed his hands deep into his pockets. "So how weird does this sound? Will you...? I mean, could we...?" His blue eyes met hers again as he tried to form his question.

Much to her chagrin, Tess couldn't fight the laughter that bubbled up inside her, even though Josh was standing before her, serious and vulnerable.

He shifted his weight and turned away. "Geez, like this isn't hard enough," he muttered as he ran his hand through his hair.

"I'm sorry," Tess managed as she stepped closer to him. "It's funny that you're in my place now, asking me..." she paused and touched his arm, hoping to reassure him. "You don't need to ask. Nothing's changed. Not since we were kids."

Josh turned back to her. He fidgeted as Tess smiled and reached for his hand. He rewarded her with his dimples as the tension melted and he laced their fingers together. "So, you will be my girlfriend? I mean that still sounds weird." He laughed and shook his head. "You'll let me take you out? In public? And you'll tell people we're together? For real?"

Tess laughed. "Yes. I will. And I will be so proud."

Josh squeezed Tess's hand tightly. "I'm the one who's proud. What you did today, Tess, it was one of the most beautiful things I've ever seen. You're such an amazing woman. Are you sure you'd want to be with a weakling like me?"

Tess laughed as she relished the warmth of their hands together. She met Josh's eyes. "I guess...I mean,

I don't have anything better to do. But if the softball team stinks I may be tempted to put a stop to this."

Josh's eyes widened in surprise. "You joined the softball team?"

Tess shrugged, trying to look bored. "I still need to watch the shoulder but I figured, why not? You in? Or are you too scared the congregation will find out you always go after the high ones?"

Josh laughed and reached out to take her other hand. He leaned forward and kissed her.

Without the reservations and fear between them, Tess finally understood what it meant to, for the first time, be kissed with a love that she'd never believed was possible.

When Josh straightened to his full height and gazed down into her eyes, he smiled.

Tess smiled too. "If you kiss me like that again I may propose to you first, Jed," she said weakly.

He laughed and rested his forehead against hers. "No one said we needed to date for a long time."

"That works for me."

"Me, too." Josh nodded toward the ladder. "We better go for that pie or your family will wonder what I did with you."

Tess nodded.

They descended to the ground.

"Jed?" she asked softly as he stepped off the last rung of the ladder.

"Hmm?" he handed her a helmet and turned to grab his own.

"Are you sure?"

Josh tucked his helmet under his arm as he turned so that he was completely facing her. He looked into Tess's eyes and reached up to cradle the back of her head with his hand. "From the minute I first saw you in Florida I knew this day was coming for us." He paused as he closed his eyes for a long moment. "I might not have known how we would get here, but I knew we'd do it."

When he opened his eyes all of Tess's fears were gone. He loved her. Completely, truly, straight-to-his-soul, loved her.

Tess gulped. Wishing for it her whole life was nothing compared to finally having Josh's love. He was once all she wanted, but now he was everything she needed.

"I love you, Tornado." He leaned down and brushed her lips with his own.

"I love you too, Jed." She paused as she stood on her tiptoes to kiss him again. "Let's go for a ride."

Epilogue

"Hey, Tornado! I need your help!" Tess smiled and started for the stairs, still loving the sound of Josh's voice reverberating through their home. Even after a year of marriage, she still tingled knowing he loved her.

A little over a year and a half had passed since her baptism, and the world was entirely different. Josh was doing well in his position at the church, and Tess transferred to a nursing job with a hospital that was closer to their home, and she'd recently brought her hours down to part-time.

After Josh proposed using sidewalk chalk outside Tess's apartment, the couple endured a very short engagement and got married in a small but beautiful ceremony conducted by Josh's dad. It was perfect. And now they were working to make their new house the home they dreamed it would be.

Miracles could happen for Tess after all.

Tess entered the bedroom.

Josh turned to smile at her. He was trying to change the diaper of their newborn, David Stuart, but wasn't having much luck. While he kept his hand on the baby, Tess noticed that the diaper lay open, covered in meconium—and Josh's crisp, button-down shirt hadn't fared any better as he was covered in it too.

"Can you help me?" he asked desperately. "I was almost done and then he…"

The scene was so hilarious and at the same time precious, that Tess could only burst into a fit of laughter. Unfortunately, since she'd only given birth two days earlier, laughing while standing hurt. She grabbed the edge of the crib and sunk to her knees while trying to compose herself.

Josh's face dissolved in horror. "Oh, my goodness! Are you OK?" he asked, looking with concern from the baby to his wife.

Tess nodded as tears spilled down her face. "I'm fine," she muttered, trying to gain control. "You're hilarious…"

Josh sighed and shook his head as he went back to cleaning his son. "Well, I'm glad I could give you your laugh for the day. Do you need help getting up?"

"No…" Tess struggled to her feet and shooed Josh away. "Go change your shirt. Everyone will be here in a minute."

Josh unbuttoned his shirt and tossed it into the hamper across the room, but he didn't move. Instead, he watched Tess swiftly and capably diaper their son, lift him from the table and kiss him.

"You little stinker. Daddy'll think you only take after me now when you cause all of this trouble." The baby kicked his feet in response making Tess laugh.

Josh reached out to hug his wife. "Oh, there's no chance of that. Not with those eyes, huh, buddy?" He grabbed David's foot and kissed Tess on the head. "And he has my dimples…" He smiled broadly to show them off and Tess playfully hit him, wondering if their effect would ever wane.

"How much time before they're here?" Josh asked.

The doorbell rang.

"About three seconds," she said, giving him a nudge toward the door. "Go. Put something on."

Josh kissed her again and sighed. "OK...want me to take him?"

Tess's heart warmed. He'd worried and taken gentle care of her from the minute she'd announced her pregnancy—and even now that she'd given birth he continued to dote on her.

"I got him," she said. "Remember they couldn't give a care about us now that he's here."

Josh started toward their bedroom. "Careful going down the steps."

"Yeah, yeah," Tess muttered as she went down the staircase they'd both fallen in love with the first time they'd entered the house. "Come in!" she yelled.

The door swung open and her entire family entered, including Grandma Vi, who was meeting her great-grandson for the first time.

Stu closed the door right at the same moment she reached the bottom of the steps.

"Where's Papa Thorne?" Brody asked, holding up a big box. "We brought a present for you guys."

Tess handed Stu the baby, as he was already over the moon for his namesake. "David, um, wasn't quite done going when Daddy tried to change the diaper and, well, now he's changing his shirt."

"What an amateur," Brody moaned as he set the box aside.

The family laughed as Tess reached out to hug her grandmother. "Come on, Gram, let's go in the living room and you can hold him."

But she was already pushing Tess away so she could go to Stu. She peered over the blanket and sighed, tears in her eyes as she gazed at her great-grandson, his dark hair and blue eyes a testament to both of his parents. "He's perfect," Vi whispered.

"He sure is," Karen said, taking her mother's arm. "Come on, Mom."

They went into the living room and got Gram to sit so she could hold David.

Tess took Brody's little boy, Michael, and entertained him while Stell lay a blanket on the floor for him to play.

"Hello, everybody," Josh said, entering a minute later.

Brody punched him in the arm. "You got christened, huh?"

Josh sighed. "Yep." He smiled at Gram, who was cooing over his son, and smiled. "And I couldn't care less."

Brody laughed, nodding. "Yeah. Me, either," he said, gazing fondly at his own family.

The friends, and now brothers-in-law, were closer now that Josh had been in town consistently for almost two years. And Stell and Tess were often calling one another and getting together. The family was closer than ever.

Josh went to Tess and kissed her quickly as he led her to sit on the couch nearby. "Put your feet up," he said. "You need to rest."

Tess playfully shoved him away. "Yeesh, Jed, I gave birth, I'm not dying."

"Take notes," Stell said to Brody, nodding toward the couple.

Brody groaned and carried the box over to his sister. "It's from all of us."

Tess turned to Josh, who shrugged.

"No idea, Tornado. Open it."

Tess tore into the paper and held out the box to Josh who lifted the lid followed by a framed picture. It was Josh when he was about fifteen years old and Tess when she was ten. He towered over her in his jean cut-offs and dirty T-shirt, a baseball bat slung over one shoulder. Tess, in overalls and pig tails—and wearing her baseball mitt—gazed up at him in adoration.

Tess laughed at the image, remembering the days they'd played ball behind the Carson home. Those were great memories. "Man, was I a loser," Tess muttered. "Nice pig tails…"

"I think it's sweet!" Stell protested.

"You have always been adorable," Josh said, putting his arm around her. "Even when you were annoying Brody and me."

Tess looked up at her husband and kissed him. "I was a dumb kid, what can I say?" She glanced at Stell. "It is sweet. I just don't want him getting a big head over it."

"Why would I do that?" he asked, raising an eyebrow and smiling broadly.

Tess elbowed him and he groaned. She reached into the box and pulled out two baseball gloves, along with a smaller one for the baby, and three matching shirts that said 'Thorne' on the back. "Aww!" Tess's eyes filled with tears.

Stu cleared his throat as Marlene gently held to his arm. It was clear he was about to cry. "We realize how hard it was when you lost softball," he said. "But if you hadn't lost that, we wondered if you would be here now—with Josh and David." He blinked several times.

Her uncle was amazing.

"God's been so good to us," he said. "We love you,

kid."

Tess went to her uncle and hugged him and then did the same to each member of her family. "I love you all, so, so much," she said thickly, not fighting the tears as they fell. "And I know that God has me just where He wants me." She sat beside Josh and kissed him as her mother set David in her arms again.

Tess wasn't just forgiven. She was fully, totally blessed.

Acknowledgements

Jim Hart – Thank you for your guidance and direction. I so appreciate all you do.

Susan Baganz – As always, this novel wouldn't be what it is without you. Thank you for continuing to make my writing better than I can imagine it can be.

Nicola Martinez and everyone at Pelican Book Group – Thank you, once again, for believing in my writing. It's a pleasure to work with you.

A Devotional Moment

Be kind and compassionate to one another, forgiving each other, just as in Christ God forgave you. ~ Ephesians 4:32

In the Bible, Jesus and the apostles talk about forgiveness many times. They speak and write about how forgiveness of others releases the forgiver from the chains of negative emotions— hate, anger, bitterness, and fear. In addition to forgiving others their transgressions, it's important to forgive ourselves when we do something horribly wrong. With our acceptance of faith in Jesus, we are cleansed of our sins. As we work through our own salvation, at some point we have to accept that while we have sinned, our sincere regret and the undertaking to amend our future behaviour is where God wants us to focus. When we ask for forgiveness, He washes away our sins and makes us new. We must be ready to accept new thoughts, new emotions, and all grace from God.

In **Forgiving Tess**, the protagonist has turned over a new leaf. She has accepted Jesus as her Saviour, and is working to pay off debt and seek forgiveness from those she's harmed. But circumstances have created distrust and she has to strain to show she's changed. Despite that, she never lets her faith waver, but soldiers on to clear her debts.

Do you have a difficult time forgiving others or yourself? Remember that we are instructed to forgive others — not for our transgressor's sake, but for our own, so we can be a burden-free, joyful beacon of Christ's love. We also need to forgive ourselves when we've chosen the wrong thing, and in forgiving ourselves to ask for forgiveness — from those we've wronged and from God. When we do this, when we extend mercy and open ourselves up to mercy from others, we'll find a peace that cannot be experienced otherwise.

LORD, GIVE ME THE STRENGTH TO RIGHT OLD WRONGS, TO FORGIVE AND BE FORGIVEN AS I WALK THIS PATH WITH YOU. IN JESUS' NAME I PRAY, AMEN.

Thank you

We appreciate you reading this Prism title. For other Christian fiction and clean-and-wholesome stories, please visit our on-line bookstore at www.prismbookgroup.com.

For questions or more information, contact us at customer@pelicanbookgroup.com.

Prism is an imprint of
Pelican Book Group
www.PelicanBookGroup.com

Connect with Us
www.facebook.com/Pelicanbookgroup
www.twitter.com/pelicanbookgrp

To receive news and specials, subscribe to our bulletin
http://pelink.us/bulletin

May God's glory shine through
this inspirational work of fiction.

AMDG

You Can Help!

At Pelican Book Group it is our mission to entertain readers with fiction that uplifts the Gospel. It is our privilege to spend time with you awhile as you read our stories.

We believe you can help us to bring Christ into the lives of people across the globe. And you don't have to open your wallet or even leave your house!

Here are 3 simple things you can do to help us bring illuminating fiction™ to people everywhere.

1) If you enjoyed this book, write a positive review. Post it at online retailers and websites where readers gather. And share your review with us at reviews@pelicanbookgroup.com (this does give us permission to reprint your review in whole or in part.)

2) If you enjoyed this book, recommend it to a friend in person, at a book club or on social media.

3) If you have suggestions on how we can improve or expand our selection, let us know. We value your opinion. Use the contact form on our web site or e-mail us at customer@pelicanbookgroup.com

God Can Help!

Are you in need? The Almighty can do great things for you. Holy is His Name! He has mercy in every generation. He can lift up the lowly and accomplish all things. Reach out today.

Do not fear: I am with you; do not be anxious: I am your God. I will strengthen you, I will help you, I will uphold you with my victorious right hand.

~Isaiah 41:10 (NAB)

We pray daily, and we especially pray for everyone connected to Pelican Book Group—that includes you! If you have a specific need, we welcome the opportunity to pray for you. Share your needs or praise reports at http://pelink.us/pray4us

Free Book Offer

We're looking for booklovers like you to partner with us! Join our team of influencers today and periodically receive free eBooks and exclusive offers.

For more information
Visit http://pelicanbookgroup.com/booklovers